Three Virgins

and Other Stories

T0083619

Three Virgins

and Other Stories

Manjula Padmanabhan

zubaan

Zubaan
an imprint of Kali for Women
128b Shahpur Jat
1st floor
New Delhi 110 049
Email: contact@zubaanbooks.com
www.zubaanbooks.com

First published by Zubaan, 2013
Copyright © Manjula Padmanabhan
Inside Illustrations and Cover Image Copyright © Manjula Padmanabhan 2013

10 9 8 7 6 5 4 3 2 1

ISBN: 978 93 83074 29 7 (hbk)
ISBN: 978 93 81017 61 6 (pbk)

Zubaan is an independent feminist publishing house based in New Delhi, India with a strong academic and general list. It was set up as an imprint of the well known feminist house Kali for Women and carries forward Kali's tradition of publishing world quality books to high editorial and production standards. 'Zubaan' means tongue, voice, language, speech in Hindustani. Zubaan is a non-profit publisher, working in the area of the humanities and social sciences, as well as in fiction, general non-fiction and books for young adults that celebrate difference, diversity and equality, especially for and about the children of India and South Asia under its imprint Young Zubaan.

Typeset in Sabon 11/13 by Jojy Philip
Printed at Gopsons Papers Ltd., A 2 & 3 Sector 64, Noida

CONTENTS

INTRODUCTION

It was going to be a simple reprint of *Hot Death Cold Soup*, my first published book. But a great deal has happened in my life between 1996 and now. A play called *Harvest*; a travel memoir called *Getting There*; two collections of *Suki* cartoons; more than a dozen illustrated books; several changes of residence; a science fiction novel called *Escape*; and a lot more besides.

I asked Zubaan if we could add new stories while dropping some of the old. In the end, we decided upon an even mix of old and new, five each. Enough to re-irritate earlier readers and plenty to spare for those who have yet to visit my somewhat freak-infested dimension. My mother asks me why I can't write about things that "normal people" can enjoy. Alas, the ideas that arrive at my desktop are all rude, unsightly wretches who belch and pick their noses and expose themselves in public.

So they are what I'm stuck with. If there's one thing I've learnt in the years since *HDCS* it's that being published is a great way To Lose Friends And Alienate People. Or maybe that's just me! My friends wish I would quit displaying my mental deficiencies by writing science fiction. Some fellow writers dismiss me as a failed cartoonist with literary pretensions. Other fellow writers would prefer to swat me off this plane of existence for refusing to praise their prose in my reviews.

But my publishers continue to believe in me. To them and to all the wonderful editors who have augmented my work through their attention and effort, I am ever grateful.

∽

When I have an idea for a story, I scribble a brief description of it on a post-it. If I manage not to lose the post-it, the idea gets entered into a folder on my computer's desktop. Usually, I will only get around to writing the story if I am invited to offer a piece to a short story collection or a magazine. Until 1984, I had been published as a journalist, cartoonist and illustrator, but not as a fiction writer. In that year *A Government of India Undertaking* appeared in *Imprint Magazine* and I wrote my first play, *Lights Out*.

For those who are interested, there's a when/where publishing history at the end of this book for all the stories here.

All the post-*HDCS* stories in this volume were commissioned except for the title story, *Three Virgins*. I wrote a first draft of it maybe ten years ago, but it was very slippery and refused to settle down. I believe a story is complete when I can read it all the way through three times without wanting to change anything. This one kept on wriggling, first this way, then that. I wanted it to be about early awakenings and yet this final version, completed just last year, is more about late-life realizations. Appropriately enough, I guess.

Exile was written for Zubaan's *Breaking the Bow*, a collection of "Speculative fiction based on the Ramayana". I set my version of the epic in the future, with all the characters gender-reversed. But joint-editors Anil Menon and Vandana Singh requested, with tremendous warmth and tact, a fresh story. They were looking for tales that expanded upon elements of the mythological world, rather than a wholesale re-telling. So I wrote *The Other Woman*, choosing one of the least central of the many characters in the entire saga. I had to look up her name on the Internet: Mandodari. She was very cooperative, I am happy to say. I really enjoyed writing about her.

I wrote *Feast* by invitation to *Tehelka*'s 2008 short story issue. Their theme was "excess" – and the word "vampire" appeared in my head even before I'd put down the phone from the briefing. I believed it was such an obvious association that I was surprised to find no-one else had chosen to write about a ravenous supernatural being on his first trip to the subcontinent.

Khajuraho first appeared in the Italian literary magazine *Storie*, in English and in Italian. The story that appears in this book is slightly longer than that original version. The inspiration for it was, of course, the guide. He was a real person. I hope his life has improved since the time I and my sister met him, in Khajuraho, thirty years ago.

∽

The drawings are what I call telephone doodles. Like many people, I scribble aimlessly while talking on the phone. A couple of years ago, I began keeping drawing pads and sketch-pens handy, with the result that a few of the drawings took on recognizable shapes and forms.

Even so, they really are small doodles, generated half-consciously, while I was talking on the phone.

It was Zubaan's idea to assign them three to a page, at the beginning of each story. A few of the creatures appear more than once. One or two definitely appear to be connected to the text. A couple of them look like characters waiting for their stories to be told.

And who knows! Maybe they will be. Some day.

Manjula Padmanabhan,
New Delhi, 2013

TEASER

Rakesh leapt onto the bus feeling like a red, hot chili. The bus was a tongue in the mouth of the world and by placing his foot upon it, he scorched it with his power.

His power resided in the fork of his pants. Most of the time it slept. But when it was awake, such as when he boarded the bus he took to college, it was vibrant. It was radiant. It generated heat, light and truth.

Some mornings, he would surface from sleep to find that the power had arisen before him and was gazing at the dawn world with its single blind-slit eye. He would feel abashed then, that he had been asleep and unaware of its presence. And relieved that he had a space to himself, a portion of the dining room, which had been walled off just for him to sleep in. He would have hated someone else to witness his miracle.

Today had been one such morning.

He believed the power to be a manifestation of the divine, made flesh upon his body. A baton passed into his keeping for a brief but sacred period. It was not given to Rakesh to understand whence the baton was passed to him, by what mechanism it lodged in that mystic, hair-bound space at the junction of his legs nor why it twanged and hummed with a life of its own. Out of the void it appeared, it trembled, fluoresced and passed onward to the void again.

He asked no questions. The priest of a one-person religion, he performed his devotions dutifully. And felt cleansed, uplifted, serene.

Thus, on this morning, as on previous mornings, his first conscious moment was of being enveloped in a fine mist of sweat and cosmic light. He washed, dressed and ate his morning meal in an electric daze. His mother nagged at him for dawdling, his father called him a lazy good-for-nothing, his elder brother teased him about some trivial thing. And all the while, he felt, safe across his lower belly, the sign of higher approval. The sign that he was blessed in ways that these minor mortals could never share.

He went downstairs, down three flights of stairs and outside to the nearest bus-stop, all in the same sparkling state. As if his feet didn't quite reach the ground. Each hair on his scalp was distinct. He could feel air moving between the strands, his nerves were bright and polished, like the ends of shiny new pins. From the place covered by the zip of his jeans, beamed a powerful invisible light. Triple-x rays, laced with dark stars, sprinkled with electrons.

Within minutes, the bus had materialised, summoned to the stop by the sheer force of his will. He entered it and immediately his potential of light and heat spread its tendrils out, not only across the entire lower deck but the upper deck as well.

He barely bothered to check with his eyes what his highly attuned senses had already revealed to him: there were several targets present on the bus.

This was not always the case. Sometimes there were none suitable to his purpose. Sometimes they sat in inaccessible places. Sometimes there was such a surfeit of choice that he was slow to select the one most ideal from among those available. There were even occasions when targets appeared in such profusion that he felt intimidated by the strength of their numbers and held himself in painful check.

But today, he knew, was going to be special. Hopping up from the boarding area to the raised floor of the lower deck, his left hand met the waiting strap as if it flew there of its own volition. The interior of the bus was still relatively uncrowded. Right away, he saw three targets.

One of them was of the tender, chubby type, with long plaits and an expression of sweet and perfect stupidity. A target who did not yet know what it was. This type would take a long time merely to register his presence, leave alone notice his flashing beam of light. Sometimes, such a target would remain innocent and unaware of him for the entire duration of their relationship. He would pity it then. Such extreme ignorance was distressing.

Of this species, even those that did become aware of him never progressed far. At most, as he pressed his attentions, they would squirm and wriggle and move themselves ineffectually about. But they remained unconscious of the source of their difficulty. They acted from instinct rather than knowledge. While Rakesh enjoyed being an agent of their education, their lack of depth afforded only a fleeting challenge.

He knew that the most he could inspire in such a target was fear. But it was a dim fear, a ten-watt fear. A fear such as one might expect to find in the mind of an animal or some other such low-born entity. And in any case, it was not fear that he sought to inspire but a submissive reverence.

Thus it was easy, today, to turn his attention to the other two targets. At first glance, they both seemed more to Rakesh's taste.

In his experience, the ideal was between the ages of 16 and 23. It would be well-dressed and smart, but not too smart. Over confident targets tended to respond in silly ways. Sometimes even causing a commotion to break out in the bus. Rakesh had developed the ability to identify and avoid such targets. He had no interest in confrontations.

His preference in clothes varied from day to day. For instance, he could never decide whether he liked short skirts or not. They were enticing, but then again, so obvious. They fairly screamed for attentions of his kind. And he didn't like to feel that he was being manipulated. Yet the sheer sight of that bare skin, those exposed lower limbs ... well. There was something to that. Something undeniable.

But in general he preferred tight clothes. A target with seams bursting under the arms, yet clad from head to foot, suggested the perfect mix of modesty and turgidity. Ripeness awaiting puncture, like cloth balloons. But kurtas only. Sari-clad targets were, as a rule, to be avoided. He didn't think it out clearly, but if he had, he would have readily admitted that they reminded him of his mother.

The positioning of the target was another important factor in determining his choice. There were three kinds of seats in the bus. The majority accommodated two passengers and faced towards the front. In some buses, the last row of seats was one long bench which could support six passengers. In other models, especially double-deckers, the boarding area was in the rear. In these, the passengers entered the lower deck by passing between a pair of seats placed across the aisle from one another. Each seat could accommodate three passengers.

The young chubby target was sitting on one of these three-seaters and the other two were further in, one by itself at a window seat and the other, sharing the seat with someone else, sat primly, with its lower limbs stuck into the aisle at an awkward angle.

The window-seat target wore a kurta and had longish hair blowing loose and open in the breeze. The hair was being held down with one slim hand. Rakesh could see a portion of the neck. He had an impression of someone gentle and refined. Such a target would tense up the moment he sat down near it, like a hi-fidelity receiver, registering his broadcast at the first tentative announcement. But it would nonetheless endure the whole journey squashed into the side of the bus rather than push at him or create a fuss of any kind.

Such targets could turn out to be angels, goddesses. That modesty, that delicacy which abhorred the slightest aggressive gesture – ah! Depending on what it was wearing, he might even get a chance to touch bare skin, with his forearm or his elbow.

Then again, the aisle-seat target seemed the most challenging of the group. The awkward pose in which it sat would provide Rakesh with the ideal opportunity to make his initial contact. To begin with he could pretend to lean against the backrest of its seat. If he timed himself just right, this could happen as the bus began to fill up. Then, unless it reached its stop, the target would effectively be pinned there while he bumped the whole side of his body against it with the motion of the bus.

Today's aisle-seat target was wearing a short-sleeved blouse and jeans. Even from where he stood, Rakesh could see that it looked plump and ripe. He was on the point of moving towards it when suddenly it turned and he caught a glimpse of its face. Glasses! He detested them. Not merely because they were disfiguring, but because they very often appeared in combination with a dangerous, pugnacious expression.

Such targets, it seemed to him, should be whipped, stripped bare and paraded in public places to teach them the error of their ways. To teach them that their true nature was to present themselves as attractively and appeasingly as possible. So that devotees of higher purpose, such as himself, could fulfil their ritual obligations.

That was his ardent quest, his daily mission. To pursue his private religion. To worship at his secret altar. He needed targets to complete his rites, in the same way that a flame needs a wick. He expected no more than submissive acceptance. It was so little to ask. Just to sit there, just to permit him to build his heat on their fuel. It always amazed and saddened him that there were those who resisted. Those who were incensed.

He stopped in his tracks, needing to make a lightning decision. The bus was moving and the other passengers who had boarded from the same stop as he, were pushing him onwards. As he turned, to buy time, the realization struck him that this was no ordinary morning. There was a wider than usual range of attractions.

The tendrils of intuition which sprang to his command whenever the power was awake in his jeans wandered ahead of him and scoured the upper deck. Now they brought to him an intimation of something still to be discovered in that area above his head, but further forward. The impression he received was so sharp and strong that he looked up reflexively. A fantasy occurred to him: of the floor of the upper deck made of clear glass, the seats padded with transparent foam, and every passenger a target! What a wonder *that* would be! The pressure beneath his belt purred aloud, just to conceive of such a sight. It was appropriate, then, to go to the upper deck.

Rakesh had to struggle through the passengers in the boarding area to reach the diminutive spiral staircase tucked into the rear corner of the bus. Grabbing the slick-steel handrail he advanced a couple of feet, feeling as he did so, the entire helical strand of shallow metal steps writhing sinuously with the headlong motion of the bus, which had, by this time, picked up momentum.

He found himself immobilized behind the rump of a large old woman who was struggling to propel herself upwards. He fancied, as he stood there, that he could smell her rancid and hanging flesh. When the bus shuddered abruptly to a standstill at a traffic light, he was pitched forward, so that his nose came within nanometres of disappearing into the unseemly depths of that ancient crevasse.

But even as his mind recoiled and the beam of solid light inside his pants wavered dangerously, the bus shuddered, groaned, hissed and in its pre-acceleration convulsion gave the antique leviathan in front of Rakesh the necessary impetus to hurtle up the last few steps to the top deck. Relieved to be spared the ghastly prospect which had briefly presented itself to him, Rakesh clung to the curving rail of the stairwell till the passenger immediately below him gave him an impatient nudge.

An open stretch of road lay supine before the bus. It charged towards its next stop at full throttle, roaring, bouncing, swinging and lolloping along so that the human flies trapped within it experienced brief spells of zero gravity. Rakesh found that he could climb effortlessly, by floating between bumps, with only his hold on the handrail keeping him from being launched into orbit.

He surfaced like a diver inside the air-lit space of a receiving hatch. It was bright upstairs. The ceiling was low, heightening the effect of a cramped, submersible vessel. Rakesh stooped slightly at the top step, to avoid bumping his head. Then he stumbled and almost fell as the bus, sighting its next stop, homed in on it, eager to devour its bait of waiting passengers.

It was at this moment, withstanding the tumultuous forces of public transport, that he saw It.

Sitting at the very front-most seat. With the windows open. Its hair streaming back in the wind. A target.

But *what* a target!

Not only was there an empty seat beside it but its shoulders were bare! Even from the back of the bus, Rakesh could see that it was wearing something utterly minimal. A confection made of thin straps and bright clingy material. In Rakesh's experience such clothing was only ever one layer deep. There would be no underclothes beneath. Such clothing revealed more than it concealed. He had seen countless examples worn by models and the type of ethereal targets who floated beyond his reach in private transports. But on a bus their presence was so rare as to be all but extinct.

He had of course seen pictures of targets wearing nothing at all. But he had found them deeply disturbing. The wanton pinkness. The predatory expressions. The incomprehensible willingness of creatures who posed in magazines conspired to make him wonder whether they were, after all, figments of some artist's fevered imagination. An artist who viewed the body as a gross physical entity, a collection of soft, moist organs. Exuding, excreting, inhaling, ingesting. A fantasist who had never actually encountered real targets in real life on real buses. Targets with their steely nubs thrusting and straining against the confines of clothing. Targets resisting, with sweet despair, the potent attentions of their natural foe and patron – these were more enticing by far than the barren, lifeless, pictures.

He moved slowly towards the front of the deck, deliberately delaying the moment of truth. There was an absolute clarity, an absolute certainty of purpose, as he propelled himself forward, hanging on to the overhead rails. No-one could challenge his claim on that empty space glinting beside the target. It was his and his alone to claim. He was a bird, his arms were wings and he glided with the lilting motion of the bus as it sped down the endless ribbon of the road.

The stiff, unbending material of his jeans relayed the movement of his legs to the wild creature which sat coiled and thudding within its den, causing it to breathe out a veritable halo of light. His whole mind became like a vast glowing bowl, his scattered thoughts scrabbling feebly at the rim. He caught himself wondering whether his light had become actually visible. Whether it was his imagination that fellow passengers seated on either side of the aisle were actually flinching as he passed. Perhaps covering their eyes, lest they be blinded.

Finally he was there. At the front seat. He had expected to savour the moment, hovering just above and beside the target, before sitting down. But the bus chose just then to come to a halt with an ungainly bump. It was almost a disaster. He was knocked forward and off balance, then tossed back again, so that he fell into the seat like a rag doll. He winced as the hard seam of his jeans tore at him. But he clenched his teeth and set his mind tight.

The moment passed without incident.

He breathed out. Opened his eyes. He was sweating and his nostrils were wide. The bus started up. Air moved in through the windows. He was in control again. And astounded.

In the sudden crisis which had almost overtaken him, he had not only sat down but had instinctively splayed his knees wide. In so doing, his right thigh had been flung against the left lower limb of the target. Practically plastered down the full length of that miraculous appendage, which, to crown everything, was bare from the ankle to just a few inches short of the hip.

And there had been no reaction!

Rakesh was dumfounded.

In all of his experience, all targets, even the most non-sentient ones, showed some response to that first touch. It might only be a vague uneasy shifting, or an unconscious recoil or a sudden flying up of the fore-limbs to bunch and constrict the top segment of the body.

That first response was one which Rakesh particularly savoured because right uptil that initial fluttering, wondering move had been made, there was no saying how the encounter would turn out. It was only after the first touch that he could foretell whether the experience ahead was going to be memorable or just mildly amusing or, as in some cases, a no-show. The difference between transcendence and failure, between brilliant, thrilling delight and mysterious, unknowable cancellation.

For there had been times aplenty when, try as he might to prevent it, the mysterious private carnival would dismantle itself and vanish into its night, leaving no trace aside from a small area of scented dampness.

But this, today, was utterly unknown and unfamiliar. The glow that had suffused Rakesh as he approached the seat wavered once more.

Was it possible that the situation was too freakish, after all? Too alien and bizarre? He did not permit his thigh to budge in any direction except for what could not be avoided on account of the motion of the bus. He was not ready to go any farther than he had already managed with the assistance of pure fate, but he wasn't ready to withdraw. His senses, all his senses, were peeled fine, like cloves of garlic. The next few moments would be of utmost consequence. Surreptitiously looking to his right, he took stock.

From the corner of his eye, he confirmed his first impressions. There was a lush bloom colouring the skin, which was pale and supple. So the target was youthful. It had made no effort to flinch away from him, which suggested that it was passive. There was something mysterious in such an extreme of non-reaction, but he let himself relax. He had encountered any number of targets who took their time to respond. None of them had ever looked like this one. But he did not question the infinite variety of fate. It might be all right after all.

The incandescence crept back into its saddle. His furtive gaze licked hungrily, slipping quickly down from the face to the chin, the neck and thence to those regions below the neck.

He wanted to groan with ecstasy. He couldn't remember ever having seen a pair of tremblies quite like the two beside him. He knew they had some other mundane name but he disdained words which would link targets to their day-to-day manifestations as women, sisters, daughters, wives. He had created his own lexicon which would never be loosed upon the air. Words which existed only to describe the relics at the shrine of his own senses.

So tremblies they were. Quivering and jittering, while their owner sat with her arms loose. The gale from the open window had reduced the cloth of her blouse to a thin, seductive film of pale blue beneath which twin light-houses beamed from twin promontories of spongy rock.

As Rakesh watched, barely breathing, he fancied that he could see a resonance. The light that streamed out from his jeans was echoing from her promontories. He was hallucinating, he was levitating. The pulsing within mirrored by the pulsing without. He would have to move soon.

The bus juddered to another halt. It had reached the peak of its route and was starting now to disgorge its contents. The passengers in the seats directly around Rakesh and the target began to vacate their positions. Within minutes Rakesh was practically alone on the top deck with his inscrutable companion.

How was it possible that she had not noticed him yet?

She had not so much as twitched. Voluntarily, that is. The bus coughed to life once more and Rakesh saw, through a screen of sparks, the promontories jump in unison. They wobbled wildly out of sync as the labouring vehicle heaved itself back onto its course. Was she blind or deaf? Had she slipped into a seated coma? Yet her body was alive and vivid with motion.

Watching her, Rakesh was barely able to contain himself. He clenched his teeth and tilted his head back, hardly daring to breathe. He spread his arms, so that the left arm spanned the aisle. The right one lay across the top edge of the seat he shared with the target. In doing this, he discovered that his right arm had inadvertently trapped some strands of the target's hair. Dimly, without seeing her, he felt her move at last. First she drew her hair out of the way. Then, beside him, along the length of his leg, he felt her shift. He shut his eyes. It was beginning. He must prepare his moves.

The classic manoeuvre required the bus to be careening

along at high speed, so that he could use its motion to lean with ever increasing insistence upon the target. It must be neither all at once nor too discrete. The quarry must not remain uncertain of his intentions for too long. Today, having started out with such an outstanding surplus, he wondered if he couldn't go much further than he normally dared. Use his hands for instance. Touch her shoulder. Her hair. Or even turn and breathe directly on her. Anything seemed possible.

He had barely finished enumerating the possibilities when he had the strangest impression that he was being looked at. He couldn't say precisely what gave him that idea, but it had to do with the movement she had made, so that her knee seemed to be digging into his leg. He was confused. He didn't dare open his eyes now. Given the position of her knee, she must have turned full-face towards him. It was a situation so unprecedented that he was paralysed. He could do nothing at all.

Now he felt her breath. Near his ear. She was saying something, but his mind refused to translate those sounds into words. Through the shut lids of his eyes he could see her.

The woman's face was harshly coloured, like a film poster or a dream. Red mouth, pink cheeks, eyes fringed thick with tar. She was not so young after all. She seemed to be smiling. But strangely. He would have liked to flinch away from her expression, but couldn't move. His skin had shrunk, pulled tight by a knot centered at the tip of his private torch. A tight knot, a bursting knot.

The bus was hurtling towards its final destination. The woman reached with her hand and touched him. Touched the curving ridge under the zip of his jeans. With the hard red talon at the end of her forefinger. Tracing the double track of stitches, up, up, towards his belt buckle.

A hoarse grunt escaped him.

And he emptied out. Heart, brain, kidneys, all. Liquefied and discharged through the geyser in the mantle of his body. One harsh pulse. No light.

He opened his eyes.

The woman was looking at him. Her mouth was twisted. She was laughing silently. He could hear the sound in his mind, over the thunder in his ears. She was looking at the damp patch that had appeared under the waist-band of his jeans, on his shirt. "Silly!" she was saying. "Silly little boy has wet his pants!"

She stood up then, stepped over his feet and was gone.

The bus roared as it sighted its terminal stop, gathered itself to make the jump to light-speed, landed at its berth with a shriek of brakes and a violent spasm. Then died. Its metal skin ticked and sighed as it gave up heat and stress.

The voices of disembarking passengers and the clangour of their feet faded as the last of them got down. The conductor far away, at the head of the stairs, agitated the clapper of his bell. Don't make me come and get you, said the conductor, clanging the clapper's strident tongue, just come on now, let's go, without a struggle.

But Rakesh remained where he was, breathing slowly. He was staring straight out at the blank sky, blinding blue and bright. Just behind his eyes, a feeling like grey rain.

A GOVERNMENT OF INDIA
UNDERTAKING

One morning I saw a balloon seller cross the street and vanish round a corner. I say "balloon seller", but he was more than that: against the bleakness of the city, its bone-grey buildings, its ragged people, its rubbish heaps and hidden rats, he had appeared as if from nowhere, a vision of youth and delight. High over his head swayed an immense bouquet of pink gas balloons, a hundred or more of them, alive, crowding together, bouncing apart, bright pink, bright with white specks. The balloon seller strode briskly along under their gay and thronging mass and, in a twinkling, had slipped from view, swallowed by the city.

So swiftly had he appeared and disappeared that I felt it my duty to run across the street and confront him again, if only to confirm the vision. But he was nowhere in sight. I wandered in and out of various little lanes and streetlets and caught nothing of him, no hint or sign that he had ever passed that way. It was on this pretext, looking for the balloon seller, that I entered a narrow gully with short squat buildings crowded one athwart the other and saw a sign which read: "Bureau of Reincarnation and Transmigration of Souls – A Government of India Undertaking". It was neatly hand-lettered in white paint on varnished wood, and contrasted strangely with the crumbling wall onto which it had been nailed.

I stood back to take a second look at the building, but no, it was just like all the rest to look at. Bleached, flaking paint, gaping doorway revealing a dark uninviting interior, a flight of worn wooden steps. There was a faint smell as of a bakery, or a urinal, perhaps. I stepped inside and noticed, once my eyes had adjusted to the gloom, an ancient chowkidar dozing on his wooden stool to the side of the door. Further in, a neat little peon sat at a small desk, staring with fixed purpose at its surface. It was covered with various objects: pencils, matchboxes, empty cigarette packets, an old glass ink-well and a paste-pot disfigured by successive encrustations of paste, and all of these arranged as for an obstacle course. I drew closer and saw that it was – for the shiny cockroach scrabbling about erratically, trying to reach the crumb of food dangled by the peon just beyond the reach of the insect's questing feelers. I saw too, that the creature's diligence would not be rewarded: down the leg of the desk, six of its brothers had been left to wriggle to their deaths skewered with government-issue straight pins. I watched in fascination, not daring to disturb the peon at his sport, to ask him where I should go and whom I should see in the Bureau of Reincarnation. But he anticipated me and said softly, not looking up from the desk, "Tea in fifteen minutes." I took this to mean that I should climb the flight of stairs, so I did.

Hardly had I reached the first floor, but I found I had joined a queue. That is, I arrived at the landing and was brought up short against a flesh-coloured room-divider which had a sign pasted on it which read: "Q this way" Further room-dividers had been laid out in a line, forming a sort of artificial corridor. I followed its length until, quite abruptly, I found I had entered a huge hall, with a vast mass of people apparently congealed along its floors and walls. Unaccountably, the building's internal dimensions had expanded and it was larger on the inside than its outside promised.

That queue was an amazing thing: not a group of individuals waiting patiently in line for something but an organic entity in itself. Physically, it was merely a more heroic version of the kind that one finds at the GPO during a sale of first-day issues. It looped backwards and forwards across that vast hall with its dingy marble chip tiling and dim, low-slung light bulbs. It passed over and under and right through itself so often that no one knew where it began or ended.

No one waiting in the queue (in my section of it, at least) could recollect having seen the waiting hall empty of people, nor was there anyone present who had been amongst the first to line up: everyone there had been waiting so long that he or she had lost all track of time and had settled into that vacuum of thought and action which is our only solace in such situations. It was in this time scale, in a place where even the finest quartz watch was reduced to a useless curiosity by its sheer irrelevance, that the queue became as one animal, living, breathing and functioning as one organism and each of us in it making up its cell wall.

Nourishment in the form of regular cycles of tepid tea and stale chutney sandwiches passed through and reached every segment of the queue as efficiently and mysteriously as it appeared. We seemed to breathe in concert, each newcomer to the queue having to adjust himself/herself to the group rhythm – asthmatics had a bad time and smokers were not tolerated – until the walls seemed to move gently in and out with our respiration The queue was constantly being depleted – as someone was finally ushered into the presence of an officer, registrar or file clerk – and constantly being replenished by newcomers and by former queue members rejoining the array in quest of yet another officer, registrar or file clerk. Since there was no distinct terminal point, each addition had to squeeze in as best he or she could, a few half-hearted grunts and tongue-clickings were raised in mild discontent, then everyone subsided once more into the vacant stupor of waiting.

For entertainment we had the endless forms, questionnaires and visiting slips to fill up, some of these transiting the length and breadth of the queue several times before being rescued by the defaulting peon and returned to the office of their origin. Sometimes we roused ourselves enough to sing bhajans and popular songs, sometimes there were a few listless bouts of gambling and once, someone who had brought a cassette recorder along, played a taping of last year's Test matches, and everyone cheered.

There were all kinds of people in that queue – you could tell at a glance from the myriad forms filled out in triplicate, the professions and personalities involved. The majority had come to check their claims for a better life the next time round: business magnates and thieves, they were each of them anxious to improve the fibre of their future lives. Others had come to look at the files of dear departed ones, to see if they could renew contact with them in the life to be; some had come to check on their antecedents, to see how well their current lives and companions matched their pasts; some had come belligerently, to demand enlightenment within the next three births or else; some had come out of idle curiosity and at least one pathetic individual I spoke to was there under the impression that he was in queue to buy tickets for *Deep Throat*. And finally, there must have been a few, like myself, who had come for dishonourable reasons. But, naturally, I never actually spoke to any of the others.

Because of the irregular nature of my request, it took even more than the ordinary number of tea-and-sandwich cycles, false leads, wrong turnings along the queue and battles with insolent peons, coffee boys, receptionists and bureaucratic vagrants before I could approach my first bonafide officer – the Assistant Registrar of Files. He was a frail, desiccated, bright-eyed little man who smelt of clean old paper and wore rimless glasses. He sat behind an enormous desk generously littered with scraps of paper, forms, questionnaires and a few odd bus tickets. Holding down the papers were a dozen or so glass paperweights, the kind which look like gobs of some unspeakable mucus, quick-frozen and injected with air to produce five (sometimes four or less) bubbles inside, arranged in such away as to keep the observer forever anxious to rearrange them more symmetrically. One of them, I noticed, a collector's item no doubt, had just one enormous tear-shaped bubble, and in it an ant had been trapped and preserved for posterity with a puzzled look on its face.

However, I had not come all the way merely to note down the details of interior decor in that musty little office. Leaning forward and putting as much earnestness as I could into my voice I said, "Sir, let me come straight to the point: ever since I saw the signboard on the building, I have been possessed with the desire to – " I paused dramatically – "change my life." I had been looking at him directly when I said this last bit and was surprised and a little disappointed to see that the little man barely blinked. In fact he seemed on the verge of stifling a yawn, so I hurried on recklessly. "Oh, I realise this is an illegal request – even criminal you might say! But I've been waiting such a long time, and no one has so much as told me one way or another whether such a thing is possible at all." I tried to change my tack from wheedling to impatience: "I am at the end of my endurance. I must know what I need to know, even if my request is denied, but I must know. I am not going to leave this office until you tell me what. ... "

But he stopped me by raising a delicate hand. For a moment I thought he was about to fob me off, as so many minions along the course of my ordeal had done, and I had my handful of tears collected and ready to throw in his face. But he pursed his lips a moment, then asked mildly, "But, have you filled out your death certificate?" I was a little irritated. "Sir," I countered briskly, "surely it is obvious that I have not died. How, therefore, can I have filled out the death certificate?"

He had been waiting for this. "And if you have not died, my dear madam," he said, with the sort of patient, understanding smile that might be reserved for conversations with the mildly insane, "then how is it you want to change your life?"

"Ah, but that is just the point," I said, feeling great relief. This was the moment I had been waiting for, to unburden the true nature of my quest at the desk of a sympathetic officer. 'You see, I am tired of my life and want to change it. But the thing is, I want to change it now, I do not want to commit suicide or go through all the mess of catching a disease or being murdered by jealous relatives or accidentally falling down mine shafts – besides, I took the trouble of bribing someone at the first floor Department of Mortality and she assured me that my dossier had not come up for review yet. As I need hardly remind you, the dossier must reach that office three full moons before a death is scheduled, in order that suitable allocations for the next life can be made." I paused for effect. "So what I thought was this: why not change it right now, in mid-life? I want to be rich. I want to be famous. I want to be absolutely indolent. And – I don't want to wait till my next life, I want it now."

He continued to be unimpressed. "Madam," he said, fidgeting daintily with his nose, "as you have stated, this is an illegal request?" He seemed to be asking for my opinion on the proposing of such requests.

"Well, yes," I said breezily, "but I don't care. I feel it can be quite simply arranged. In fact it is so simple that I'm absolutely certain other people must be doing this right now, that it must already be part of your system." I didn't want to come right out into the open and say that, since all government concerns are corrupt, this one must be equally so. I sincerely felt that it was just a question of understanding in what dimension it was corrupt and how the cogs of reincarnation had been realigned to suit the flavour of the corruption. "All that I'm asking is that I, with my lease on life, inhabit the body of someone else, preferably someone rich and comfortable, whose number has come up. Someone whose body is intact and in working condition but whose life has run its course. Don't you see how easily it could be done?"

A blink of light played about the bare rims of the Assistant Registrar's spectacles. "And your body, madam? What will happen to that?"

"Oh come now," I said, my confidence growing. "Surely

it is of little concern – the rich person dies. I discard this body like a sweaty track suit and impinge upon the other one before its mechanism shuts down forever. Perhaps it could be one of those cases of coma in which a person who has been all but pronounced dead, miraculously revives. The only difference would be that instead of the original occupant returning to life there would be – me! So I don't care what you do with my body – keep it in coma perhaps? Loan it out to some soul kicking its heels about waiting to be reborn? To visiting extra-terrestrials?" I had spent my time in the queue fruitfully, I thought, and had actually advanced my scheme to include a scope of operations wider than my petty little life. I had the notion that, if I could only discover the actual process of transferring souls from corpse to new embryo, I could set up a sort of transmigrational banking system.

After all, I reasoned, this was just another government department: therefore there must be some sort of quota system, a waiting list of souls, a roster of lives waiting to be reborn. I imagined that there might even be a regular state-wise system of making allocations of how many lives could be legally issued per month or year or whatever – in fact I was amazed that the family planning programme had not set up permanent headquarters here. What I hoped to offer was in the way of a side attraction; a short trip to life while a soul awaited its legitimate birth. I did not feel any guilt at what I planned to do. If anything, I felt quite virtuous as I thought this might be the ideal way in which to bring home the point that it is really worthwhile to strive for release from the cycle of birth-death-rebirth. I had always felt that the system as I understood it was far too cumbersome: by the time a soul has done with being born, growing to maturity, struggling through childhood traumas and neuroses, the original purpose – that is, of leaving the cycle entirely, by attaining enlightenment – is inevitably lost sight of. It seemed to be so unfair, so undemocratic. Under my system, a soul would be able to experience life without the confusing preamble of childhood and adolescence (especially adolescence) and perhaps, thereby, understand more clearly about the sorts of lives which lead to better results in the next. Maybe these visiting souls could even be trained to be a source of inspiration to their fellows doing time on earth, like freelancing messiahs, perhaps. All in all, I thought I had a fairly wonderful scheme worked out.

And still the Assistant Registrar was unimpressed! "Madam," he said, "do you think no one has considered this subject before?" He knew nothing, of course, of my grand vision, only of the basic request. He did not wait for my response. "So many people have approached us but we have always had to turn them down." He assumed a slightly professorial tone, leaning back and attempting to bring the tips of his fingers together in the classical posture of pedantry, but not succeeding very well because the arms of his chair were too wide apart for him to rest the elbows of his meagre little forelimbs. "Firstly, this is only the Department of Files: we make records, that is all. We have no direct jurisdiction over lives. Secondly ... have you seen the files?"

For the first time, I looked up and around me, to take in the shelves which lined the room. I saw that the shelves were filled with files, then realised with a little start that the shelves were not exactly against the walls of the room, but that they were themselves the walls of the room, that behind them lay the possibility of further such glass-fronted filing cabinets; that the chamber in which they were housed could now be of entirely arbitrary proportions. I got up and went closer to one of the cabinets and saw that the files within were alphabetically marked – they were the same tatty old box files that one sees in bureaucratic concerns around the country, with papers spilling out, edges scuffed and dust-bitten, mouldering under the excrement of generations of spiders. But the alphabets were not all in English. In fact some of them seemed barely human "What are these files?" I asked, knowing that it was expected of me.

"All the births. All the deaths. We record everything," said that sage and prune-like man, with modest satisfaction. "Every birth, every death, every centimetre of every soul's journey along its personal path of release. Do you understand, madam, how many lives and deaths, progressions and regressions, we must be recording?"

"But…" I said, a vague sense of unease setting in, "I thought only people subscribing to a certain highly popular religion – only Hindus, in short – were eligible for rebirth?" I must admit that I had never really given the subject a thought until the moment of seeing the signboard. And then too, I had roughly generalised, thinking it unlikely that the government of one country would be entrusted with the reincarnation of the world's peoples. I just assumed therefore, that the Bureau's operations must be restricted to those people whose religion explictly upheld such a belief.

"According to the propaganda, that is so," said the Assistant Registrar, "But in fact it is not of the least concern to the celestial office. And of course, you realise, madam, that I am not talking of human beings alone, but all living things!" And he smiled suddenly, a frugal, neat-toothed and wrinkle-wreathed smile, because he saw that I was amazed.

"Everything?" I asked, awed in spite of myself.

". . . including plants," he said.

For a few moments, my mind reeled, processing the thought: stag-beetles; crocuses; Eskimos; pangolins; wandering albatrosses; Saint Bernards; mindless strands of seaweed; Bengalis; hammerhead sharks and ruby-throated hummingbirds; microbes and monsters.

"... though we stop short of single celled organisms," he said, as if intercepting the drift of my truncated survey of life. "In fact, even now a case is being fought by an amoeba and will shortly be brought up in Parliament. Depending on that decision, we will change the rule perhaps."

"Why discriminate against amoebas?" I said still a little dazed at the revelation he had made.

"Of course," he said, "because it is not clear that they die. How to issue a death certificate for a life form which simply subdivides," he mused, almost to himself, sucking pensively on a scrap of food caught between his premolars. Obviously, this was the subject of feverish debate, the argument that raised factions and stoked the furnaces of human ire along the tube-lit corridors of the Bureau of Reincarnation. "It is not clear-cut with them," he said. "It will make a nuisance of the filing system. Already we are overworked. The stenotypists have threatened a protest march."

But by this time I had been recalled to the purpose of my visit and the issue at hand. "Meanwhile," I said, breaking into his argumentative reverie, "coming back to me. Consider how simple my case is, compared with that of a hydra or paramecium: here I sit, healthy and plump with life, entirely unlikely to subdivide or encystate. Isn't there any way to grant me my meagre request? Isn't it possible to slip someone a little consideration, grease a willing palm?"

The little man sighed gently and trained his eyes back

on me. "Madam," he said, "that is what I have been trying to explain to you. This is only the office of files, of documented records; I could tell you which lives are eligible for enlightenment, which lives are vacant, which ripe for transfers, which doomed to a thousand rebirths. You could have the whole cosmos opened to you if you wished to know what was going to happen to which life. But the *actual* allocations, the *actual* decisions – " he shrugged poetically, "that is not for us to worry about. That is done at the Transmigration Department."

I snorted at that. "The Transmigration Department! Don't speak to me of transmigration – I think that's just a convenient excuse you people have cooked up to avoid explaining what really goes on here." I was absolutely sure of my ground now because I had repeatedly been assured that my request could be dealt with at the Transmigration Department, but try as I might, I had been unable to find it.

"But yes, madam," said the Assistant Registrar, eyebrows atwitter with the agitation of having to prove his point, "it is on the seventh floor."

"Vicious libel," I said bitterly, "because there is no seventh floor. The stairs stop short at the fifth floor and when you try to climb any further you reach the terrace. I agree, there is some cause for confusion, because there is a mezzanine floor somewhere else and no one seems quite certain just how many floors the building has, but so far I have not had any reason to believe in the existence of a floor above the sixth."

"I am telling you, madam, there is," said the man. A new expression had entered his eyes, a conspiratorial look, as of something overheard in the lavatory. "There *is* a seventh floor, but I will tell you a secret – it is not easy to go there. Permission restricted, secret passwords.

In fact, we ourselves do not know how to go there. We only get the messages and the directives. There is a rumour that some people have found a way to go there, but I cannot tell you myself, I do not know it." A note of embarrassment had crept in. "We have only a small part to play, madam. Keeping records, that is all. The rest we do not know."

A fly nattered by, I felt a tickle in my nose and the storm warnings of an imminent depression. It looked like the end of the road. There are some people who like to hammer on about what they want even when it is obvious that theirs is a hopeless case. Sometimes they even manage to get their way, merely because the other person cannot bear to hear their arguments any longer. Well, I have never been that sort. I will persevere upto a point, but as soon as pursuing my goal requires me to lose my reasonableness I accept that I have been beaten and back down quietly. This point, I felt, had been reached in the Assistant Registrar's office and I resigned myself to the loss of a great expanse of time. I got up to leave and said, "I'll be going then."

In a gesture of courtesy which surprised me, the diminutive officer hopped out of his chair, escorted me to the door of his cubby-hole amidst the filing shelves and held it open for me. As I passed through it, I heard a whisper, the merest breeze of speech: "Find the peon Gopal! He knows something." I turned in astonishment, but the door had closed irrevocably and though I knocked and hammered for ten minutes on it there was no response from within.

I will not document the course of my search for the peon. It seemed I wandered about that miserable building for hours, days or weeks, it was hard to tell. There was little or no variation whatsoever in the routines of the place from one day to the next. The lights remained on continuously and the staff worked non-stop shifts. The innards of the building were labyrinthine and it was rare to catch even so much as a glimpse of the outside world. I gave up searching for the peon at one point, only to find that it was equally impossible to relocate the entrance through which I had discovered this nightmarish place. It was therefore with considerable surprise and relief that, turning a corner at random, I discovered a lonely passageway, innocent of tube lights, with a row of windows down one wall.

The peon sat perched on a window-ledge, etched against the beams of dusty sunlight forcing their way in from between the loose slats of the shutters. He was sitting there, doing nothing at all and looked up languidly as I approached him. I recognised him at once from the descriptions and I lost no time in confronting him with my needs.

"You are Gopal the peon," I said to him. "You know something about the Transmigration Department and how to reach it. I have been looking desperately for that same department but cannot seem to find it." I had thought enough about what I would say to the peon and said it, now, almost easily. "If you can tell me this that I need to know, I will give you whatever of value I have with me now – my four gold bangles, my diamond earrings, my gold ring with the sovereign and, if they are not enough, I can – I can offer myself." Truly, I was desperate.

He looked up with that cynical all-seeing, all-knowing expression of peons who work in the halls of the mighty. With one glance he assayed the worth of my possessions, briefly considered the attractions of my person, weighed the true nature of my quest against his scale of values and made a spot decision. "I'll show you for nothing," he said, and got up to lead the way.

The route was, predictably, circuitous. We went down the deserted corridor, descended a flight of wooden stairs, crossed a fetid latrine crawling with unspeakable life-forms over a small wrought-iron bridge connecting two sections of the building – I had long since ceased to understand what manner of architect had been responsible for this monstrosity, it seemed to have expanded out of control. We passed by kitchens and warehouses, file clerks and laundry women, rooms full of Japanese tourists and bandicoots, rooms filled with windows, rooms empty with pigeons ...

And along the way Gopal spoke to me about my quest. "You want to change your life," said the peon, as easily as if it were a switch in toothpaste brands. "You want to overturn the progression of reincarnation. You want to jump your place in the queue." He shrugged, worldly-wise. "It can be done."

He spoke as one who has learnt to see creation from a slightly remote and favoured position. "As for bribes, there are many ways to make them: sometimes a little incense, sometimes a few flowers, sometimes a handful of gold coins, sometimes a river of blood. They are easily bribed, on the seventh floor," he said, a little contemptuously, "Still," he continued, "they are only a different kind of clerk to the ordinary human ones. They can adjust a life here, a life there, but they cannot change the rules."

"But who can change the rules?" I asked, bewildered. I had thought that the seventh floor held all the answers, but annoyingly and like in any other outsize concern, one could never seem to get to the real epicentre of things, no final resolution to one's curiosity. "What are the rules?"

The slight sense of unease that had first set in at the Assistant Registrar's cubby-hole had, by this time, settled into a compact mass of unhappiness. I knew, as I sprinted to keep up with the peon, that I was swiftly losing my grip on the situation. Running a specialised sort of travel agency for souls or changing your own life is all very well as long as it is under your own control but I was beginning to suspect that I would never really be shown or instructed in the actual process of the transfer. I had imagined some sort of machine, something like a large, friendly computer, with the Bureau's staff acting as its maintenance team. But with every passing second, the chances of ever reaching the machine or ever understanding how to operate it, were growing dimmer. I began to regret having got involved in this thing.

Also, I hated all the information that Gopal was giving me about the seventh floor. Whenever I asked him where the rules were set down and who could change them he would merely smile his dazzling smile and sweep on with his discourse, in the manner of someone who rarely gets a chance to hold forth on his favourite fixation. "Everyone knows they are terribly careless," he said. "One extra digit on the forwarding letter to the Registry of Rebirth and a pious zebra is reborn as a lusty dandelion, saints reborn as coral polyps in the Great Barrier Reef. They play terrible jokes: an incestuous couple reborn as kissing gourami, lovers reborn as Siamese twins, oysters reborn as misers."

"But," I said weakly and plaintively, as we negotiated yet another dark and slimy passage, "Why are you telling me all this? I don't want to know. I don't want to hear about how corrupt they are in heaven and how meaningless it is to struggle on earth and how futile it is to live a decent life. I already know all that. It's within this futile life that I would, at the very least, like to live a rich and comfortable one – by whatever flea-bitten standards we have for such things back in the place where I live. I'm not interested in the larger issues – I just want this life, this one which I know about at this moment, to be vastly improved."

"Yes, yes," he said impatiently, running fleetly up a down-moving escalator, "that's where I am taking you, to the place where you will get a chance to improve your life." And he told me about angels and demons, ghouls and sprites, mountains of human ash, mansions of perfumed ice, pickled crab genitals and the thousand petalled lotus.

A green door, a gust of wind and suddenly we were there at the seventh floor.

I gasped and said, "It's not at all as I expected it to be." But Gopal bustled me through, talking crisply all the time. "What I am going to do is this," he said finally approaching the specific area of my interest. "I am taking you to the – I call it the departure lounge. This is something I discovered for myself. I found the place where it actually happens, the exchange of life essence, from soul to flesh, and flesh back to soul."

I was amazed. "Aren't there any formalities to complete?" I asked, refusing to accept the truth about my situation, at the mercy of the peon. I wanted something reassuring to sign, something to guarantee me my own life back if I weren't satisfied, something to ensure that I wasn't being taken for a fatal ride by a power-hungry underling in an empire whose horizons now seemed to stretch from dawn to dusk. "How do I know you are not fooling me? How do I know you are not dying of cancer and are only awaiting your opportunity to grab my nice healthy body? How do I know you will not loan it out to your friends – perhaps dead friends – for free rides?" My mind had begun to fill with the various obscene and exotic horrors that this bureaucracy, beyond all others, seemed to offer. "How do I know you are who you say you are?"

But it was long past the time for second thoughts. The peon merely smiled lightly and ushered me into a corridor whose walls seemed to curve and melt and cease to hold their substance stable. Immediately and subtly, the atmosphere of an airport was created by a sense of current and urgency around us, by the blandness of the corridor and the impression of hosts of fellow travellers crowding alongside us in patient yet determined strides. I could see no one except Gopal and myself but all around me I could feel the pressure, though not physical, of others. I was frightened then. I could smell them, these fellow travellers: seaweed and nasturtiums, warm cubs, hot butter, the pages of a new book. It was as if each one of them carried its own personal identity in the form of a distinctive scent. I felt arctic waters close about my stomach and my flesh begin to shimmer in an atmosphere dense with metaphysical beings. How do I smell, I wondered within me, what is my scent! Will I ever know it!

"What you have to do is very simple," Gopal was saying, matter of fact as ever, "I will show you where to go. You go there and then you wait, just as you might wait for the next airbus to Cochin. You won't have long to go."

"Just a moment," I said, terror flooding my inner ear. "I had very specific desires about the ways in which I wanted my life changed. What you suggest – I'm not even very sure what you suggest – sounds extremely haphazard. You've not explained anything about how the exchange is to take place, or what choices I am to get or by what means I am to make my selection. You haven't given me forms to fill or tickets to hold on to, or life jackets or airsick pills." The terror had reached my tonsils and was spilling out in little sparks and flashes, leaving a taste like ozone in my mouth. It seemed that the atmosphere around us grew increasingly thick with the passage of souls and I fancied I could feel them eddying irritatedly about me, confused at my physical presence yet fundamentally disinterested, hurrying onward to their embarkation gates. Every so often I would feel one push straight through me, leaving behind it an aftersmell of itself and my fear would increase a hundredfold. I felt the weight of each blood cell as it fled in panic through my arteries and I felt the labour of each separate bronchiole as it processed the heavy air I breathed.

My mind began to fill, slowly, with the red and throbbing manifestation of my own life. Dimly, as if at a distance, I could feel Gopal the peon take my hand and pat it comfortingly and say, "It's so simple: you wait a short space of time and then a moment will come when you will know you have to make your choice. At that moment all you have to do is to wish. Just wish. As you used to on falling stars and rabbits' paws." I clung dumbly to his hand, so friendly and solid in this concourse of odours and spirits and he repeated his advice. I looked at him, or tried to – I could not focus clearly. He had receded from sight, to become a dark figure, vaguely beside me. All around us, the silent traffic of spirits, souls in transit; throbbing in my head, throbbing in my hands and feet, in my blood.

We were almost there. I could see a haze ahead of me, as if the corridor (now barely perceivable in terms of walls and floors) were widening out, then suddenly we were in a vast hall, perhaps, a vast space, blinding white. I shut my eyes and abandoned myself to my terror, now flowing out freely in glowing lines from my ears, nose, eyes and navel.

I could feel my blood, red and hot with life, pounding through the lacework of my veins and arteries I could feel it in my neck and earlobes, across my belly and in the calves of my legs. I could feel, like distinct and terrible drumbeats, the double-clapping thunder of my heart's valves as they powered the life substance across the span of the small, warm and fragile world of my body.

It seemed as if that whole vast hall were filled with this thunder, the thunder of blood and life, the air vibrated with it. The boundaries of my body seemed to have already dissolved into the space around me so that the whole hall and all its spectral beings pulsed in rhythm to my drum-beat. I cannot say that I was truly conscious, but I could still feel Gopal pushing me firmly onwards, disengaging my hand and saying, "Don't worry, I will stay by your side. I will stay by you."

But of course he did not or I think he did not, because after a point my mind vaulted too far out of its normal orbit to know or care much longer. I heard him say, "You need only wait a short while and then you will step out of your own accord and when the moment comes, you will wish."

I had become a live and sparking bundle of fear, so clear and pure that it defined my entire existence. I did what I had to do, without question. Stepping out, I experienced what may have been a short wait or a long one. Then, as Gopal had explained, a moment came and silence fell about me like thunderbolts. I looked around me and meteors scarred and seared my eyes, stars shot away on either side of me like hailstones and my mind reeled with radiance. I felt the mouths of a billion billion billion souls suck me in, assimilate me within their experience, renew themselves upon my life – then breathe me out with a whistling, steaming roar from their billion billion

billion gorges. At that instant I knew I had to make my wish. I wished.

A SECOND'S BLINKING

I looked up and saw the hot and shining sky. I looked down and saw – nothing. Nothing.

I was not there.

Perhaps, if I had had a body then I could have recorded the emotions that I felt at that moment in physical terms: the betrayal, the shock, the foolishness, the self-reproach. But instead, just like the lack of body, there was a lack of any feeling in the place where I would normally have registered emotions.

Already the Bureau, the people in it, the peon and the star-studded place were vanishing like a lazy dream and I would surely have dismissed it as one if it were not for my conspicuous loss of body. I knew then that I had been cheated and been made a spectre of; but I did not feel in the least concerned as I hung suspended in the heavy air of mid-afernoon, people bustling about and through me. I drifted gently around, not caring where I went, sometimes passing through people, sometimes through buildings, sometimes through trees and dogs. I felt like a polite visitor at the art exhibition of a friend, neither moved by nor critical of the array of minds and lives presented to me.

Towards evening I found myself approaching the place where I used to live. I remained dispassionate and allowed the current to take me there of its own accord. I entered through the walls and settled into my own room.

As I sat there, lulled into a calm and peaceful mood by all the familiar artefacts of my distant life, I gradually became aware of a sensation at my feet – I suddenly became aware of my feet, the tingle of flesh and bone against the floor. I looked down to the place where I had been used to find them and felt an odd pleasure as I recognised them thickening slowly into substance.

My feet, my hands, my head and navel, all of these and all that lay between them were, very gently and unhurriedly rematerialising from the void. And in a short space of time I could sense all of myself, from the humblest capillary and hair root, to the muscles powering my heart, the small compact planet of my existence once more bonded together and ticking with its own familiar rhythms. I sat there in the gathering twilight of my room, with the warm thudding comfort of my life marking time within me, without me; and I felt, at that moment, a deep and savage bliss.

THE OTHER WOMAN

Mandodari stirred in her bed of crocus petals. She opened her eyes, sat up and looked around. *Something had changed.* But she could not tell what it was.

She got out of bed, bathed in pigeon's blood, ate a breakfast of dolphin milk curds and stepped out onto her terrace. From the highest level of the great iron palace, she could see the island nation spreading away on all sides like a living carpet: emerald fields fragrant under the sun, coconut palms nodding in the light breeze, peasants bent over and toiling. Then her pet black peacock sprang up onto the parapet wall in front of her and began to dance. He had not done that for many centuries.

Yes!

Something had changed.

But what?

Throwing on a peignoir of silk and opals, she went to find her husband. He was in his apartments, surrounded by glowing wall-charts, speaking with someone on a small device attached to one of his ears and tapping with the fingers of both hands on a flat tablet supported on the back of a slave crouching in front of him. His multiple heads each had their own headsets. He smiled at Mandodari and reached out to pat her rump, but was clearly in no mood to talk. She left him and wandered slowly through the hundreds of rooms of her home, her expression thoughtful.

Her in-laws and co-wives were in residence, but she neither felt like disturbing them nor did she believe any of them would be in a position to answer her question. The brothers-in-law weren't famed for their intellect, the sisters-in-law were fawningly affectionate but could not be trusted to be sincere. And the co-wives? Well, their attention spans extended about as far as their TV remotes and worked only on their own children. Yet even had she known someone who might have been interested in hearing her out, the realization was growing within her that this message, or feeling, or whatever it was, was aimed specifically at her.

She could not remember anything like this having happened before. Her position had always been one of the spouse-in-the-background, the faceless bed-warmer who had less than a walk-on part in the great dramas of the age. If ever she made an appearance, it was as a snivelling nag or noble not-quite-cuckoldee. There were even some dramas in which she had the joyous position of offering counselling services to a husband whose desired mistress remained obstinately unavailable!

Any changes to this unfortunate situation were welcome to her. Harnessing her swans, she made arrangements for an extended journey to the mortal dimension. As the one most likely to benefit from a makeover, she might as well do her own investigation.

☙

She visited shopping malls and amusements parks, stepped into homes and hotels, playgrounds and prisons, factories and sweat-shops. She traversed the diverse regions of the planet and experienced a range of cultures, climates and eco-systems. Eventually, she even found the answer to her question.

But the more she travelled, the more she found herself craving company. Initially she was careful to avoid manifesting herself physically. She told herself that it took too much effort, that she didn't enjoy the sensations of being confined within a simple physical body, that being embedded in time was cumbersome and potentially dangerous. It was the sight of such teeming hordes of mortal beings that fascinated her. There had not been so many of them in the past. When millions of them congregated for parades or riots the sight was sometimes breathtaking. She wasn't sure whether or not she approved. Still there were times when, watching them, she found herself experiencing something very close to envy. Which was surely perverse and bizarre. As a divine being, she should feel nothing but pity or disgust or amusement. Envy was unheard of.

Once, twice, she succumbed to temptation.

By the third time, she had to admit she found it pleasurable. Not that she had anyone to admit this *to*. There was an unspoken belief amongst her fellow-divines that descents into the flesh-dimension were at best an indulgence, at worst a vice. Those who practised regular visitations did so furtively. No records were kept. None she was aware of, at any rate. It was understood that whatever the activities, they should not result in major disruptions of mortal time-space.

She did what she could to be discreet. She took care over her choice of locale, the clothes she wore and the mortal forms she adopted. There were conventions that she was aware of. For instance, it was always best to perform the actual manifestation in secret because of the dismay and confusion it caused amongst mortals. Another one was to avoid assuming a form that would cause alarm or fear. Of course, once solidity had been achieved, she found moving around in the physical dimension immensely cumbersome. Her first two efforts, for instance, had been in the midst of deep forests. Each time, she had been close to mortal habitations, but of the kind where the concerned individuals were so steeped in their beliefs about the spirit world that intelligible conversation was not possible. More than anything else, they recognized her as an immortal and for that reason did not dare to say or do anything that might offend her. But travelling away through these remote regions using unfamiliar mortal equipment towards more habited areas took so long that she became frustrated and returned to her own dimension unfulfilled.

The third time, after intense deliberation, she selected a location of high population density but at a time of low occupancy: a changing room, after closing hours, in a shopping mall in what mortals thought of as the western hemisphere.

It was the dead of night by the time her manifestation was complete. She had done her homework well, she thought: Mandodari chose to appear like a seven-foot tall version of a mortal whose face and figure appeared in huge paintings called billboards, displayed in street-galleries around the world. In her view, this popularity meant that the face was regarded not merely as attractive but also common enough that perhaps many mortals had the same one. She could never have imagined that the pop-rock singer Lady GooGoo's appearance was in some way unique or that for her to appear with no advance publicity in a mall in rural Pennsylvania would constitute a media event on a par with seeing the northern lights over Bangalore.

Of course it was darker than a moonless night in the tiny changing room. The lights and the ventilation were both off. The divine tourist was unclothed, having thought she could help herself to an outfit straight off the clothes racks directly outside the changing rooms. While choosing a clothing store in the mall, however, Mandodari had not paid close attention to the section of the shop in which she had chosen her changing stall. She hurried out of the stall, only to find herself surrounded by miles of racks devoted to tiny frilly dresses, stretchable sleep-suits, socks the size of new-born kittens and endless pairs of woolly booties.

Weak, watery light seeped into the main section of Sear's via skylights, from the neon signs on the exterior of the mall. She was grateful for the illumination, however. She was nervous of using electricity and preferred not having to figure out how to switch things on or off. There was only just enough light to enable her to find her way around the silent, darkened store. She had to assume there was some logic to the way that the merchandize in the store was organized but it was absolutely opaque to her. Clothes racks extended in neat lines in all directions and there were disconcertingly life-like statues poking up from the mass of merchandise, draped in clothes that represented some of the styles and cuts available in that section. But Mandodari had as yet only a rudimentary understanding of mortal languages and certainly no desire to memorize all the hundreds of different scripts available. The signs and labels made no sense to her. She had no choice but to stumble her way around until she was in an area where the clothes looked as if they might fit her.

Her research had shown that most women these days, at least going by their representations in the street-side galleries, wore a combination of leggings and short, tight tops. Once she had found the jeans-section, she removed a pair from its hanger, struggled with the fastenings and then, to her consternation, discovered that they were at least four sizes too small. In the course of the next half hour she discovered exactly how hard it was to find a pair suitable to her size and taste. Some were the right length but too tight in the waist. Some were the right width but were covered in rivets. Others were ripped at the knee. Still more were smothered in zippers and pockets. In the semi-darkness, it was a relief that the colours of the fabric were not obvious, because otherwise that would have been yet another feature to consider.

The plastic hangers on which the clothes were displayed made an extremely annoying tinkling sound as she tried to riffle through them. An extraordinary assortment of paper labels and dangling price tabs had been variously stapled, tacked on, glued and stitched into place on the pants so that she found herself snarling out loud as she tore into them. She spat like an angry cat each time the unfamiliar zippered fastenings caught in her pubic hair when she tried to do them up. Eventually she took to simply ripping them apart when removing them. That was easier than finding the tab of the zip then guiding it down and getting it stuck in the hair yet again.

By the time she heard the sounds of approaching security guards and saw the beams of torchlight stabbing into the depths of the store, she had managed to surround herself with a mountain of discards. It was not in her nature to feel afraid, so when the two uniformed men approached her, she made no effort to hide or run away. Instead she turned towards them, naked, her long blonde hair disshevelled and towering a foot taller than either of them. In her hands was a pair of Levi's Loose 'N' Easy Cargoes ripped to shreds. In her carefully enunciated though archaic Sanskrit, she explained that she was only looking for something suitable to wear and wondered if they would care to help her.

The men began to jibber excitedly while waving their arms about. This caused the light from their torches to career wildly, casting fantastic shadows this way and that across the ceilings and floors of the vast showroom. Mandodari could not follow a word of what they said. Kicking aside a couple of clothes racks that toppled over with a satisfying crash, she strode towards the guards. She had been fully prepared to reward them for their services. Instead of behaving with decorum however, or showing the least respect, the two idiots began shrieking and retreating, like baboons in the presence of a spitting cobra.

Recognizing then that there was no point wasting time, she reached out, grabbed one man in either hand and dashed their heads together. The instant silence was wonderful. Then she sucked out their still-warm blood, dismembered them with clinical precision and ate them slowly and methodically. She started with the limbs, moving onto the squishy but delicious internal organs, ending with the tongue, the eyes and the brains.

Being manifested in a physical body was hard, hungry work.

❦

Basra Dott, the famous television anchor was single. Whenever someone pestered her about her marital status she grinned and said, "Every night I go to bed with eighty million people!" And counting. Her current ratings were so high that she was seriously considering hiring a second security detail for herself. She knew some celebrities who had two lines of defence, one visible and obvious, the other dressed to merge with the crowd while continuing to perform their duties.

Nevertheless, she did not actually live alone. There was a middle-aged couple who looked after her daily needs. Lal cooked and did the grocery shopping while Renu, his wife, did the laundry and the floor swabbing. There was a separate person, a scrawny young girl connected in some way to the local presswallah, who came in once a day to do the dusting, the toilet-cleaning and the garbage clearance. Another two men, both young and interchangeable in terms of height, size and general deportment shared the task of being her drivers. On account of the unpredictable nature of her work and her hours, she could never have less than continuous chauffeuring. Indeed, these two formed part of her security network, having been supplied by the same agency that provided her with a permanent on-site sentry outside her front gate and with bodyguards when she was away at work.

She owned a two-storey private home, in a quiet residential colony with tall, nodding asoka trees along its boundary wall. There were so many individual sentry boxes outside each of the mini-mansions in the colony that the Residents' Association had repeatedly had to turn down suggestions to set up a modest clubhouse for the men. The reason the suggestion could not be entertained was that there was no vacant plot of land available for situating such a facility.

Ms Dott often had house-guests, many of them members of her extended family, some of them staying for several months. However, it so happened that she had just seen off her younger brother and his wife the day before. In the lull before the next visitors arrived a week from today, she enjoyed the luxury of sitting up in bed drinking her first cup of coffee undisturbed. It was brought to her by Renu, who also brought in the stack of newspapers that was delivered to the door. Right beside her she kept her DingleByte, a handheld device that permitted her to watch TV while surfing the net while playing Mahjongg Solitaire, while answering e-mail and sending SMSes. But like so many other public personalities, Ms Dott greatly cherished the few hours of her time when she was truly alone. So the device was switched to silent at night and however much it hummed and flashed and cavorted there on her bedside table, which it did with monotonous predictability, she ignored it and would continue ignoring it until after she'd had her shower and was ready to face the world.

So it was during this glorious lull, while she was still calm and listening to jazz on her room stereo, the coffee cup still warm in her hands and the air conditioner humming sweetly, that with no warning, her DingleByte sprang to life. First there was an ear-shattering screech, such as might be made by a transcontinental airliner revving its engines prior to take-off, then a stranger's face appeared on the device's small, glowing screen. A woman. Her voice scythed through the air as she said, in a peculiar mixture of old and new languages, none of them English, "Good morning! Welcome! I am needful of an audience. I shall come now, yes?" It was not really a question.

Basra was so shocked she had no time to spare on being angry. "Wha-?" she stammered, before instantly recovering her famous poise. "Wait! Who are you?" There was no point asking her how she'd got the number.

If she could have crashed through the silence-barrier on the handheld then obviously she had access to some extremely sophisticated software-overriding capability. That made her instantly a force to reckon with.

By way of an answer, the air above Basra's armchair began to shimmer as if with heat-haze. It would take fifteen minutes for the whole body of her unexpected guest to fully materialize but since she had helpfully arranged for her own head to appear first, she was able to talk within the first minute or so. "I am Mandodari," she said, speaking slowly and sounding each syllable with care. "You is hear of me many times. I will appear on TV show, with your help. It is time to tell my side of the story. But first you must interview me. In exchange for this I am filled your empty womb with half dozen sons." She paused now, as her mid-section made the transition to physicality. "Also, though I am not yet hungry, soon I will be. It will be best to keep some goats ready. De-horned and de-hooved is best, but I am not fussy. And some clothes too. Your room is too cold. What is wrong with it?"

Basra had always been nimble-witted, able to sort within seconds of being shown options between what she *had* to accept about reality and what she could push into place to suit her needs. Even before Mandodari – "Call me Mandy!" – had fully downloaded her mortal frame, Basra had (a) accepted that her guest really was a supernatural entity, (b) had the potential to provide viewer-cocaine for at least a couple of weeks (c) would undoubtedly be a towering pain in the butt. In the short term, the house was big enough to provide space for the goats, Lal and Renu's silence could be bought at the rate of one gold bangle per day, the dusting-maiden would be a problem and would have to be sent away, while the drivers were naturally laconic and would neither notice nor talk about anything they encountered in the course of their work.

That was in the short term. In the long term, well ...

Basra decided to ignore for the moment the knowledge that interviewing an immortal would be fraught with dangers of an otherworldly kind. "All right," she said, when the initial shock had settled down. "Let's get started on why you're here, what it means for you, what it means for our viewers and what it means for our country."

Mandy said, "What it means for *world*. Silly."

The two women were sitting on Basra's patio. The divine was facing out towards the hedge that screened the carefully tended lawn from the common gaze of the street. The seasoned journalist, veteran of four general elections, a woman in her late thirties who had been called everything from "hard-boiled idealist" to "crypto-fascist" faced her guest. She could see her own reflection in the sliding doors of the glass-fronted sitting room: short hair, tawny eyes and the type of smooth, wrinkle-free skin that signalled good health and an even temper. She was attractive in a friendly, street-wise way and her viewers trusted her because she looked like one of them. From where she sat, she could enjoy the play of sunlight falling through the slats of the wooden trellis overhead, the leaves of a healthy bougainvillea poking through, and a back-view of the crimson silk kimono she had given her unexpected guest to wear.

Though at first glance Mandy could pass for human, at second glance it was impossible not to want to recoil from her. It wasn't just that her dimensions were a couple of inches larger than life-size. It was also the peculiar hue of the skin: pearly white – not blue, not brown, not even green – but nacreous, echoing the sea, not the land. It was the hair that was black but with fiery streaks that appeared and disappeared disconcertingly. The eyes that weren't merely dark, but impenetrably so and with no discernible pupils. The mouth was lush and warm and curved upwards in a permanent smile. But when she smiled – which was often – her teeth were all identical, very white and a tad larger than was comfortable. Behind them, flickering just out of view, was a long black tongue.

So she was beautiful, yes. In a repellent way.

She was talking animatedly, holding the gorgeous silk around her full, lush body. "Until two months before," she said, referring to mortal time, "I am invisible. I am waking up and sleeping and waking and sleeping, but there is nothing for me to do. Nothing for me to *be*." She tried to explain what it was like to live outside the four dimensions of the mortal sphere. "We do not die. So there is not wear, not tear. Not today, not tomorrow. Yet also there is morning and evening. There is variation. There is pleasure and failure. My peacock is dancing for me, for instance: he is not do that since the time of my marriage. Which is many mortal centuries past. It is wonderful that I am see him. But I think you is too stupid to understand. You must not try." Her speech was fluent but contained many anomalies of grammar and syntax. Basra could not tell whether her own grasp of Sanskrit was too weak to make sense of her guest's speech or whether the divine's knowledge of mortal language was too outdated.

The thing Mandy most wanted to talk about was of course the answer to the question that had brought her to the physical dimension. "You is not see it, I am sure?" she asked Basra, who shook her head politely, knowing it was expected of her. "I am look for long times, before I did work it out. It is the high court. There is some case about property."

While trying to tease out meanings from the mass of information available in the physical world, she had stumbled upon the internet. Apparently the one really significant technological breakthrough that had occurred since the early days, she said, was the proliferation of electronic media. "I am not idea how it will works," she confessed, "but it is works. My husband is have fast connection. So I am return home to palace, I am go online and am Google my name. And by clicking, clicking, clicking, I am begin to understand what is change, what is happen in some very near months that is make different for every of us. Not just Them – " she meant the royal couple whose names were synonymous with the epic to which she was so intimately connected " – but even me also, even my husband also and all mortals also." She stopped. "What is problem? You is frown."

"Oh!" said Basra as if caught by surprise, though this was just one of her ploys to add a little variety during an interview, the carefully positioned frown. "I was just wondering, you know – you've mentioned your husband several times already – and the fact is, I mean, I hope you'll excuse me if what I ask seems impertinent or ... or ... you know, *rude* – "

" – you is mean his so-called *death*?" cut in Mandy. She held both her hands up with her fingers curled over, making the sign for air-quotes. Apparently she had spent more than enough of her spare time watching mortal television. "Pooh! I am just *told* to you: we is not die. It is like you mortals enjoy playing battles – you is call them sports? – you know, like kicking head made of cow-leather from one side of battlefield to the other, for example, or two men is stand in platform and beating each other – "

According to her, engagements between divines took

a form similar to football, but with less goodwill. "My husband is never agree to lose. He is disgusted, insulted, humiliated. He is always great warrior, he is always great genius, he is invincible. There is no ever doubt he will win." The features of the beautiful face knotted together in a fierce sneer. "Of course he is not die."

"What are you saying?" said Basra, leaning forward with her eyes all agog. She was so practised at feigning emotions in order to get her subjects to talk that she could do it now without even noticing that she was putting it on. It was a shame that all this amazing raw footage was being lost in what was after all only a private conversation. She was recording it, discreetly of course, on her DingleByte, so that she'd have evidence to take to her CEO. But an audio-tape would not have news value. Besides which, she was starting to worry that Mandy's version of events was too far removed from the popular one. "Are you saying that the battle – the one that's been the high point of every recreation of the epic since it was first written up – the battle was *rigged*?"

"Not *happen at all*. You tell me: how else it can be for the immortal warrior to lose? And that too, when his enemy is so small king, so short, so thin and having only one head? Huh! It is a lie, a sham, a nonsense. That is why I am here. To tell the truth. To tell my side. To change the story. At last."

As the divine rambled on, Basra's mind was ticking, ticking, ticking. Eventually, she claimed she needed a break from the information overload. She showed Mandy the room in which the goats were tethered and a few rudiments of using the facilities of a modern home. Then she left for work.

☙❧

A hurried conference was called in the inner sanctum of ENDO-TV. Basra's CEO was a grizzled powerhouse of a man called Ved Mentor, who had been in the news business for over forty years. He and the only other senior news anchor Ornob Gosh listened in silence to what Basra told them. Their expressions morphed from mild amusement, to annoyance at what they believed to be a childish prank, to distaste and finally dismay. They listened to the recorded conversation in grey silence.

Mentor was standing with his back to the room, his hands on his hips, facing towards the picture window that showed him the urban sprawl of South Delhi, a rambunctious jumble of rooftops, satellite dishes and trees, spreading out as far as the eye could see. Several minutes ticked by. He said nothing. Then: "How long can you stall her?"

"A couple of days," said Basra. "A week at most. I don't really know."

Ornob, who was Basra's contemporary in age as well as ambition and fervour, said, "It's interesting how she locates the source of the 'change', as she calls it, to the court case in which an epic hero's birthplace was established." He glanced up at the other two. "I mean, for us here in the so-called 'mortal dimension', it was all about land and settlements, riots and victims, who won, who lost. Meanwhile?" he shook his head and raised his hands towards the ceiling. "Up there? *An entire pantheon stirs to life!*" He ghosted a chuckle. "I don't know about the two of you but I've … I've … never had faith. In anything. Not gods, not devils, not four-leaved clovers. Along comes a court judgement and that's it! The entire game changes! And suddenly we're battling the demon hordes with our little matchstick ideals."

Mentor raised his shoulders high and spread his palms

wide. He was a tall man, clean-shaven, with a square jaw and a quirk of hair that fell over his forehead. "Ornob – I disagree: you *did* believe in something. You believed in the courts and the rule of law. What we have here is the result of the courts' ruling on something that had always remained outside their purview: the verification of a mythological character. Until that point, for those who had faith, that character was as real and as physical as you or I. Those who had faith did not need to know where he was born in order to believe in him. In fact, NOT having a precise spot made it possible to locate him everywhere: on earth as well as in the hearts of the faithful.

"But once the courts mark a spot purporting to be a real birthplace, with a real X on a real map of a real city, ah! That changes everything. The stuff of pure faith is dragged down into the muck of who-said-this and I-said-that." He gestured as he spoke, raising his hands high over his head, then plunging them down, to emphasize his point. "What was once mystical, magical and divine comes tumbling down. And we are left to argue about how many demons can dance on the head of a journalist."

He hauled up the belt of his pants, a familiar mannerism of his. "Basra, for better or worse, that journalist is you. We'll air the broadcast, but I suggest you take a week to prepare for it. There's a Supreme Court decision coming up that could overturn the high court's ruling. The fate of the Universe may depend on how we present our material."

❦

"At my marriage," said Mandodari, looking straight into the cameras as she spoke, "the path to the wedding platform is lit with one hundred living candles. It is a glory sight: one hundred human beings, chained inside iron cages, and set on fire. Our slaves is so happy to die for us. This is how we celebrate. This is how we show we are strong.

"Centuries is pass since that time. Nobody is look in my direction. But here I am now." The full red lips curved up in a feral smile. "My time is come," she said, with no attempt at false humility, as she turned both her hands towards her full body. Though tightly encased within an outfit in green and orange cheetah-spot velour with fluorescent blue organdy flounces at the elbows and knees, there were no unsightly bulges. "I am tell the true story of the war against my people."

Basra Dott drew in a breath, reminding herself to pace her questions carefully. "So ... Mandy," said the famous television anchor, "ever since you made your presence known to me – for which I must tell you, I am extremely flattered – the one question that's been at the top of my mind is, Why now? You've had – literally – centuries in which to make yourself known to the world of ... of ..."

"Mortals," said the divine, nodding her head as if encouraging a child.

"... mortals," repeated Basra, allowing herself a little smile which managed to convey a sense of amazement alongside a dose of judicious skepticism. "So ... why today? Why now? Has something *changed*?"

Mandy blinked and flexed her shoulders. "I am want to set record straight. For instance: my husband is not have ten heads. Why is mortals believe such kind of nonsense? Five is maximum. And it is must be odd number only: one main head and then one or two on sides. Ten heads is means five this side, five that side and nothing in middle! It is total-foolish. But to get back to wedding night ..."

"We'll do that, Mandy, we'll do that," said Basra, "but

first our viewers need to know what brought you here, to the mortal dimension – "

"Is too boring," said the divine. "Wedding night is much more thrill. For example, I am want to show how nonsense it is, this claim that my husband is lose interest in me because of mistress. He cannot! It is all lies of their side. There is not ever any mistress – "

"Who?" interjected Basra.

"You know it is who," said Mandy, her forehead starting to bunch together in a frown. "I am not insult my mouth by speak her rubbish name." Throwing her head back, she howled in a high falsetto, "*Oh she whose perfumed face rivals the full-moon! She who makes the stars tremble with desire!*" For an instant, there was a disturbing flicker in the region of the guest's throat, as if a second mouth gaping open or a curved and toothy beak poking out. "After all, you tell me: why is *I* am here? And not *she?*"

Basra's tawny eyes glittered. "Yes, Mandy, tell our viewers what that reason is …"

"Because," said Mandodari, "because for all this time, I am sitting in background of this so-called big story, feeling this hurt, this pain, this agony in my heart. The whole world is say, Look! Look! Your husband is running after that woman! Look-look – he is catch her! He is bring her to your house, he is feed her honey and dolphin cream! And all this time, all this many, many years, where am I in the picture? Where do I hide my head? Huh! NOWHERE!"

The huge, ugly-beautiful face reared up, seeming to grow livid with the stored memory of this ancient, deathless enmity. "I tell you, it is ALL LIES!! Everything. First lie is, why is they come to forest? To steal, of course!

It is our forest. Second lie is, how is my sister-in-law lose her nose? Because that man and his brother – I will not say they's name – they is see her take bath, they is grow hot, then they is chase-chase-chase, until she is fall. Her nose is break, but still they have fun with her. Third lie is, who is win the war? My husband of course. He is bring army to avenge his sister, and they is chase this man and his brother away. The end! That is whole story. There is no wife and she is not come to forest. At all. She is total imaginary. That is why in final end, she is not even stay with so-called hubby-bubby, but vanish into earth. Hahaha! Big joke. She is imaginary from start to finish."

Basra could see, around the edges of her field of vision that a type of slow pandemonium was in progress. One of the light boys had fainted. The sound recordist had whipped off his headphones. To her right, someone – she couldn't see who exactly – was gesturing. But she nodded, arranging her features in a sympathetic expression and ignored all distraction. "All right, Mandy," she said. "All right. The problem is, we here in the mortal dimension have for centuries been given a completely different version of events – "

"I am know," cut in Mandy. "That is why I am come. To explain. To show the truth. This is an age when womans is free to speak out her heart. This is my heart."

"Yes, yes," said Basra, "but being free to speak isn't the same as being free to lie – "

"I am not lie," said Mandy, starting to look angry.

"And," continued Basra, "in our dimension it isn't enough to just state a fact. In order to believe it, we have to see evidence – "

"Wrong!" cut in the divine at once. "The court is show no evidence of birthplace!" A note of triumph had entered her voice. "They cannot. Is not surprise. We is divine, after all. Neither is we die, *neither is we born ...*"

❦

Back in her bedroom, Mandodari, the wife of the ten-headed demon king settled into her saffron-scented mattress. For all the time she had been away, there had been a hum of unrest and uncertainty. Rumours were flying around of changes and restructuring, of new currents in the flux of reality. And then, just as suddenly as it had begun, the disturbance or irregularity or discontinuity, or whatever it was began to subside. She returned with her swans as if nothing had happened. She told no-one of where she had been and returned to her quarters as if nothing had happened. Her eyes began to close once more. Her time in the mortal dimension was already fading from consciousness. No records had been kept of it, and the unprecedented broadcast that had been aired with such fanfare by ENDO-TV was shown to have been some type of extraordinary scam. No hard copies were made and all references to the interview were erased. Gradually the entire episode passed into the un-memory of forgetting.

But not all change is for the worse.

Even the most transitory incidents leave traces.

On a parapet wall of a vast iron palace, for instance.

A black peacock is dancing.

KHAJURAHO

Carol and Robert Delaney had not planned to visit
the erotic temples at Khajuraho. Their flight to
Kathmandu from Bangkok was diverted to New Delhi
and then cancelled altogether due to political tensions in
the mountain kingdom. The airline gave passengers the
option of remaining one or two nights in India before
being reconnected to their onward destinations.

The Delaneys had three days left on their Asia-Pacific
tour. They were loathe to allow mere politics, of all tedious
reasons, to ruin their careful planning. So they chose to
stay on in India.

The local American Express agent, an Indian who
spoke English surprisingly well, made a number of
suggestions. When he mentioned the temples with the
X-rated sculpture Robert immediately brightened. He'd
heard about them he said, though Carol couldn't imagine
when or where. He'd certainly never mentioned them to
her before. Those two words, "erotic" and "temple", just
didn't go well together, in Carol's view. Then again, as
their tour had shown them, there were almost as many

different views of reaality as there are airline booking clerks. Three weeks of zigzagging around from Easter Island to New Zealand to Australia to Indonesia then Japan and on to Cambodia and Thailand had left her weary of the outlandish, the astonishing and the outright bizarre. She wouldn't have minded something just a tad ordinary or at the very least, famous. That white tomb for instance, the Taj Mahal. Wouldn't that be something?

Robert just went on grinning like a goofy schoolboy, saying he'd set his mind on the weird temples. Carol shrugged and said she didn't care either way. He was six years older than her. She often let him have his way. He'd be retiring soon. He was a tall man, handsome if you ignored the deep ravines creasing his forehead, the pouches under his eyes and the silver-gray hair thinning on the crown of his head. Carol was short, blonde and trim, with the same flat stomach she'd had as a secretary, when she'd joined the firm where she'd met and married her husband. It had been a good match. They had two children, both boys. One was in college, one headed his own software unit. Whatever that meant. Carol didn't ask questions to which she couldn't understand the answers.

The bookings were made. Robert and Carol checked into the nearest Holiday Inn. Early the next morning, they were on their way.

It was a small town, Khajuraho. *Ka-zhoo-ra-ho*. Carol practised saying it out loud and found it wasn't too difficult. Half the reason she had resisted coming to Asia all these years was that she didn't like those impossible names! And now here she was. She'd enjoyed Thailand best so far, names and all. India seemed less easy to like. Maybe it was because they had gotten here out of necessity, not choice. The poverty was more visible. The climate was definitely worse. Then again maybe it only felt that way because their taxi from the airport had not been airconditioned. *Ka-zhoo-ra-ho*. Well, the names were easier. That was something.

Carol often talked out loud in a rolling tide of comments about everything happening around her. Robert had grown used to it. He joked about it sometimes. Called her his Universal Reporter.

The agent suggested spending the entire first day resting in the hotel with perhaps a brief stroll through the market in the evening. The temples, according to him, were best seen at dawn. "It'll be cooler too: the site opens at six. Believe me, once the sun is properly up –" he smiled in a nudge-nudge, wink-wink manner "– it might get *too* hot if you know what I mean!" Robert snickered. Carol ignored the dirty-joke silliness. She didn't mind looking at pornography now and then, just to please Bob, but it was never something she sought out.

She and Robert checked in at the Khajuraho Sheraton and spent the day blobbing out by the swimming pool. In the evening they met the guide, arranged by the hotel, who would take them around the temples. He seemed pleasant enough. He was of medium height, had light skin for an Indian and a warm, sensuous mouth. His English was passable. It wasn't *what* he said but *how* he said it that was difficult to understand, Carol remarked to Robert later. His first name was Rajesh, he said. Carol had to see it spelled out before she would try saying it. *Raahzh-* she said, tentatively. *Raahzh...Esh*. Not bad. She said it a few more times to fix it in her mind.

The couple had a light snack and went to bed. Robert put his arm around Carol, drew her to him and nuzzled her ear, but she patted his hand in an "I'm asleep!" way. He took the hint. After thirty years of marriage, they knew one another's signals.

The next morning the hotel had arranged a taxi to take them to the site. It was just before sunrise. Rajesh was already there. He was carrying a full-length black umbrella with him, tightly furled. *Must be against the sun?* thought Carol. There certainly had not been any talk of rain. Perhaps he was unusually fastidious. He wore a white short-sleeved shirt tucked into his black pants, everything neatly pressed. *Who does his laundry?* wondered Carol. He was so very thin. There was something hungry and underfed about him that suggested chronic loneliness. How much did a tourist guide earn, after all? Enough to support a family? Unlikely.

He greeted them warmly but with reserve. Carol liked that. She preferred foreigners to remain at a decent distance, where she could keep her eye on them. He had already bought the tickets to enter the complex. She guessed they would reimburse him at the end of the day. "Are you ready?" he asked, "Shall we go in?" Rather silly question, all considered, thought Carol. *Maybe he's a little simple-witted?* Perhaps it was just his professional patter.

A part of what they were about to see was visible from outside: tall, tapering structures, pale with dark patches, covered with intense carving. They were perhaps ten storeys high, thrusting straight up into the mauve morning. Carol recognized them as temples from the vaguely similar buildings elsewhere on the tour. In Bali, for instance and in Angkor Wat. She found it to be a complete waste of time to visit such buildings. It was simply ridiculous to think there might be more than one deity, after all. She believed that even the most determined pagan must know, in his secret heart, that he was wrong.

The iron turnstile through which they entered the complex shrieked piteously as it turned on its single metal pin. Within the low boundary walls, they found themselves in a stone courtyard perhaps two football fields in size. Emerald green grass carpeted the earth wherever it was not covered by granite flagstones. The jutting structures were situated atop platforms which were about the same height as Robert's head. There were four temples in clear view but there were other, lesser mounds, suggesting ruins. Along the periphery, forming a continuous boundary, were trees, dark green, seemingly uniform.

Rajesh began. "This group of temples is part of a complex that once numbered 85 altogether. They date from the mid-tenth century to the mid-eleventh. They were built by the Chandella dynasty, that lasted for five centuries before succumbing to ..."

The words pouring effortlessly out of Rajesh rolled right over Carol. She couldn't even pretend an interest. It was all so bleak, so impossibly alien. She looked around, trying to locate even one thing in the surroundings that actually attracted her, but found nothing. In the distance she noticed a group of fellow visitors. Indians. The women wore bright, fluttering saris, their colour a relief from the dreary stones around them. Carol herself wore a thin white GAP tee-shirt, a pair of pale cream Dockers, sensible walking shoes and a floppy hat over her shoulder-length hair. In her Tote she carried her waterbottle, a sun-umbrella, an automatic camera and an emergency bottle of sun-tan lotion. Robert wore khakhi Bermudas, a blue Hawaiian shirt and a bush-hat bought in Sydney.

Now Rajesh was inviting them to come forward. They ascended a flight of stone stairs. Using the spike of his umbrella as a pointer, the guide indicated small details of stonework. Carol wondered what sort of *pourboire* he was going to expect. He certainly knew his stuff, whatever it was. She wondered where the pornography was hidden.

She had told herself she'd let the men go in and gape at it without her. She disliked perversity in any form.

Then they were standing in front of one of the friezes decorating the sides of the platform on which the nearest temple stood. Every surface of every temple was heavily embellished with figures carved in stone. Carol's eyes had grown tired of looking at this type of sculpture, with the inevitable stylized flowers here, the folds of cloth there, the boneless writhing of the limbs, as if all the characters had been, inexplicably, modelled on octopuses. If not for the young man whose services had been engaged for the day, she would certainly have excused herself to go and sit somewhere, while Bob went slowly around, looking for the smut.

Instead, however, she focused on what was directly in front of them. Then her eyes widened. She suddenly realized it wasn't either flowers or mythical beasts she was looking at.

"Here," said Rajesh, flourishing his umbrella, "we see a couple in a typical embrace–typical for Khajuraho, that is." He pronounced it *Kha-j'-RA-ho*. "For the normal people, this type of pose might be on the challenging side. From the ornaments that the lady is wearing, she is clearly a courtesan or a princess. The man clasps her waist while she holds his erect member in her left hand. With his right hand he caresses her breast, gripping the nipple between his thumb and forefinger. With his left hand, he is stimulating her genital area from the rear. His eyes are shut, from which we can guess that he is experiencing the celestial pleasure. Her left limb is raised up and similarly his left limb and each limb is placed on the partner's shoulder. This is so that the man can achieve the greater penetration. On either side of the lady, we can see her two companions and they are smiling. They are giving the couple support. Additionally, this lady on the right is giving herself the stimulation with her left hand."

Nothing in Carol's life so far had prepared her for this moment.

No word described what she felt.

It was not embarrassment or disgust. It was not pain or pleasure. Instead, it was like having her normal, everyday self peeled away like a banana skin, leaving the fruit of her being exposed to the world. In one instant, something she had never known before was revealed with the suddenness of a peal of thunder ringing out of a cloudless sky: that there is, in this world, a cosmic *otherness* that separates one culture from the next. It is so extreme and so outrageous, that even something utterly mundane, such as the act of love, when depicted in an exotic idiom becomes an assault. An assault that could savage her cultural awareness. That could rape her ignorance.

Looking at that sandstone thumb and sandstone forefinger as it pulled on that sandstone nipple, she did not merely see a highly stylized carving, half-life-size and eroded by time but she felt it on her own skin. The ancient lust that animated the sculptor's hand was preserved here intact, in the silent stone. It reached out now, across the centuries, and pawed at her own white Anglo-Saxon flesh, with its rude, ungentle fingers, so that she felt like wincing. She stepped back a pace, covering her own breast involutarily with her own hand, protecting it. Even so, she felt an unholy wetness flood her genital area. She felt scorpions of fury and shame riding up her thighs. She felt the core of her dignity unravelling like a great white snake within her.

Rajesh glanced at Carol, his eyes alert. Robert saw nothing but the statues.

Perhaps the guide had seen reactions of this sort

before. Perhaps he had words to comfort her or at the very least to show her that she was not alone. But in the east, the sun arose abruptly from a bank of clouds that had till that moment been frowning on the horizon. The change of light changed the mood. The three visitors moved on.

With fastidious thoroughness, Rajesh took them to each of the friezes. "Here we see the couple surrounded by ladies. The woman is astride the man. Her both legs are supported by her companions. The man balances on his head. With his each hands, he stimulates the genital organs of the companions on either side." He pointed elsewhere. "Here, again we see a happy couple joined by their companions. And here, we see the lady has taken the man's member in her mouth while another man gives her pleasure from behind. Here, a woman is shown with her eyes shut, signifying the moment of orgasm." He pronounced the word as *or-gaah-z'm*, orientalizing it. "And here we see that the lovers are joined by a lustful horse ... "

He showed them the scorpions riding up the heaving thighs of lustful maidens, signifying rising passion. He showed them maidens writing love letters, their bodies twisted around in positions of longing. Maidens removing thorns from their feet while revealing their pudenda. Maidens washing their hair. Maidens pleasuring other maidens. He showed them everything he could. Only towards the end, did he spare them the details, being content to say, as he pointed with his umbrella, "And here, as you can see, they are *busy* ..."

When the tour was over, the three of them sat at a tiny, open-air café close to the temple enclosure, with tin-topped folding tables and metal folding chairs. It was modest as eateries go, but its excellent situation guaranteed prosperity and clean, hygienic food. Though it was past lunchtime no-one was hungry. Or if they were, they did not admit it. Robert ordered cups of sticky-sweet coffee for the three of them. He had said very little all morning.

Carol fingered the Tote bag on her lap feeling curiously empty. She could not remember the last time she had felt no need to make comments. It was almost unnatural, like ceasing to breathe or to think.

Rajesh seemed relaxed rather than tired. Obviously, he was used to this. It was his livelihood. He allowed a decent interval of time to pass before posing a question of the sort that he must have asked countless times before. It had a practised, well-worn feel to it. "So?" he asked, his tone neither too curious nor too intrusive, "do you have any questions?"

Robert stirred and smiled. He massaged his face with his fingers. Then said, "Well! I guess you pretty much talked all the questions out of us, huh? My gosh. Quite something. I'd never have believed it if I hadn't seen it with my own eyes."

Rajesh turned to Carol. "And what about you, Madam? You are feeling satisfaction?"

Carol had been looking away towards the horizon where an untidy jumble of flat rooftops marked the presence of the village of Khajuraho, distinct from the temple-site. The coffee was untouched after the first sip. She was neither smiling, nor scowling nor doing anything at all with her features. Her lipstick had faded away, leaving her mouth a soft, naked, coral pink.

Her gaze was disconnected as she turned her face towards him and said, "Raj...Esh?" He nodded. "Raj-Esh. You seem very young to be a guide," she said.

It wasn't a question and the young man stammered, trying to respond. "I ... I ..."

"Have you been doing this a long time? One year? Two years?"

Rajesh was not used to answering questions about himself. "No, no," he said, shaking his head from side to side. "Many more years. Too many."

Carol raised her eyebrows. "Oh! How many?"

"Ten," said Rajesh, then pausing to reflect. "Maybe eleven. Yes. Eleven years."

"That *is* a long time," murmured Robert.

"And ... has it always been here? Only here?"

Rajesh nodded.

There was a silence during which three people, each in their different ways, chewed over this information. A young man had spent eleven years, six days a week, describing scenes of fornication in solemn detail, to battalions of snickering tourists. What had this done to him? How had it affected his personal life? What would it do to any human being?

"I see," said Carol, staring at the guide. She felt she was seeing him for the first time. The totality of him, the shiny black hair, the little moustache, the scrawny wrists, the skin stretched like canvas across the bones of his face, the lack of physical bulk. She had never before consciously connected concave cheeks and slender hips with a scarcity of food. "I mean, do you enjoy it?"

He had expressive, heavy-lidded eyes and deep brown irises. "It is a job only," he said. "I am from this area. There is no any work, you see. Only tourism."

Carol continued staring.

"Do you have a family? A wife?"

Ordinarily, she would never dream of asking a stranger such questions. But there was nothing ordinary about this morning. Never in her life had she spent three hours listening to a stranger describe oral, anal and bestial sex in a soft, professorial voice. By opening one door in her social inhibitions, all such doors had yawned open.

Rajesh dropped his eyes. "No," he said. There was a quality of terrible humility in his voice. "That is to say, yes, I was having family but not now. She – my wife, that is – left after two months. She is left to her home." A tiny pause. "One week back, she is left me."

One week?

Carol could not make sense of the information. She knew nothing about this culture or its customs. She had no idea whether abrupt departures were typical for married women or bizarre.

"Why?" she asked. "Why did she leave you?"

Robert said, discomfort colouring his voice, *"Honey – "*

Rajesh glanced up, blinking rapidly, but he answered Carol. "It is very rare, you see. In my country we ... that is, everyone ... we are not having the divorces. Parents will decide who will get married. Then marriage is fixed. Then it is forever. But I ... you see, I ..." He swallowed hard. "I am having some difficulty, you see. It is not easy to describe." He could name each of the three stages by which a scorpion's progress revealed passion: the ankle for teasing, the knee for arousal and the thigh for abandonment. But when it came to the mundane sorrows of conjugal failure, he had no vocabulary.

"My wife is go to her family, saying that she ... that I ..." His lips fluttered with the effort of forming the correct words. "I have never been, you see, with a ... with a ..."

Carol nodded understandingly, prompting him, "... a woman?" She did not especially approve of homosexuality but she liked to think of herself as broadminded.

"With…with *anyone*," said Rajesh.

There could be no response to this. Both Carol and Robert looked away now.

But the effort of confession had calmed the young man. He brightened and changed the subject. "There is one more thing I can show you," he said to the couple. "It is in the Archaeological Museum. It is very close."

The Delaneys would both have preferred to go back to the hotel, to wash up and get ready for the evening flight back to New Delhi. Out of sympathy for the guide however, they agreed to follow him.

In the museum, in a corner with a strong overhead light, was a carved stone panel that had been recovered from one of the ruined temples. It was about one foot high and five feet long.

"Here," said Rajesh, pointing with the tip of his umbrella, "we see the sculptor at work."

Sure enough, there he was, with a chisel in one hand, a mallet in the other.

"Here," pointed Rajesh, "you can see all the life of the world, posing for the sculptor."

Horses and noblemen, dwarves and traders, wives and mistresses, priests and beggars, monkeys, birds and flowers.

"And here," said Rajesh, "you can see one couple is … *busy*."

Entwined and naked, at the far end of the tableau was a pair of lovers. Each figure had one leg raised up and placed on the partner's shoulder. On each face was a miniature version of the ritualized smirk of sexual bliss that was carved onto countless full-size counterparts on the temple walls. The element of parody was unmistakeable.

Now Rajesh was pointing again, back to the figure of the sculptor.

"Look," he said. "Can you see his face?"

The head of the little effigy was not much larger than a chicken's egg.

Carol leaned in close. She stared for several minutes.

But Robert was bored and tired and asked to be told what there was to see.

Carol looked over her shoulder and said, "He's laughing!"

"Who?"

Carol turned her back on her husband, to look at the stone.

She felt a desperate urge to giggle.

Culture, faith and language separated that nameless sculptor from Carol. Yet he had reached across the iron curtain of time to carve a smile upon her living face. Wasn't that a miracle? His personality filled her being. His ancient mirth shook her feet loose from the earth and struck sparks in her hair.

She glanced at Rajesh as she straightened up. He appeared to understand what she felt. Or maybe not. She could never be entirely sure of what he did or didn't understand, but it didn't matter. She strode out of the building, walking ahead of the men, feeling like a helium balloon.

The sunlight outside was, as expected, blinding.

The heat was intense.

The temples thrust upward majestic and priapic, piercing the boundless sky.

HOT DEATH, COLD SOUP

Sally excused herself after showing me to the guest room, saying that we'd talk over lunch. I unpacked my overnight case and arranged my clothes inside the two empty shelves of a voluminous linen cupboard. Then I called my editor in Delhi to tell him that I'd be away for three days in the wilds of northern U.P. He asked me what kind of story it was going to be and I told him I couldn't talk about it yet. He sounded tired. He told me to avoid getting into any scrapes. "We try to report news here," he said, "not create it." Then he wished me luck.

I'm the seniormost woman journalist on the paper, my weekly column is syndicated in four languages and twenty papers around the country and I can turn in a 2000 word lead story in one hour flat. I think he misses me when I'm out on a job.

The house had been designed by Sally's husband, Subhash. It had no windows. It had been built in concentric circles around a courtyard which it enclosed completely. The outer walls overlapped slightly to let in air and light but no glimpse of the outside world. Radial walls cut through the inner curves. All the rooms had contoured furniture fitted immovably into place.

If I could have met Subhash, I would have asked him whether he had been inspired by an onion or a nautilus shell. But I couldn't meet him, because he was dead. That's why I'd come to this little hamlet, this nowhere called Udhampur. Finding the house had been simple: I asked for the "Amriki" Memsahib. Even if I hadn't, though, I would have been led to this house. It was the only house to which I, so obviously urban, would have come. If a spaceship had settled down amidst the wheatfields it could not have looked more outlandish than that house.

I had been invited by Sally, whom I had never met prior to that morning. She had called me at the newspaper to tell me that she was an American married to an Indian who had only just passed away. She needed help urgently. She was planning to commit sati ("Satty", she called it) and the reason she had thought of me to help her was that she had read somewhere that I was a widow. She had thought that I would understand her plight.

She wanted me to come instantly. Noone in her husband's family knew yet that he was dead, she said, adding that she was anxious to "'join him in the next life" before anyone found out her plan. She didn't sound hysterical or even mildly distraught. When I said I would come at once, she wasn't surprised. "Good!" is what she said, and started to give me directions for getting there. She asked me not to tell anybody about it till it was over. Her tone was absolutely matter-of-fact. She may have been discussing the itinerary of a tour with her travel agent. She said she'd pay my expenses there and back, and that of course I would stay in her house.

It was so extraordinary that I didn't pause to think twice. I cancelled everything for three days ahead, sent the peon to buy tickets and left a message on my Significant Other's answering machine to tell him that he would be relieved to hear I was going away for a few days. He was always complaining that I wore him out, poor man. Both my daughters were away in college so I did not need to worry about them. I wondered briefly about confiding in someone at the paper about my assignment, then decided against it. The story was too hot. I was bursting to ask Sally what arrangements she had made, whether she'd already bought the wood, how she imagined she could get away with it.

But when we sat down to lunch, at a table so ornately carved as to make seating uncomfortable, it became clear that questions would have to wait till milady was ready to answer them.

Sally was around seventy, I estimated. She was the type of woman whose adjustment to India includes the wearing of saris. So she wore an organdie sari, pristinely white, icy-crisp. Her hair was dark silver, oiled and plaited into a tight metallic braid that swung stiffly some two inches away from the ram-rod straightness of her back. She wore no jewellery and the vertical slits in her ear-lobes looked faintly obscene. On her forehead was a tiny bindi, like an apology. I supposed it signified that spiritually she was still married. I wondered where her husband's body was kept and marvelled at her composure. Even assuming that she had called me the instant the man had expired, it meant he had been dead at least twenty-six hours. Her plan to "join" him must surely be implemented very soon. Yet there was no urgency in her manner, no sense of the seconds fleeting past.

Her skin, heavily lined, had a desiccated quality, as

if the climate of North India had sucked out whatever there must once have been of her pink-cheeked freshness. She told me that she had married Subhash when she was twenty. They had met in Harvard. "I was the junior assistant librarian there," she said. "He used to come to me to help him find books. He had such beautiful hands! So graceful?" Her voice, with the rolling "r" and the drawl had a way of raising up the ends of sentences to form a chain of rhetorical questions.

There were pictures of Subhash in the drawing room. It was difficult to reconcile the person in the pictures with a library in Harvard – or a romance with a twenty year-old Sally for that matter. They were formal studio portraits, taken by Mohd. Shaqeel and Sons, in Delhi, each inscribed in a quaint and ornate hand. They were near life-size prints, the way that no-one makes them any more. Subhash looked very young, his eyes boring holes into the photographer's plate.

He had that expression of poignant concentration that one sees only in early photographs, when subjects had not yet learnt to flirt with the camera's faithful but cruel eye. His ears stuck out, his skin had the burnished quality of patent leather, his shoulders were pinioned back and he seemed to be holding his breath. In some pictures he wore Traditional Indian Dress and in others he wore Western Three-piece Suit. In either case, he looked as if he were about to leave for a costume party.

He had been a prodigy, a rich landowning villager's boy, so bright that his light had shone all the way to Delhi. Once there, he had easily won scholarships enabling him to cross the caste-polluting seas, his slender bird-boned body arching out across the planet, a tiny human bridge connecting one world and the next, his medieval village with the pre-war US.

"He was a philanthropist," said Sally, her dry face lighting up with reverence. "His whole family depended upon him! You should have seen the way they used to come – his nephews-in-law, his uncles and cousins! And he was a philosopher. He read all the time – he was what we call, back in the US, a polymath. Do you know the word?" She paused to look at me and waited till I nodded. "There wasn't anything he couldn't do if he once put his mind to it!" She sat back again. "He was an industrialist, an engineer, a chemist, a photographer ... He was interested in *everything*! Even astronomy!" She said the word as if expecting that I would find it as astounding as she did.

We had finished lunch by this time and were sitting in the drawing-room which curved around the central courtyard. I could see, through the floor-to-ceiling glass, sparrows hopping about the painstakingly groomed pebbles and boulders of a Zen garden. There were plants in there too, huge leaved and tropical, their glossy edges glinting dangerously in the strong sun, like green scimitars, swords, daggers. Most of the natural light in the house came from this hidden courtyard. It produced the curious effect of living underwater, around a bubble of trapped air.

I wanted to ask Sally what she had thought when she first met Subhash. Had he still looked like the awkward boy of the photographs by the time she met him? Had she been the one to tame his staring eyes, tuck in his ears and fold away his untrimmed edges? Or had he come to her already sanitized and house-broken by the West?

But Sally quickly established that she answered only those questions which were worthwhile according to her private canon. It was not, for instance, worthwhile for me to hear that, for all his skills, what Subhash finally became was a highly successful merchant. I had to discover that for myself, later on. "I never really asked him," is what she said, when I raised the question of how he had afforded himself a twentieth century lifestyle in the midst of seventeenth century rural India. When I expressed amazement at her ignorance, she looked bewildered and said, "But Indian wives never ask their husbands direct questions!" It took several dodgy passes over the subject before she faced it as squarely as she ever would. "He was a finance man," she finally conceded, "a wizard with numbers."

They had had no children. "Oh no!" she said. "How could we?" I stared at her, wondering what she meant. "They would have been such a – a – *distraction*! Such a mess!"

I was surprised. In my experience, her generation of women had held motherhood to be a sacred calling. I found myself wondering what her religious background was and when it would be appropriate to ask. I felt I should wait till her need to speak obsessively about a partner so recently deceased had abated.

"He was a wonderful musician," she was saying, "he played all kinds of instruments – "

"Indian or western?" I asked.

Sally gave me the kind of look which made me realize that living in village India as she had, Sally was perhaps unused to Indians who actually interrupted when a white skin was talking. "Indian instruments," she said finally. "The sitar and tabla. The flute." Then after a bit of a pause, "He studied the harpsichord in America – but the Government wouldn't let him import one so he had to give up on that." Another pause. "And of course he liked to listen to music from all over the world."

There was a silence. I was looking at her just then, so

I remember that there was no change in her expression when she said, "He still enjoys it."

"What?" I said.

"He still enjoys music," said Sally, looking away now, and into the sunlit courtyard. The house was very silent. Outside, the sparrows were hopping manically from rock to rock. "It's always on. There are two, you see – "

I couldn't understand what any of this was. "Two what?"

"Tape-recorders," said Sally.

I still didn't understand. "Tape-recorders?" I repeated.

"It's piped into his room, of course, and because there are two machines, there's never a break in the music," said Sally, as if the subject of her conversation were obvious, "so he doesn't have to do a thing." Faint smile. "Except listen! – And he was always good at that – "

"Just a minute," I said. "Are you talking about your husband?"

She looked at me as if I had asked how to use a flush toilet. A combination of sorrow at my stupidity and embarrassment on behalf of my ignorance. "Yes," she said, nodding vigorously. "Subhash."

I composed my face to show no alarm. "You feel he can hear the music?"

"Of course he can," said Sally. "He enjoys it!" She smiled and bobbed her head.

"How do you know that?" I asked. I didn't smile. I was wondering whether her husband's death had left her seriously deranged.

"Oh he's *always* liked listening to music – " she said, the expression of reverence reappearing.

I said, "No, I meant – how do you know *now* that he's enjoying it?"

Sally frowned, as if concentrating very hard. "We were

very, very close," she said, "unlike you Indian ladies! I know you're brought up to be formal with your husbands ... But we, my husband and I – we had a *wonderful* marriage! There wasn't a thing I didn't know about Subhash – nor he of I!"

I resisted the urge to correct her grammar. "Are you saying that you are still in ... communication with him?"

She opened her eyes very wide. "Of *course* we are!" she said. "Well, *he* can't talk – not really, I mean, poor sweetie – though he does try! But I speak with him all the time! Whenever I can. And when I can't, when I'm not actually there, like right now, you know?, there's always the music playing. I chose it all for him. So it's like me trickling into him through his ears!"

I took a deep breath. "Sally," I said, "where is the body right now?"

She looked ingenuously at me. "Why ... here, in our bedroom, in our bed! When he got sick we had a bed made up, you know, with the pulleys and things? but queen-size, so that I could lie near him too – "

"I need to understand," I said. "The body is in your bedroom, in your bed?"

She wetted her lips before answering and tucked a stray wisp of hair away from her face, as if vaguely embarrassed. "Well...I – I'm sorry, Mrs Sen, but I have some difficulty with..." Then she rearranged herself, starting her statement afresh. "Back where I come from," she said, brightly, "we *never* refer to someone as, you know, a 'body' unless he's actually dead!"

"Do you mean ..." I said, speaking slowly and carefully, "that your husband is *still alive?*"

And she said, nodding as if to a deaf-mute, "Oh yes!"

Just then, one of the servants came to whisper something to Sally which caused her to sprint out of the room without time for excuses. The night nurse was mentioned, drips, oxygen cylinders. But I returned to my room without waiting for her to reappear. There was a buzzing in my ears.

Rummaging in my file, I found the notes I had taken in Delhi, when Sally and I had spoken on the phone. And there it was: "My husband has passed away ... passed away just now ..."

It was extraordinary to think that she had lied outright. I realized with chagrin that I had not doubted Sally's word for even an instant. I had endured the dusty, sooty discomfort of the eight hour trip and one change of train, without having performed the most routine check for authenticity. It was no joy to have to admit to myself that my reason for not doubting her was that she was a foreigner. Even fifty years after Independence, I had found it impossible to resist a direct appeal from a Westerner and an elderly woman at that.

Not only had I sped off without confirming the story, but I had told nobody about it, wanting to hoard it all to myself. Such a fool, such a fool as I felt! I tried to blame it on Sally and the urgency she had put into her voice, but it didn't help. I am the seasoned professional; I am the one who knows only too well just how many publicity-hungry cranks there are who would sell their own right hands if they could get a journalist to record the event. And not just cranks. There are enough sophisticated intellectuals who chase after the transient immortality of the Sunday magazines, as to make one wonder what advantage their extra grey cells have afforded them.

I allowed myself half an hour to tear out my hair strand by strand in contrition. Then I settled down to try and work out what to do next.

I didn't want to slink home empty-handed. That would

merely increase the acreage of time and expense I had already wasted in getting there.

But what kinds of story-options did I have? Now that Subhash was alive, I could conceivably interview him. Quiz him about the relevance of curvilinear architecture in the Indo-Gangetic plains. The decline of Homo Harpsichordensis on the subcontinent. Whatever.

But it was Sally's story that would be the more interesting one, for our readers at least. They're always ravenous for news of aliens in our midst. The very idea of someone choosing to leave the fabled comforts of the First World to live in the rank and sweaty confines of the Third, creates a flush of confidence amongst us. We long to hear how these cultural transplants are getting along, we rejoice at the news that they are healthy and happy, against all odds. And whenever one of them dares to complain, we frown and tell them that they haven't understood India. So, yes, Sally would make a predictably successful human interest story, whether she was planning to commit sati or not.

Had that been just a bizarre hook she had used to lure me to her house in the wilderness? I marvelled now at the chance she had taken. I could so easily have arrived with a battalion of news photographers, video cameras, police and red-faced US embassy officials in hot pursuit! I wondered if she knew that sati, despite its adherents amongst the poor, the ignorant and the politically motivated, did not have the blessings of the Government.

The more I thought about it, the more idiotic my earlier willingness to believe in her stated intention now seemed. Sati is, above all, a public spectacle, a socially sanctioned "gynicide". It demands the presence of an officiating family, bloated with pride at their scion's so-called martyrdom. It requires planning and pomp to avoid becoming just another murder. How would Sally manage any of that? Over the phone anything had seemed possible, but now, having met her, having understood her isolation and lack of visible family, I could see that it had to be beyond her means.

Telling myself that the least I owed myself was an understanding of why she had called me to Udhampur, I spent the rest of the afternoon taking notes about details of interior decor and reading a gory Paul Theroux thriller set in New York.

∞

There were three live-in servants: the cook, Shammi; her husband, the bearer, Salim; and an unnaturally short, dim-witted creature with dark skin and glassy grey eyes called Laxman. He did the cleaning and "top-work".

I didn't see Sally again till dinner. When we were seated, Salim padded silently in from the kitchen, carrying a stoneware tureen. He served me first. When he bent to reveal the soup to me, I saw ice-cubes floating in it. Cold cucumber soup. I detest cold soups. I think they are a perversion of the logic of soup. Like hot ice-cream or egg-free omelettes.

Sally said, "It's cucumber and dahi with just a teensy bit of pudina!" She had the highly mannered style of a mime artist. Each item of the dinner was announced with a fanfare of raised eyebrows and moue of lips, suggesting some thrilling, astounding event.

The soup was followed by two cuts of mutton, each embalmed in coconut chutney and wrapped in individual shrouds of limp banana leaf. Daal in small glass bowls, pickled onions and pappad completed the ill-assorted meal. I found myself wondering why anyone felt constrained to experiment with the tried and tested combinations of Indian food. There was, I felt, an element of cultural arrogance involved. Like interior designers who use cult-objects from New Guinea as lamp bases in fashionable drawing rooms. The underlying logic being that no-one to whom the objects were sacred would ever enter such a drawing room. Or, if they did, would be too intimidated to protest.

The dining table had an ornamental skirting which extended so far down from its edge that a diner's knees were effectively clamped into position, either uncomfortably apart or squeezed together between hard, projecting coils of carved rosewood. It was like a very genteel version of prison stocks.

Perhaps noticing my discomfort, Sally rapped her knuckles on the wood and said, "Isn't this a *wonderful* table? Subhash found it! You should have *seen* it when he had it delivered! Such a mess? All the legs were off and it was covered in some kind of white *muck* – I don't know *how* he saw through it all – "

I smiled sourly. "It's not very comfortable though, is it?"

Sally's pale eyebrows touched the ceiling in disbelief. "You don't find it comfortable? My *goodness!* You must be the *only one!* All our guests have always just *loved* it!" She had been nibbling delicately at her pappad, with her lips drawn back from her teeth, using only her incisors. I am not sure why this should have produced such a charge of irritation in me, but it provoked me into lancing the boil of composure which had kept both of us pretending that my presence at her table was a commonplace occurrence. "Sally," I said, putting down my fork, having just despatched the mutton. "I think you need to explain something to me."

She cocked her head to one side. "Oh?" she said.

"In your conversation with me on the phone, in Delhi," I said, "you made it clear that your ... that Subhash had, ah, passed away. Why did you do that?"

She widened her eyes out in the way she did when she wanted to convey an emotion set to maximum strength. "Because he *had* passed away!" she said.

"I see," I said. "And then he came back alive, did he?"

"That's it," she said, her face radiating light. "He couldn't *bear* to leave me!"

"Sally," I said, "I find that a little hard to believe – " However, even as the words left my mouth, I knew they had been a mistake.

Sally's face fluoresced with pride. "Well, as I told you, Mrs Sen, Subhash was a – *is* a – very special man – "

"Of course," I said, "but surely – "

"We held a mirror to his mouth and it didn't mist up, not even a little bit – " she said.

"What is he suffering from?" I asked, changing tack.

She simpered, "Oh he's not *suffering,* Mrs Sen! We have pain-killers to take care of him!"

"No, I meant, what *disease* is he suffering from?"

"It's not a disease – " she said in her slow, deliberate way. "It's a *condition.* That's what the doctor told me. He said, the cells multiply on their own, just like humans or, you know, any other creatures which multiply ... and sometimes they like the body they're in so much that they multiply *real fast* – and that doesn't do *us* any good, or our bodies, anyhow – "

"You mean – it's ... cancer?"

"Well," she said, "it's a *form* of cancer. It's in the intestine – you know – " she made a coiling motion in the air " – the big snake-like thing in our tummies – "

"Yes! I know what intestines are!" I said, annoyed to

notice that I was starting to nod too. "All right. He has cancer! So when he lost consciousness – "

"He didn't lose consciousness, Mrs Sen! He died! The *nurse* said he died – "

I took a deep breath. "Okay. Let's even accept that he died. But are you telling me, Sally, that your husband passed away – and the first thing you did was to grab the phone and call me? You found my telephone number and everything – all in the space of the few moments during which he was ... declared dead?"

Now she shook her head from side to side, a quick fluttering motion. "Oh no-o-o! I had your number long before he died. I'd been worrying about what to do, you see and I – "

"But when you called me was he – conscious?"

"I've just told you, Mrs Sen, he was *dead*!" There was an air of triumph. "He didn't have a *pulse*. He wasn't *breathing*. He –"

"All right!" I said, "just tell me – how *long* did that condition last?"

She paused a nanosecond, considering her answer. "Well," she said, carefully, "... 'course, as soon as I saw he had died, I – I – flew to the telephone – and – and – I called you, like I said – "

"Sally," I said, "I don't believe you!" The walls seemed to shudder slightly. "I don't believe *anyone* would dash to call a complete stranger, the instant the nurse tells her that her husband has died!" I leaned forward. "Maybe he did have a near-death episode – but I'm willing to bet that when you called me, he had already revived from it." I took a deep breath. "You knew I wouldn't come unless you said he was dead-and you're right! I wouldn't have dropped everything to rush right over if I hadn't believed there was a real story here. But okay. I'm here now. And your husband's still alive and maybe I've wasted a lot of time. But let's be honest with one another, please! At the time you called me, Subhash was alive – and you had some reason for wanting me to come which you didn't want to state over the phone – "

She grew still. Her animated expressions dropped away like plaster masks, revealing a quite different face underneath. Gaunt and pinched. "We all have to make our plans, Mrs Sen," she began.

"And please," I said, interrupting her, "call me by my first name! Everyone knows me as Shona – "

" – and I had made mine," she continued, implacably. "I made them at the time that the doctor explained to me that Subhash might not survive. I made them more than three years ago – "

"Did they include me, three years ago?"

"No," she said, coolly. "But that's when I started to read the magazines and newspapers – Subhash gets them from all over, you know, he was a great one for the newspapers – at one time we used even to get the *Herald Tribune* – 'course, it came ten days late to Udhampur – "

"But what were you looking for?"

She concentrated inwards. "I was looking for someone who would help me in the proper way. An Indian woman, but someone who would speak English, someone who would understand – "

"Understand *what*, Sally?"

She sighed. "Well ... I just thought ... if I found a woman who had lost her husband ... someone who must also have longed to join him on his last journey ..."

"Sally – " I said, "Sally – women *don't* long to join their husbands – "

"Oh yes they do!" she reared up. "You read about it in

the papers every *day* practically – how they want to jump into the fires, how the police struggle to stop them – "

"That's not true!" I said. "In the last ten years, it's happened only once or twice and then, only when they were forced by their relatives!"

"No!" she said, "You're wrong!" She spanked the surface of the table smartly for emphasis. "I bet you – if a survey was done, almost *any* woman would prefer death to widowhood!"

Her voice seemed to echo right around the house. I felt momentarily that I was in the presence of some elmental force. Woman Rampant With Dying Husband.

"Well, *I* didn't!" I said, harshly. "When *my* husband had his heart attack the last thing I wanted was to die with him – "

She had started to shake her head, from the opening words of my statement. She was smirking in a conspiratorial way, "Oh come now, Mrs Sen! You've just allowed yourself to be brain-washed!"

I wanted to hit her.

I don't think of myself as a feminist. I belong to the generation before the movement took to the streets and the market-place. But in the face of Sally's gloating conservatism, I felt like a one-person shock troop. I felt her very presence, the very fact of her existence, was a threat to all that I stood for, the freedoms I had come to recognize and appreciate as my right. It maddened me that she should choose to flaunt as jewellery, the very chains that have bound and curtailed the lives of so many women in centuries past.

"Let me finish my statement, Sally," I said, keeping my voice as reasonable as possible. I wanted the logic of what I said to come through, not the emotion. "I was going to tell you that I was actually delighted when my husband died. I wanted to dance on his ashes! I felt released! I felt unbound – !"

She cut in quickly, "Well maybe you weren't lucky enough to have a happy marriage, Mrs Sen?"

I said, "I was married at eighteen to a man twenty years my senior, who drank himself to death and left me with two small daughters – "

A pitying leer now appeared. "Oh, *that* explains *everything!*" she said. "*Poor* you! How *sad*!" She shook her head from side to side and clucked. "A good marriage is the best thing in the world for a woman! – and the *worst* thing, is an unhappy one. That's too bad! Well – then. You *can't* understand, can you?"

She had skewered me on my own rhetoric. I wriggled grimly on the spit. "I can understand a good relationship," I said, "and the value of a man's company if that's what you mean – "

"You mean – you remarried?" With her head cocked.

"No, I – "

"Oh well," she said, sweeping all argument aside airily, "then you just don't *know*, do you? Because there's really nothing to compare with a *marriage* – all these *other flings* that some women have these days, they're really nothing, you know, they're just *a joke* – "

"Sally – I'm actually involved with a man right now," I said, praying that I would never have to stand by my next few statements in a court of law. My friend is a man so reserved that he would choose castration before any public exhibition of his private life. "We have a wonderful relationship – "

She lifted a shoulder and a lip in naked disdain. I was fascinated by this quality of nakedness. This elaborate pantomime which I had seen previously only in American soap operas. "So why doesn't he marry you then, if it's all so wonderful?"

"It's me – it's I who don't want to marry him," I said, "because I don't believe in the institution – " But I knew it was useless.

She allowed herself a little nod. A neat summation. "Men like to have their freedom, honey!" she said. "It's a law of nature!"

"Sally," I said, keen to change the subject, "let's get back to why you called me here, me specifically – "

She was still glowing slightly from her last remarks. "Well," she said. "I talked to a few ladies before you, on the phone, you know? Without really saying why. But none of them – oh, I don't know, Mrs Sen! None of them seemed right."

Salim came in to clear the dinner dishes away. "And I did?" I said. "Just another name you'd read in the newspapers?"

She gazed inward before answering. "I was looking for someone who had a sense of style ... *and* someone who had lost her own husband!" She looked up at me, her masks once more in place. "I don't want to be just any old Satty, Mrs Sen! I want to be a Satty who will stand as an example for years and years ahead! You see? So I wanted a lady with me who would understand what it means to do something well, something beautiful and perfect- like in the West!" She was smiling. "And ... and ... I thought about it, I planned it, but I didn't really get panicked until just a couple of months ago. Silly me! But up until then, *He* could talk. And I could discuss everything with him – "

"Even this?" I interrupted.

That blank look again, as if I had said something

disgusting or objectionable. "Hhhoh – *yes*! I used to discuss *everything* with him! – "

I asked, "Was it your idea? The sati, I mean?"

"It was *our* idea!"

I shrugged. "It's an extreme step to take – "

"It is *not*!" she said, flashing. "I'm telling you – to those of us who know what a good marriage is, there is *no better choice*!" Two spots of heightened colour appeared on her powdery cheeks. "From – from the *moment* I knew that there was even a *chance* that Subhash might – you know, *pass* on before me ... it's been the *only thing* I've had, to hold on to. That I wouldn't have to endure the lonely years ahead without Him! That there was a way *out*!"

I said, "Sally – do you realize that it isn't legal? To commit sati?"

Salim appeared with the pudding. China grass. I loathe China grass yet had to admire its presentation this time. We had each been given a perfect little rosette, de-molded onto a tiny glass plate, with two fragile wine biscuits alongside.

She waited before answering me, allowing the daintiness of the pudding to calm and soothe her. Then. "What exactly do you mean, Mrs Sen?" Her voice was cold, cold. "Where is the question of ... *legality*?"

"Committing sati is a crime," I said. "You won't be able to just get up onto the pyre with your husband, it isn't that simple."

Her voice was like a serpent's tongue, flickering. "What did I call you here for, Mrs Sen?" She was staring down at her plate, her hands coiled into her lap. "Didn't I make it clear? When we talked on the phone? That you were to *assist* me? That you were to help me with the details?"

It was my turn to stall, teasing out an opal fragment of

the pudding with a tiny spoon designed for people whose lips had scalloped edges, before answering. "Yes, Sally," I said presently. "You did make that clear – but I couldn't believe that you really planned to do it...." I finished, sounding lame even to my ears. What I meant was that I didn't believe she understood the implications of what she had planned.

Her eyes had gone opaque.

I quirked a glance at her. "I mean – surely you guessed that I would try to argue you out of it?" She did not answer. "That – that I might have my own views?"

Her mouth convulsed. It was a couple of seconds before she could get any words out. "Views? *Views?* Mrs Sen – we explicitly *agreed* on the phone – you gave me your *word* that you'd help me!"

"I certainly did *not*!" I said. "I was very careful to avoid doing that. I never actually agreed to help you – "

"But you let me think you would!"

" – Just like you let me think your husband was dead!" I countered, tranquilly.

Her hands fluttered like a pair of agitated birds now, released from the cage of her lap. To her mouth, to the table mat, to her hair. She had gone pale again. "Why did you come, then?" she gasped out, suddenly. Two commas of angry red appeared at her nostrils, framing her nose. "If you didn't plan to help? Don't you understand? I can't do it all on my own! I must have someone with me to ... to ... do the last few things! But that's all I want! No advice, no argument, no – *opinions*!"

The polyp of China grass slithered coldly down my gullet. "I came because I ... I felt that someone in your position is badly in need of – " I groped for a word " – guidance. I thought that you had been suddenly bereaved and were all alone in India. I was sure you were confused and – "

She bent to it like a striking cobra. 'You thought I was *mad*!" The last word was practically a shriek. Her face was now parti-colored, her mouth distorted with anger.

"Well ..." I said, cautiously, "well ... I thought – it would have been quite natural if you were ... disturbed." I hacked at the rosette of pudding, to steady my nerves. I made four irregular sections so that I could swallow each one whole. "I *do* think anyone who wants to die on her husband's funeral pyre is ... confused," I said, "and I thought – "

She was nodding her head fast and her breath was jerky. "Yes ... Yes ... *I* know what you thought! You Indians are all the same! Deceitful! Sneaky! Oh yes! Now I see your type! I should have known it from the start – but I was desperate! I had no choice! And you thought you'd exploit me! You thought you'd come here and snuffle up some hot gossip and run back with it and ... and blurt it out to the *world*! – "

Isn't it astonishing the number of people who are certain that the entire planet is panting for news of them? "Well, Sally – " I said, "if you were actually preparing to commit sati, I grant you, the world might be interested. But instead, you've called me here, imagining that I've nothing better to do than to report on a semi-conscious husband in rural U.P. – "

She threw down her serviette. "That's quite enough, Mrs Sen! Finish your dessert and I'll have Laxman fetch a tonga for you – you'll spend the rest of the night in the Railway Waiting Hall – the bathroom has glazed tiles – "

It was my turn to stare at her in supercilious amazement. 'You *must* be joking, Sally! I'm not planning to leave!"

"Mrs Sen – after *deceiving* me like this! – Really! – The *cheek* of you! And eating my food! – I'm *ordering* you to *leave*! I don't want you in my house!"

"I see! – And what about the time and money I've spent, following up on *your* little deceit? About your husband's death, I mean."

She had closed shop. "I am not prepared to speak to you any further," she said.

"Yes, but I *am*. You haven't answered me. Who is to pay for my expenses getting here? – "

"What is the amount? I'll have Salim deliver it to you in the morning – "

I said, "Sally – I am *not* leaving!"

Her face was rigid. "Well then. I'll have to call the police."

"You do that," I said, "and I guarantee you'll have the entire police force of North India around your house by lunch time – don't forget: what you want to do isn't legal!" I had finished my pudding by now. "Who do you think I *am*, Sally? Some little cub reporter with a leaking pen? What gave you the right to mislead me about your husband's – "

"I tell you he was DEAD!" she screamed, suddenly. The force with which she expelled the words brought her to her feet, bending over the table towards me. "Gone! Forever! I didn't think I had any time! I thought I'd have to move as fast as possible! Before anyone came, before he was taken away, before … before …" She began to jerk and shudder, sobbing. I've never seen tears like hers. Her face was close to mine and I could see them, leaping out from between her eyelids, jet-propelled by her anguish. Her face was like a Noh mask, her lips drawn back from her teeth in a tragic snarl and it was seconds before she could gain enough control over them to speak. "Before his family came to turn me into a … a … a …" her whole frame was shuddering and her mouth, disobedient to her will, contorted to form the word, "WIDOW!"

I thought she was about to throw up. Holding her hand to her mouth she made a low guttural sound, as if her vocal cords were in convulsion and ran out of the room. She vanished beyond one of the curving corridors, still spurting tears. I continued sitting at the table, as Salim and then Shammi cleared things away. They affected to be automatons who had seen and heard nothing, but I could feel their tension. Salim kept dropping cutlery and I could hear the two of them speaking in low voices once they were no longer in my presence.

When Salim came back into the dining room, I asked for tea at seven o'clock the next morning and went to my bedroom.

∽

I slept well and when I awoke it was to the sound of birds chirping. Cool grey light welled into the room from a walk-through window which opened onto a charming little rockery. It had obviously been created just so that the room and its adjoining bathroom had access to fresh air and light without being exposed to the world beyond these womb-like walls.

It was late enough in the year to be very fresh outside, when I stepped through the window. My skin prickled deliciously. Looking up at the irregular quadrilateral formed by the pebbled walls I still couldn't decide whether I approved of the design of the house. But there was a certain guilty pleasure in being able to stand under the open sky completely naked, secure in the belief that no-one could see me!

It was eight by the time I left my room. The house was silent. The dining table had been set for breakfast, two places. I sat down, took a banana from the fruit bowl and ate it, wondering what Sally's move would be. I was relieved that we had had it out, the night before. And at the same time, I felt a little abashed, a little cruel.

I could see the headlines: *American Woman Prepares To Join Husband On Funeral Pyre! Attempt foiled by Police! Feminists Up In Arms!* Yet in the clean light of morning the raw torment of Sally's final words touched something in me. I couldn't agree with it and yet ....

And yet.

She had lived all her adult life in a universe lit by just one star: Subhash. How was I to judge her, I who belonged under a crowded sky? How could I know the desolation that must have overtaken her when she understood that her potentiator, her radiant heater, her solitary sun, lay dying?

Sally appeared so silently that I didn't notice her till she drew her chair back to sit down. She didn't look at me. She didn't look anywhere. If possible, her face was even more frigidly white than before. Her pupils had contracted to needle-points. She didn't move towards the covered dish at her place or to her glass of mosambi juice. She just sat.

She was wearing a loose white kimono over a floor-length nightie. Her hair, though still neat, seemed not to have been replaited from the day before. As the silence extended, my mind began to race about like a rabbit in a room full of caged, baying hounds, as I tried to formulate suitable conversational gambits. I even considered apologizing and leaving meekly. But she pre-empted me.

"He's sinking fast," is what she said, finally. "The night-nurse knows the signs – there's fever and restlessness, the feet and hands swell – she says it could be a matter of hours. 'Course, she's gone home now and the day nurse, well – her name's Juliet – they're Christian girls, you know? – she's not so experienced, she's young, I think, so she's seen less than the other one – "

It took me a few seconds to understand from the dull monotone issuing from Sally that she was not going to refer to the previous night's altercation at all. I was speechless. It was the perfect solution. Me still in Udhampur, Sally still in charge of the situation. And the simple device? Total amnesia.

"... he was breathing sort of steadily, and then I said to Juliet, 'Have you got a swab ready? I think I'll just take a look at that sore on his' – "

I said, "Sally – what about last night?"

Her head jerked up. She looked at me, but seemed not to really see me. Her mouth groped for words. She said, "That's what I'm *telling* you about – last night – "

I shook my head. "No, Sally – I meant, what about *our* conversation of last night?" She looked blank. "You know ... about my reasons for coming to Udhampur? Your reasons for having me here? Don't you remember?" It was bizarre. I was almost pleading. "Don't you remember you told me to leave this house?"

Her eyes were wide open and her eyebrows were at the quarter-way mark, between "astonished" and "bewildered". "Oohhh ... that's right," she said, without much conviction. "*You* were here at dinner. I was filling in my diary, this morning – and you know – I just *couldn't* think *who*'d been with me at the table! – " She was smiling now, wide but with a touch of uncertainty. "Isn't that shocking?"

Well, if it was a performance it was an award-winning one. And it accomplished her purpose so well that my only course lay in shrugging the whole thing away, forced to accept that I had been reduced to a faint hum of random noise on the compact disk of Sally's life! It certainly wasn't a role that I was used to playing. But she seemed so genuinely befuddled and helpless that I felt sorry for her.

There was a sudden pattering sound, then the nurse Juliet appeared.

"Madam!" she said, "please, you come – " It was astonishing how fast Sally moved when she wanted to. In a twinkling, they were out of sight. I left my half-drunk coffee cup in mid-air and ran in the direction they had gone.

I hadn't been in that quadrant of the house before. Sally and Juliet were nowhere. The corridor curved silently along then abruptly admitted a door. It was closed. I opened it.

A large room, brightly lit. Salim, Shammi, Laxman were all there. Sally herself was at the epi-centre and Juliet too, with a thin weedy looking woman, an ayah. The room was clumsy with equipment. The bed was vast, just as Sally had described it, the kind that can be folded in three sections, or rotated around its central axis. A glucose-drip stand dangled awkwardly to one side. A cylinder of oxygen was being used just now, while Sally, Juliet and the ayah fussed with it. Trolleys were parked at strategic locations, one piled with kidney dishes, another spilling over with hypodermic needle packets and yet another stacked solid with cassettes and books. At the foot of the bed was a trolley bearing a television. The piped music was tinkling on, bright and irrelevant.

And then, Subhash.

He was naked, skeletal and bound together by thick blue cords. I thought they were holding his bones together, those cords. Then I realized they were veins. His skin, so dark in the photographs, now looked like shiny parchment. There was no flesh. At every joint, loose skin lay in bruise-brown folds like bunched drapery. The abdomen was a bowl-like depression in which the shrunken organs bumped up like furniture under dust-sheets. In the chasm between his wasted thighs, the genitals flopped, flaccid and meaningless, dusky flounces. There was no hair. Transparent tubes carried coloured fluids into and out of him, with unseemly alacrity.

Tacked onto this skeletal frame were the head, the hands and the feet. I could not see his face at all, because of the oxygen mask. The extremities had swollen, looking obscenely plump. And then the ribs. I've kept them till the last.

Expanding ... contracting, expanding ... contracting, like some huge, crouching bird, shackled by the earth, shackled by life. Its wings were tied down, shuddering helplessly against their bonds. Unable to soar. A tired quality to the struggle. The bird was tired. It was losing the will to struggle. Soon it would drop down, defeated.

I shut the door again. No-one had noticed me.

I walked slowly back to the dining room, breathing with deliberate care. As if trying to avoid hyper-ventilating. No question of interviewing Subhash now, I thought.

Seeing him, the bed, the music system, the nurse, had over-turned my incredulity instantly. I no longer had the slightest doubt that Sally meant to do as she had promised on the telephone. The moment Subhash died, she would swing into action.

That meant that I had to move fast, move immediately to report the situation to my newspaper. The longer I delayed doing that, the more I would implicate myself in her actions, if she actually managed to achieve her ends.

In a sense, it didn't matter whether or not she succeeded. From the moment Sally's story entered the media reactor, it would mushroom across the world's news networks.

Her intention alone, the sheer spectacle of her albino silhouette on her husband's funeral pyre would be sensational. I could already hear the motorized shutters of the press cameras, chattering ferociously, vying for the award-winning frame. And oh, what it would do for the pro-sati lobbyists around the country! What a boon from the gods of media heaven! What a bludgeon with which to belabour widows, young and old, who were less willing to follow her example!

I won't pretend that discretion is my normal diet. I came to Udhampur on the spoor of what promised to be a big kill and if someone had spoken to me about repercussions then, I would have laughed their contentions aside. Journalists can't afford to worry about repercussions, I would have said. We assume that our ends justify our means, as we stampede towards a banner headline. Never mind the blood puddling in our tracks. Never mind the thin screams of victims trampled underfoot.

But Sally had been too efficient. She had called me early enough that I had had time to reflect. Time to imagine the long shadow that would dangle from the cursor of my computer's screen if I chose to file the report.

Sitting once more at that monstrous dining table, drawing what warmth I could from my coffee-cup, I asked myself a difficult question: should I suppress the story?

Twelve years on the news desk screamed out at me, "No!" But I silenced them.

I tried to look at the option for what it was. Walking away wouldn't achieve much by itself. There would be nothing to stop Sally from whipping around and calling someone else. Someone whose career might depend on being the first to by-line a story like this one. She must have had at least three failsafe options in case I didn't match up to her expectations.

That meant I had to be willing not only to suppress the story, but to shove a spoke in Sally's entire plan. Visions of pyre-side combat arose in my head, or of keeping Sally confined while disposing of Subhash's body and of having to contend with the hostile reaction of the servants. Of creating so much pandemonium that the police would be called in anyway, thus negating the whole purpose of my effort.

My conscience wrestled with my common sense. Just then, Laxman emerged from the corridor and crossed the room, not glancing at me. He seemed like a wind-up toy, the way he moved around, a piece of human clockwork. Or rather, not human at all, because the normal response to seeing another member of one's species is to acknowledge its presence. Whereas he had walked past me, glassy-eyed.

I told myself that I needed to get out of the house. I needed to stand at a short distance, to see things in perspective. And to find the cremation site perhaps.

I believed that it had to be somewhere on the premises. From everything else I had seen, Sally wasn't one to leave much to chance. A public cremation would involve too many variables. So it had to be here, it had to be as cosy and accessible as a private swimming pool.

Going to the front door, I turned the latch and stepped outdoors. Fresh air and fathomless sky! I felt reassured. I remember wondering, as I crossed the threshold, whether I would have trouble getting back in. But the sunshine was too inviting. Pulling the door shut behind me, I went forward.

The compound was girdled by high walls, whose buckle was a black sheet-metal gate. I went to it with the intention of taking a quick peek outside but by the time I had actually reached it, the spirit of adventure had a firm grip on me. I left the compound and walked a short distance up the dirt road to the tarred highway. There was a tonga already hunched and waiting at the corner. I took it to be a good omen and stepped up into it.

The soft green velvet of the winter wheat crop clothed the fields on either side, their flatness broken here and there by stunted trees and diminutive pump-houses. There was a clean smell of dung in the air. We set off. Sitting next to the tonga driver was a little boy wearing a cobalt blue shirt. He spent the whole journey looking over his shoulder at me. He didn't smile. After a while, I stopped looking at him.

In half an hour, we had reached Udhampur, a town the colour of flies and fatigue. It was as crammed full of people as the surrounding flatness was empty of them. Cycle-rickshaws tringled their bells, heavy-browed bulls ambled about. I saw a dog so covered in sores that it looked like a piece of flayed meat walking around. No-one else looked at it.

I got down from the tonga and told the man to wait. I walked in to the bazaar and wandered slowly from shop to shop. Most of the stores were built so that a flight of three high steps led in through a pair of narrow folding doors to an unlit interior. I went into a cloth store and looked at the virulent colours of the printed textiles. Two ladies came in behind me and bought ten metres of black nylon. I felt painfully conspicuous in my orange border sari, my arm-load of silver bangles, the rupee-sized tikka on my forehead and brilliant pink Kulu shawl. I felt like an apparition from another dimension. I wanted to tie back my bush of defiantly greying hair, I wanted to shrink down from my five-foot seven, tuck in my middle-aged flab and become unremarkable. I felt people staring at me in the unabashed way that I might stare at a statue in a public park.

Further down the road, there was a vegetable market. Inevitably, near it, there was also a garbage dump. Sitting in the middle of the garbage dump was – someone. A vagrant. When I passed the first time, she was just sitting there, immersed in the rotting garbage with a blank expression on her face. I use female pronouns now, because somewhere in my mind the information had been processed that the figure had had no facial hair. But at the time that I saw her, no pronouns had appeared. I had thought of her as "it", because that shielded me from the horror of identifying with her.

I walked down the length of the market, then began walking back. As I passed the garbage dump on my return, my eyes moved of their own volition to locate the garbage-dweller. It is with the same instinct that we pick at a scab.

She had changed her position. She was kneeling so that her naked rump was high in the air, her face down at knee level. Yet her sex was in no way revealed. In the place where one could have expected to see an anus, there was instead a bulging growth, bright red and shiny, the sun winking on its surface. It was easily the size of a cricket ball. I felt my own anus tighten reflexively, and my throat go rigid, as I walked back to the tonga fighting tears of disgust, of hate, for the nightmares that inhabit our streets. And hate, too, towards myself, for having no compassion, for being helpless, for having no response but flight.

All the way back to the house, I could see that glabrous, diseased redness in my mind's eye. I cursed myself for having looked, I cursed the world for the cruelty in it. I paid the tonga driver twice what he asked, as if to clean the sight from my memory. He took it without comment and trotted off quickly, fearing perhaps that I might change my mind.

I shut the gate behind me, conscious of a visceral trembling. I couldn't bear to return to the confines of the house just yet. I told myself that I still had the compound to explore, which gave me an excuse to remain outside.

The land had apparently been untended for some years. The estate sprawled over a good six or seven acres, of which at least one was accounted for by the house. At one time, the grounds had been landscaped. There were threadbare patches of lawn, there were marble benches. But the wilderness had triumphed. Venerable neems and sombre mango trees competed for attention amongst spindly-armed mulberries, bared for the winter. Knolls of reddish earth sprouted eager adolescent peepuls. A winding ditch with fallen-in sides suggesting an abandoned watercourse, led away from a stone-lipped well. Fragments of statuary punctuated the land, a marmoreal rump here, a headless torso. In one spot, a plump sandstone arm, suitably beringed and braceleted, had been placed coyly around a blackened tree stump.

Towards the rear was a neat bungalow with a red-tiled roof. A child sat at the entrance in his school uniform. Salim and Shammi's quarters, no doubt. Away to the side, inside open sheds, were two Ambassadors and a Jeep.

Nothing I saw suggested the possible site of a cremation. I stumbled and tripped through the scratchy undergrowth, reckless of snakes and scorpions, till I was exhausted. Then I sat down on a mossy bench and felt, unnaturally for my years, lost and forlorn. Behind me was the ugly little town, before me was Sally's designer prison. I felt like a grain of wheat caught between two mutually exclusive traditions: the pitiless squalor of the antique world and the glittering sterility of the modern one. I longed to escape back to my dimension where, it seemed, there was scope for creativity.

But I couldn't.

Being in Udhampur and reporting Sally's story was part of all that I had worked to achieve in my life. I reminded myself that a story like this would be on CNN, on the Beeb. I could not afford to let it slip from my fingers. I could not walk away.

I got up to go back inside the house. But when I rang the doorbell there was no response. I walked around, hammering at the two other doors I found in the smooth, unyielding skin of the house. Silence. I went up to the servants' bungalow but the boy had vanished and didn't respond when I called to him.

I returned to the house. The lack of windows, which had earlier seemed a minor idiosyncrasy was now revealed to be an act of aggression, an insult to the warmth of human curiosity. Had I been a villager living in the surrounding fields, I would have wanted to tear down this mean-spirited mansion which did not share so much as a window with my world.

I started around for the front door again, feeling, by this time, an angry desperation. I checked in my handbag to see if, at a pinch I had enough money to get to the station to buy myself a ticket back to Delhi. I was relieved to see that I did. Sally might have decided, on a whim, to refuse me entry to the house. She might have regained her memory of last night's fight for instance. Or disapproved of my perfume. It would mean nothing to her to leave me stranded outside, sans travelling case and dignity.

My bladder began to whine its familiar complaint at

the prospect of being denied relief indefinitely. My legs were tired from walking on uneven ground.

Then I reached the front of the house and there was Sally standing at the threshold. It was a little strange to see her in the open air. She was frowning. "Mrs Sen!" she said sternly. "Where have you been? It was highly irresponsible of you to leave the house at a time like this! I gave the servants strict instructions that no-one is to leave without my permission!"

I entered without saying a word. I felt numb and defeated.

We lunched in silence. I was grateful that it was a simple affair of daal and rice. At the end of it Sally turned to me and said, "I need to speak to you about the arrangements. I need to show you where they've been made." I saw that the dazed and semi-coherent personality of breakfast had been replaced by a confident dictator, bullet-bright with purpose.

I said, "I'd like to make a phone call."

"To whom?" she said.

"To the paper," I replied. "I must tell them where I am and what I'm doing here." As I said the words I realized that the telephone had been removed.

"No need for that, Mrs Sen," said Sally. 'You can tell them when we're through."

"They'll want photographs," I said. "They'll ask for proof."

With an air of cool triumph she countered, "Will a video tape do?"

I said, "Sally, you don't understand – it's imperative that I call the newspaper. They won't believe me otherwise – "

"They'll believe you, when they see the video." She had cut her banana into neat slices, the cream-yellow disks arranged around the rim of her plate like tiny cartwheels. Holding each one down with a fruit fork, she peeled the skin off with her knife and ate the flesh. "It's all set up. There's nothing for you to do but press the switch."

I said, bluntly, "If I don't tell the newspaper at once, it'll look as if I've been your accomplice, Sally."

She looked at me and allowed a tiny pause before saying, "I think you'll find your way around that."

"Are you saying," I asked, "that you'd prevent me from leaving?"

"It doesn't matter what I say, Mrs Sen!" said Sally, almost smiling. "Once it's over, you can tell them what you like."

" ... or not tell them anything," I said.

She was so very sure. "Oh, no," she beamed, "you won't do that! It won't be in your interest!"

I peeled myself a banana in silence. I marvelled at the change that had come over her. I guessed that this was closer to her normal self. When she had the energy to maintain a front.

"All right," I said, presently. "It's three o'clock now. Do I have time to rest before you show me?"

She nodded and suggested that we meet at four-thirty. "In the drawing room," she said, tilting her head in its direction. "The light's just right at that time."

∽◌◌∾

I had a hot shower and changed into a caftan. I lay on my bed and thought I wouldn't sleep but I must have because it was five by the time I was conscious again. I was late for Sally. I wondered why she hadn't summoned me. Dressing once more, I left my room and went to the kitchen.

Shammi was alone. She was sitting on the floor and folding paan. A short stack of pale green packets had already accumulated in the center of a grubby handkerchief spread for that purpose. She heard me, gave a guilty start, saw me and relaxed.

"Where is Sally-Madam?" I asked without preamble, speaking in Hindi.

"In the room," said Shammi, "the hospital." She got to her feet. There was a tired quality to her actions. "Tea Memsahib?"

"If it's not a trouble," I said, automatically, not really thinking of the words.

She turned her face slightly in my direction and her professional-servant's veil was put aside. She said, with a faint smile on her face, "Trouble!" And she shook her head, a movement so delicate, that it did little more than cause the dupatta to tremble where it left the back of her head to meet her shoulders. Meaning to say, she was bound to make the tea at my bidding.

There was a stool in the room. I went to it and sat down while she lit the gas on the range.

It was a large kitchen, a mixture of Indian and European. At head level there were white-painted wooden shelves extending all the way around the walls. A new and efficient-looking refrigerator purred in one corner. In another, there was a glazed-tile mori circling around a tap where utensils were scrubbed. Near the ceiling there was an air-vent. There was no external window.

"Shammi," I said, adopting the tone of voice that signals a request for confidences, "tell me something – "

She looked up, throwing two spoons of tea into a white pot.

"How long have you worked in this house?" I asked.

"Since I was born," she said.

I murmured my surprise. She looked around twenty-three.

"My mother worked here," she volunteered. "I used to stand by the fire. Then I helped with the cutting. Then I helped with the washing. Little by little I began to work." She looked up at me and smiled again.

She had pleasant features. Her mouth was dark and full, her teeth white and perfectly regular. Her dupatta was midnight blue, transparent, tiny spangles scattered through it, rippling silently down and over her shoulders. Her kurta-pajama was livid green and she wore a short tight cardigan, turquoise with white stripes. She had luminous eyes, a trace of kajal glistening at the base of her lashes, culminating in a dusky comma at the outer corners. A flat brass star rode the plump swell of one nostril.

"So you grew up here," I said, thoughtfully. "Just you?"

The water had come to a boil. She did not answer, as she lifted the vessel off the fire using tongs. Then she said, "Yes. Just me." And she threw me a complex glance. I was puzzled but did not pursue it.

"And what about your mother?" I asked.

"She died," said Shammi. "Six, eight years ago." She poured the water into the tea-pot, unfurling a plume of white steam.

"That's very sad," I said. "How?"

She capped the column of vapour rising from the pot by fitting its lid over its gaping mouth. From the spout now, a purling streamer arose, languid, yet relentless. Heat escaping. She plucked down from the shelf a quilted pink cosy and fitted it onto the pot. I thought, abstractedly, about the effort we go to, to bring heat under our control. Despite which it finds ways to escape. We rarely do more than delay the inevitable. Shammi placed the pot and its cosy on a dark-wood tray. "Oh," she said, finally, her mouth tightening very delicately. "What to say, Memsahib? She died." Her tone implied that the lives of the poor are weak, sputtering things. Easily snuffed out. Then she added as an afterthought. "I was sixteen and already married three months. She was only thirty."

Thirty! I felt a current of sympathy course through me. That meant she had been fourteen when Shammi was born. Even allowing a year or two for exaggeration, that was still very young. "And your father?" I asked, while she organized a cup and matching saucer, a spoon, a sugar bowl. Two strainers, each with its own drip-stand. Milk in a pan from the fridge.

"He left," she said. I waited for her to continue. But she poured the milk into a smaller pan, long-handled, and placed it on the fire, saying nothing. Then, once more as an afterthought, she added, "As soon as I was born."

The starkness of her story left no place for sorrow. The mother, a child herself, abandoned with a baby. How had Sally reacted? It was hard to imagine these throbbing dramas taking place in a house with fitted furniture, where nothing moved except by rigid design. "So you've never seen your father?" I asked.

Shammi said, "No." The milk hissed on the sides of the pan. She turned the gas off.

"What was it like to grow up in this house?" I asked, wondering whether she would be able to answer me.

She turned around, the pan of milk in one hand, the milk jug positioned in the other, her eyes wide with surprise. "What was it like, Memsahib?" she said, "Why – it was good! Such a big house, such a good family – !" Into the jug went the milk, its hot scent pungent with cream.

"But without your father?" I persisted, "And your mother, so young?"

Putting down the milk container, Shammi took the cosy off the tea-pot now and poured a slender amber arc through a strainer, into my cup, before she answered me. "Sahibji was there," she said evenly. "He was kind to us." She handed me the cup. "Milk?" she asked.

"Yes," I said. She poured from the little jug, through the second strainer. "Enough. But how did your mother raise you? How did she look after you?" She turned to get the sugar, and brought it to my reach. I helped myself.

"Sahibji was there," she repeated.

She looked up into my eyes, the sugar bowl in her hand. She held my gaze, challenging me to understand. "He was always there." Then she turned aside, putting the bowl away. The spangles in her dupatta winked. "My mother was ... beautiful," she said, her eyes averted.

It was the way she said it, nothing else. But I heard the hiss of heat escaping, human heat. I felt slightly breathless and would have liked to gasp, but didn't. So! A secret had flowered even in the antiseptic core of Sally's private fortress!

Shammi busied herself with her own glass of tea. She mixed water into the milk, threw in a teaspoon of leaves from a small stainless steel container by the range and turned on the gas. There was a scalding rasp as the milk responded at once.

I blew on the surface of the tea in my cup, thinking that there are no simple lives.

When she had her glass in hand she sat on the floor and told me about Subhash's family. That he had four sisters, two brothers. There were five nephews. Subhash had settled all of them one by one. Far away. They used to come to the house and make endless demands. Subhash had taken care of all of them. But none was as wealthy as he. This land that the house was on had belonged to Subhash's father. When the father died, Subhash had razed the old building to the ground and constructed this new one.

I found it difficult to understand how it was possible that Subhash lay dying with none of his family around him. Shammi said that they weren't allowed to come.

"Why not?" I asked.

She swept a glance at me and said, "Sahibji put a stop to it."

I was taken aback. I had been so sure a decision like that would have come from Sally, not Subhash. I said, "But – why? His own family!"

Shammi shrugged. I was surprised to see that her expression had snapped shut. As if all my questions so far had been acceptable but this one now, for no reason that I could understand, had crossed some boundary of reserve beyond which she would not go. I yearned to explore it, but she did not give me the option. Instead, she got up, sighing, "What to say, Memsahib? At one time they used to come."

The audience was over. I thanked her and went back to my room. I paced the floor.

Subhash, Subhash. The idea that he might have lusted after his servant girl brought him into such sharp focus that it was almost hard to look at him any more. Sally's version of their life together was revealed to be a thin nursery rhyme laid over a dense and solid mass of – what? What must their life have actually been like? Why did he hide himself in this nowhere called Udhampur? If he had been the genius Sally described, why had he chosen to do so little with his capacities?

Then I remembered with annoyance that one of my

aims in seeking Shammi out had been to ask her to tell me where the telephone was kept. But I had forgotten. I opened my door intending to go back to her but was distracted from my purpose by the sight of Laxman, dawdling in the corridor.

I turned toward the drawing room.

The house was eerily quiet.

From the drawing room, there was a narrow corridor, glassed-in on its courtyard side, along whose length were three or four doors, with a final one at the end of it. The full extent of the curving wall was solid with framed photographs but I didn't pay attention to them till I had reached the end of the corridor, to find that the door there was locked. I walked slowly back, looking at the pictures.

There was Subhash as a young graduate. Subhash on the ship out of India. Subhash at the gates of Harvard. Subhash receiving some prize, the shirt-collar of his formal dress-suit cutting a painful white line into his tender sepia neck.

I found myself looking for pictures of Sally as a young woman. There were none, initially. Then the first few appeared. Sally at her First Holy Communion, fresh-faced, squinting in the sunlight of some impossibly corn-scented summer's day. Sally with her blonde hair in bright pigtails reading a book. Sally at the wheel of her father's old Dodge, and someone, her brother perhaps, beside her, pretending to be a terror-struck passenger. Sally as a young woman, serious and flat-stomached, standing by the front door of the library where she had met Subhash's "beautiful hands". She herself wasn't beautiful but had a quality of health and youth, of fifties-style, guileless American confidence, Pears-soap-scented, clean and wholesome.

Then there were four or five, pitifully small pictures, taken apparently at the registry office where they must have been married, Sally and Subhash.

She had worn a white lacy dress, not a gown and a face-net which reached just the tip of her nose. Subhash had worn a dark suit and a hat. There was no indication of who had taken the photographs. Sally seemed to have been smiling continuously: when they reached the desk, while Subhash signed, when she was handed the pen and finally looking back at the camera, her net thrown aside, making a We-Did-It! face. But for all her gaiety, the pictures were forlorn. Her smiles had been the only ones they had had on that day from which other faces, her family's faces, had been absent.

Then she disappeared again. The pictures which followed could only have been taken exclusively by the hand of an adoring wife. Subhash at a telescope ... drinking a glass of wine under the Eiffel Tower ... standing at the Parthenon. In the middle of the European tour they had afforded themselves colour film and taken a shy sprinkling of coloured pictures: roses, tulips, Subhash posing beside a Dutch cow, Subhash posturing alongside a Flamenco dancer, Subhash reflected in a distorting mirror at Brighton Beach.

And then they were in India.

Subtly the mood changed. Black and white film again, brutal highlights on polished skin, the edges of teeth, hairpins, fingernails. There were stiff, posed photographs of various elders taken individually. Then a rash of group pictures.

How strange Subhash looked surrounded by his own family! He had become an outsider. His skin was visibly lighter than that of all his relatives now. While they scowled, uncomprehending and hostile, he sat forward, mobile, vital. While the others stared fixedly at the camera itself, he looked beyond it, aiming his gaze at the future and at those who would see the imprint, left in silver crystals, of a flicker of light from the past.

There was only one noteworthy picture amongst these, of Sally. It was quite a large one, a studio portrait, hand-coloured. She was sitting in an ornate chair, wearing a dark blue brocade-silk sari, with the pallu over her head, a large bindi on her forehead and the full armoury of jewellery. The scenery behind her showed a wind-mill and a weeping willow. Her skin seemed unnaturally white and there was a curious expression on her face, as if she had attempted to pack into that one exposure the whole trousseau of qualities expected of a Perfect Wife. There was Faith and Trust there, Obedience, Virtue, Hard Work, Loyalty, you name it, it was there. I looked at it for a long while, thinking about the many, many women whose only aim was to earn the privilege of posing for a portrait such as this one, women whose only ambition was to be living showcases for their husbands' financial clout.

"It's beautiful, isn't it?" said Sally, from behind me.

I jumped. "Oh!" I said, practically shouting. "Sally! You gave me a shock!" A wave of guilt washed over me, as if I had been caught reading private letters.

She seemed hardly to hear me. "Yes," she said, in a dreamy voice, going towards the photograph. She put out her hand and touched it very lightly. "What a long time ago."

She had evidently come from Subhash's bedside. The well-coordinated quality of the lunch-time persona had evaporated. "It's all happening so fast," she whispered. "He's slipping away. He's leaving us." Heat escaping, I thought. She turned to me, her eyes unseeing, reaching for a portion of the wall just behind me. I jerked aside.

She lifted a photograph up, behind which was concealed a small niche in the wall. She extracted a bunch of keys hanging there. "Come," she said to me and proceeded towards the door I had been unable to open.

Behind it was a spiral staircase, at the top of which was another door. Opening it, Sally stepped out and waited as I followed her.

The view was breath-taking. The day had ended and from the dense blackness of the surrounding fields golden fire-flies of light from village homes twinkled as the earth released the sun's energy in rippling currents of air. Above us, the rich canopy of stars danced in resonance. We stood still a few moments, two small human buoys, awash in a tide of night.

The terrace sloped towards the central courtyard. There was no moon, so I couldn't make out very much. Bulky shapes covered in tarpaulin or plastic sheets crouched here and there. I thought of vast captive animals, tethered to the roof, covered in blankets. Waiting to be fed.

From the inner edge of the roof, another spiral staircase led down into the central courtyard. In the darkness, the mass of foliage obscured the floor. Off-centre and not far from the foot of the staircase was a pale structure which I took to be a fountain. From where I stood, its shape suggested that of a sauce-boat.

Soon we were inside the courtyard and walking across a pebbled path towards the fountain. When we reached it, Sally stopped and turned. "This is where it's going to be," she said.

I looked at the basin in front of us, glowing faintly in the dark, the way that marble does. The top of it was not quite head high. It was an oval, eight feet narrow and maybe ten feet from pole to pole. "In ... in the *fountain*?" I asked, stupidly.

"It's not a fountain, Mrs Sen," she said. "It's a Well of Infinity. Subhash's name for it." She moved around to the right and I saw that a short wooden step-ladder had been leaned against the pristine whiteness of the "Well". She started to climb up it, bunching momentarily against the star-bright sky as she stepped over the rim of the structure and dropped out of sight. I started up the ladder myself.

Inside the well, about three feet below the rim, was a flat surface, mildly inclined and wide enough for two bodies to lie side by side. Poking up from the centre was a dark spike. Sally was already lying down, to the left of the spike, her feet lower than her head. "We'll lie facing East," she said. "First I'll settle him in, then I'll arrange myself next to him – like I am right now. But I'll need some help with organizing my pleats – I'll need you for that, Mrs Sen!"

I heard myself mumble, "I see."

"Once I'm lying down, you could pin everything into place so that even if there's a breeze or something, I'll still look neat."

"Okay," I said, feeling that instead of my brain there was an empty ice box. Now that I was getting answers to the questions which had been knocking around my head ever since reaching Udhampur, I couldn't seem to understand what they were. The wood, a voice kept saying in my head, how will the wood be stacked? Who will pile it around you and Subhash? And where *is* the wood? There was even one part of my mind which was unreasonably annoyed to find that Sally wasn't going about her sati in the traditional way. I found myself thinking, *Why can't she just do what we do?*

It had been Subhash's idea, Sally was explaining, to invent a form of sati which would be quick, painless and elegant. Instead of the nuisance of a wood-burning fire, they would both be soaked in a shallow pool of petrol. Just under the rim of the well were holes spaced neatly five inches apart through which the fuel would pour. The sloping floor of the well ensured that their faces would not be submerged. The spike in the middle of the well was designed to release a spark which would ignite the fumes.

"We timed the filling with no-one lying inside here and it took less than ten minutes – " she said, "so it should take even less time when we are in place, don't you think?"

I murmured assent.

"You'll have to see to the camera, Mrs Sen," she said. "We'll get settled and then once everything's just right, you can start it rolling."

Camera?

"You know, the video?" She had mentioned it, now I recalled. Of course, the video. "It's on the roof," she said, pointing upwards, "it's all set up. You won't have to do anything but switch it on. We've tried it dozens of times just to be sure that it works. There's really nothing to it – you settle me in, go back up to the roof and turn the switch on. Then, while I'm reciting verses from the Bible, the Gita and the Koran – oh! And of course, before you go back up, you'll turn on the gas, you know, there's a sort of a valve down here at the base of the Well – "

"Will there be enough?" I asked. "Petrol, I mean."

"Oh yes," said Sally, "it's always ready. And the music too! You'll have to do the music! There's a switch right by the camera – it's really quite easy, but I – do you think you'll be able to manage Mrs Sen?"

"I think so," I said. "You've chosen what to play?"

But of course. A recording of Mozart's Requiem Mass, rendered by Subhash on his sitar. He had taped it years ago, she said, "when we first had our idea about the Well. Can you imagine? He thought of it way back then!"

"Amazing," I said. "When was that?"

"In '85" she said, "that's when he first became keen that we should control not only our lives but our deaths as well. He's that kind of man. He thinks of everything."

"Did he plan to die first?" I asked.

"No ... " said Sally, her voice flattening very slightly, at having to confess to one godlike power that Subhash had not possessed. "But he planned it so that whoever went first, the other could follow without pain." There was a tiny pause. "I'm glad it was me, anyway," she said. "My chance to prove my feelings for him!" Then she was glowing up at me. "Do you see now what it means to have a Real Marriage, Mrs Sen?"

"I'm surprised that you need anyone's help, Sally," I said, "it's all so ... complete."

"Oh but you're really important!" said Sally, quickly. "You'll be the one to tell the rest!"

"What?" I said.

There was a tiny pause. "Subhash used to say that I mustn't talk about it like this – but he was always so modest, you know? He never liked the publicity. You see, he meant this to be our gift to – to *humanity*!"

I said, "I'm not sure what you mean, Sally – "

"The Well, Mrs Sen," she said. "It's just the perfect answer, don't you see? For married people who die, and leave someone behind. Satty was one answer, but it just wasn't good enough! Because you needed so many other people to help, you needed so much wood and there was the discomfort too, of burning. And not just married people, Mrs Sen! Even those who aren't married, lonely people or – or – you know, *others* – who need to die and need to think of ways to, you know, dispose of their mortal remains and they just *can't*, can they? I mean, they can't be sure that what they want is what they'll get. This way, you can control *everything*! You can choose the date, you can settle your affairs, you can say your goodbyes – and then you can just climb into your own little well and *poof*! It's over!"

I thought how fortunate it is for all of us ordinary mortals that a majority of celebrated thinkers are frustrated in their efforts to "improve" existence to suit their own bizarre notions of perfection.

"Subhash always had such wonderful plans, so many things he wanted to do. But nobody was ready to listen, were they? The Well was the only idea he could easily share with others. So he thought it all out, how to make it work and then how to be sure that everyone could hear about it. He knew that the newspapers would be thrilled to print a true story and we planned it so that whoever came to write about us would become famous too. That way, we'd all be happy!" I couldn't see her face clearly but felt sure she was smiling broadly as she said this. The afternoon's clash of wills at lunch had not been forgotten. "So aren't you glad you stayed? Don't you see how it's all going to be worth it?"

I nodded thoughtfully, though she probably couldn't see me. "How do you turn on the spark?" I asked.

"It's right here, a little button, in the middle where I can reach it," said Sally. "It's like that thing they use in the kitchen, you know, to light the gas? All I have to do is push it down."

I had been sitting on the rim of the fountain so far. Sally patted the space beside her, the space reserved for Subhash and said, "Come in here, Mrs Sen, why don't you? You can see for yourself, how easy it is."

So I stepped into the Well, feeling resistance crawling up and down my skin. Both to being in such close proximity to Sally, whom I couldn't pretend to like, and to having been manipulated so shamelessly.

Carved into the floor of the structure was a body-shaped cavity, contoured, said Sally, for Subhash's dimensions. I struggled to bring my head and shoulders into alignment with the space available, while compressing my back so that my tail-bone could slot into the groove assigned for Subhash's. I did not succeed very well and had to be content with an uncomfortable compromise, my heels extending beyond Subhash's, the small of my back arched out of shape where Subhash's spine rose in the taut curve of a well-carried back. I wondered to myself, how long ago this shallow furrow had been excavated and whether it had been adjusted for the changes wrought on a body by age. I didn't need to ask. Sally volunteered that it had been up-dated only months ago, before Subhash became bed-ridden.

She talked about their marriage, their life. The stuff of publicity hand-outs. According to her, it was an idyll of sweet domesticity, marred only by a tiresome family and a millennium too dull and crude to recognize the genius of a man born before his time. That's why, she said, he had no choice but to gradually shut himself in and concentrate on those things he really cared for: his music, his thoughts and her.

I was looking straight up at the sky. I picked out two satellites dawdling along. And then I saw an aircraft, like a miniature constellation, moving purposefully before a backdrop of distant suns. That modest delta of lights, so tiny and inconspicuous, nevertheless carried a payload of human lives, maybe three hundred or more, within it. What kinds of cargoes – of what kinds of lives! – rode around the stars in the fathomless space beyond the aircraft's familiar twinkle?

"We didn't want children," Sally said. "The family was so furious? They wanted Subhash to take another wife! But he told them it was his decision. He told them I could have ten children if I wished but that he didn't want me to, because it would spoil our lives to have children. Babies are so messy, you know? And they take up so much time? And effort? – "

It was tempting to just lie back and listen passively. To avoid caring that Shammi had shown me a different reality to the one that Sally was hoping I would record. She and Subhash had deliberately created a kink in the warp of reality, then chosen me to be a shuttle for their weft. Who can say why I decided to knot their skein? Was it with the noble intention of establishing Truth? Or simple spite?

I waited till there was a check in the flood of Sally's consciousness. Then I heard myself ask, as if from a long way off, "By the way, Sally – " Not bothering to apologize for the lack of context. "What happened to ... Shammi's mother?"

She said, "Huh?"

I said, "You know – the cook?"

Sally said, "Oh. Well. She's quite good. Lazy though. I really had to train her."

I said, "No, I meant – the mother."

There was a strain in her voice. "The mother?" she said. "What ... mother?"

The marble was cold to lie on and I was starting to shiver. I said, "Shammi – " Then I paused, wondering whether it was indiscreet to reveal what Shammi had said to me. But overruled my concern. "Shammi was born here. She said that her mother died very young."

Sally made a strange sound. I couldn't tell at once whether she was clearing her throat or gasping. But it was just the words stumbling on their way out. "These ... *servants*!" she managed, finally. "How they *talk*! That woman didn't *die*! I mean, she just ... *went away*!"

"Left the house?" I asked. "Leaving her child behind?"

"Huh!" said Sally. "No child! We had to get her married!"

"Just sixteen – " I started.

"Old enough!" snapped Sally. "And the mother – she was a – a – *slut*! We took her in off the streets! Pregnant!" She said the word like a curse. There was a moment's silence. I said nothing. The cold was getting to me. Then she said, struggling to maintain her composure, "Subhash was always too kind to her. Like he was to everyone. She used him. She twisted him ... She distracted him, my *goodness*! She made it hard for him to work. In the end, I – I had to tell her to go!"

I said, *"You* told her to leave ... ?"

There was a sharp intake of breath. "I don't understand why we're talking about my cook's mother, Mrs Sen!" said Sally.

"I was just interested," I said innocently, "because Shammi mentioned her – "

"No! She was forbidden! – Her mother was nobody. Nobody!" The words shot out before she could control them. "She should never have been here. That's what I said right from the start! She was pure trouble, from the moment she set foot in this house. And I wouldn't have it any more! No wife would've! Not after she ... they ..." Her voice faltered. She fell silent in confusion.

"Who?" I said. "What?" The cold was seeping into my bones and a trembling was starting up deep in my marrow.

"She did it on purpose," said Sally, unsteadily. "To keep her hold on him ... and ... I *warned* him. But he didn't see it, did he? No! He was *too kind*! Always so ... so ... *concerned* about other people!"

"Sally – " I said, "what did she do?"

"Nothing!" Her voice grew momentarily firm. "I didn't see it! I didn't hear about it! It never bothered me!" Then her voice dropped away again. "I knew it was all just ... just ... lies. Lies ! It wasn't his problem at all! But he made it his, didn't he? Oh yes. And everyone whispering ... such *stories*. They drove me mad with their stories! So in the end – she ... had to ... *go* ... "

My teeth were starting to chatter. "How, Sally?" I said, trying to keep my voice from skidding. There was a high-frequency vibration taking place deep inside my gut. I couldn't tell if it was due to the cold or my fear that I knew what Sally's answer would be. Whether she told me or not.

"It doesn't matter!" said Sally, "it doesn't matter what happened – and it didn't – I mean, *nothing* happened. Nothing. That's ... that's what we decided. People like her don't matter, Mrs Sen, not compared to Subhash, not compared to genius. That's what I kept telling him."

"And what did he say?" I asked.

"He said ... he said ... " Her voice faltered again and she stopped, painfully. "I can't tell you what he said."

I was silent. Like most journalists, I had learnt years ago that it's more difficult to stop someone talking than to start them.

"He was cruel! He was rude!"

I said nothing.

When she spoke, her voice was hoarse with bitterness from a wound which spat and quivered, even now, even after all these years. "He said an Indian wife does not ... answer back."

I waited.

"That I was too Western. That I didn't know my place. That I didn't understand how to care for a ... for a ...

man." A dry sob escaped her. "That I ... I ... I ... " But she couldn't say that last one. She succumbed to a spasm of weeping.

It was true, what Subhash had said. An Indian wife would have been a pedestal for him, inert. Sally, by contrast, could only perform her devotions as an elaborate ritual. She drew attention to herself by the very act of proclaiming her selflessness. When it came to biting a real bullet, with real teeth, she had cracked. And why not? The only people who benefit from the behaviour of typical Indian wives, are typical Indian husbands.

When she had regained her poise, she said, "But I stayed in the end. Didn't I? Because I was so sure it was all just *foolish*. It wouldn't *last*. And he needed me. So I stayed. And ... And in the end she ... went."

I asked, very softly, "How, Sally?"

There was a silence on the side where she lay.

She said, "While he was away. On tour."

I said, "Okay." I was barely breathing. A person will talk and talk and then, when it comes to the crucial admission, the final one or two words which will cement a quote into the front page of history, they will pull away and bowdlerize.

Sally said, "She ... vanished. No-one knows how." She had pulled away.

I said, "Really? No-one?"

"No-one who mattered," she said, whispering. "When he came back, he didn't get angry. He said ... that I must put it out of my head and never talk about it. That nothing had happened. And that it would be all right. He would make it all right. And he did. He fixed everything. Even his family. They tried to hurt me but he *fixed* them!" She essayed a little rough laugh. "He fixed me too, in a way. But different. 'Cause – 'cause – " her voice faded briefly.

"'Cause he stayed by me, not them. He was *mine*. Mine! And no-one could change that. No-one."

She stopped. I could hear her breathing hard. I could hear the engine of truth labouring within her against the deadweight of silence that Subhash had tried to smother it under. For his own sake as much as for hers, I imagined.

"He used to tell me, Reality is ... only what gets recorded. So when it happened ..." The engine strained. "When it ... it ... happened, he said the only important thing was to see that there was no ... record. Anywhere. Even in our minds."

I swallowed against the cold that was rising up in my throat.

"So ... there *isn't*." Her voice became mechanical, like a trained parrot. "There's no record. Really. Nothing at all. No record." But her voice was hollow. The engine had still not come to rest.

"Except one. Not a record, really. Just one thing I had to accept, as a, as a price," she was whispering again. Her breath rose like a thin grey spectre that I could see from the corner of my eye, in the tense night air. I didn't have the courage to turn my head to look at her. I felt my neck might break if I tried, just then. "A price. For making her ... go. Only one thing, one small thing." She was speaking as if to herself, barely audible. "I didn't even have to say who he really was or ... or ... anything. And *he* never would, because he's dumb! And stupid. And ... and ... *ugly*. But I must keep him in the house, Subhash said. Keep him close to us. Care for him. Keep him like our ... *own*." Her voice failed.

Laxman.

I don't believe she even said the name. It dropped into my mind like a feather through vacuum, soundless. My skin was growing numb from the cold. A vision formed of myself, frozen solid to the floor of the Well, having to be chipped away by masons, to vacate the site created for Subhash. I imagined I could feel my lips cracking, as I framed one last question. "How old is he?" I asked.

"I don't know, Mrs Sen," said Sally dreamily, "It was never important. Like so many other things."

She sat up. "I can hear the cook calling us," she said. I heard nothing, but did not have the energy to contradict her. "It must be time for dinner."

∞

The table was set for dinner when we re-entered the house. But Sally insisted that she must change and wash before we sat down. It was dark inside and the silence oppressive. I waited in the drawing room, deliberately refusing to think. When Sally returned I took my place at the table feeling subdued and colourless. She by contrast, had revived and was resplendent in white. Her sari, organdy as ever, was shadow-worked with a pattern of white doves. Her hair had been oiled and replaited. The bindi on her forehead glowed like a drop of new blood.

We had a peasant omelette with toast, followed by fruit. Sally talked about the arrangements that had been made to dispose of the house and property after she and Subhash "passed on." Apparently plans had been set in motion through accountants and lawyers, to turn the house into some sort of educational trust and museum. She talked animatedly about showing me Subhash's study and the papers and books she expected would be published posthumously.

Salim brought coffee in a silver service. There was only one cup. Sally waited till I had filled it, then rose graciously from the table telling me that she had to get back to Subhash. I remained where I was, wondering what to do.

The coffee was still warm in my cup when Shammi came into the dining room, her eyes wide.

"Memsahib!" she said, whispering "you come now!"

My heart sank. I had hoped I would have at least the space of one night in which to recover from the shocks of the recent day. But it was barely nine-thirty. "The nurse is saying, he can go any minute now – " said Shammi.

I went back with her to the hospital room and stayed till he died, which was at dawn. I remember glancing at my watch.

The crisis of a life's passage is a peculiar one because all those concerned know that the struggle against it is futile, yet no-one dares be the one to call halt. So, yes, I held the oxygen mask in place as the night nurse drained fluid from his lungs. I supported his fragile, fleshless body, still surprisingly heavy, as Sally changed the sweaty sheets from beneath him and sponged his back. I arranged pillows, I insisted that the saline drip be maintained despite the swelling in his hands and feet, I agreed that the dose of anti-pyretic should be doubled to bring his fever down. I am not at all accustomed to hospital scenes, but in this case I was there and doing it, all through that endless night.

Oddly enough, for a man who had been largely unconscious for weeks, in those final hours Subhash was with us. He spoke in an unintelligible mumble, between raucous breaths. His eyes were open and able to focus. I will never know what he could understand of what he saw, but on the one or two occasions that he fixed his gaze on me, I could feel his mind, inquisitive, probing, wanting to know more. Sally seemed to understand what he said and he kept her scurrying to follow instructions and requests right uptil the last moment. He wanted his orange juice to be chilled, he wanted to hear her read "Tithonus" to him. He wanted the bed raised. Then he wanted it lowered.

Twice it seemed that he had slipped away, only to shudder back to life. His hands moved recklessly wherever they could, huge bony crabs, plucking at the tubes, the sheets, the air. His desire to live was insatiable. Standing near him I could feel it sucking hungrily at my own life and at the lives of all those near him. He filled the room with his presence and his needs. When he died, it was as if a crowd had departed, not just one man.

It happened at a moment when Sally had turned away and I was looking at his face, thinking that strength of character can transform even the ugliest features. His forehead was high and his eyebrows were long and delicately arched. Even in old age and in sickness his mouth was firm and full. I was looking at his face when he opened his eyes, widened them as if in mild surprise, breathed out and ... was gone.

A great stillness descended upon the room. The rest of us froze as if in a tableau, while Sally came slowly forward. She nodded a couple of times, expressionless. Then she passed her hand over his face, shutting his eyes. It was so final. She looked up at me. "We'll wash him and dress him," she said. "Then I'll get dressed myself."

From the foot of the bed, there was a sound.

Laxman was standing there, making a broken, guttural noise, like a donkey braying. I had never heard his voice before. I had assumed that he was completely mute, not merely inarticulate. He was crying. I was surprised that he was sentient enough to feel this kind of emotion. His quartzy eyes were spilling over with heavy tears and he was holding on to the bars at the end of the bed, sobbing helplessly.

Then I looked up at Sally and her face was so distorted with rage, with violence, that I stepped back a pace.

"Take him away!" she hissed, to no-one in particular, "take him – take him – AWAY!"

Salim came forward, wrenched the small dark figure away, still braying pathetically and bore him from the room. Sally was rigid, her eyes shut and the muscles around her mouth jerked. I thought she might be about to have a fit, but she brought herself under control. When she opened her eyes again, she was calm. Her voice was taut but steady. "You have four hours, Mrs Sen, to make yourself ready."

I went back to my room, bathed and packed. Outside, the sky from my walk-through window showed pink with promise.

I lay down on the bed in my caftan and dozed fitfully. At eleven o'clock, there was a knock on the door.

Shammi was standing there. "Madam is calling you," she said.

I told her to wait, because I had to put my sari on. I am ashamed to confess that I had brought a stylish black and white patola to wear, anticipating breezily that sartorial conventions in Udhampur would be mine to invent. I dressed quickly and stepped outside. Shammi was squatting on the floor by my door. I asked her what she thought about what was happening.

She shrugged. "What to say, Memsahib? All must go some day."

"But do you know that it's a crime? What Sally-Madam is doing is a crime?" I was ad-libbing. I had no clear intention behind my questions, aside from wanting to stall events till the mist in my head, which prevented me from thinking, lifted. I had still not located the telephone, after all. I still had no access to the outside world.

Shammi didn't react to my questions, but looked at me with big eyes, as if to say, What relevance can such a question have to me, a servant? She had gone into that state of fatalistic shock that her class of people entered in the presence of the Great Leveller.

I asked her, "What will happen to Laxman?"

She said, "What happens to every one."

"I meant, who will look after him? Who will care for him?" I asked, knowing that such questions were senseless in the context. "Do you think of him as your brother?" The muscles of her face twitched. She looked up at me with a tortured expression. She would much rather drift back into her comforting limbo. She said nothing. "Is he simple-witted? Or only mute?" I asked, desperate to elicit some response. "What will happen to him now? Where will he go? Where will all of you go?"

She continued to look into space. I bent over and shook her shoulder. "Shammi?"

She flinched slightly. In a dead voice, she said, "Sahib-ji loved him very much." Then she clapped her hands to her ears and shook her head, her tongue between her teeth, deflecting invisible anathemas. "Don't ask me! Don't ask me to say!"

"Shammi!" I said, "How did she die?"

She stared at me for a moment, then she covered her face with her hands. "No, no!" she said. "I won't say! I won't say!" And then from behind her hands, she said, "She was sick, often. Bleeding, bleeding. One day it was too much. Sahibji was away. Sally-madam locked her in a room. Didn't call the doctor. So she ... died. When Sahibji came back, he carried her out with his own hands. Burnt the body. Didn't let anyone come near. Used the ashes for the plants. Then he built that thing, the white one."

The Well.

I tried to pry her hands away from her face. "And no-one did anything!" I cried. "No-one said anything! The police –"

Shammi lifted her head up. "Memsahib – she is waiting! We must go!"

"Shammi! Listen to me! I'm not going to let Sally-Madam die today!" Actually, it came as a surprise to me to hear my own words. Up until that instant, I hadn't realized that I was going to say them.

"Memsahib – " her eyes were pleading with me to not ask anything of her. To leave her sealed into the social time-capsule that had swallowed her mother.

Footsteps were running in from the direction of the drawing room. Salim appeared, out of breath.

"Where are you!" he gasped, angrily. "Everything is ready! Come on!" He was speaking to Shammi, but of course his words were actually directed at me.

"I'm coming," I said, closing the door of my room.

I followed him till we reached the end of the corridor before the stairway to the roof, Shammi trailing behind me. When Salim had started up the stairs ahead of me, I turned to Shammi. I said, "Look. I want you to do exactly as I say. I want you to stay back here. If you hear me calling your name don't come to me – go straight to the phone and call the police – are you listening? – Don't ask questions." I had to use the obedience codes. "Just do it!"

She started to shake her head, but she remained standing where she was.

Salim was half-way up the stairs. I followed him. On the roof, he stopped and realized that Shammi was not with us. But I didn't let him fetch her. "Look," I said, "this has nothing to do with you! Stay out of it."

"Madam-ji will insist that she is there, everyone must be there – " he began.

"Even Laxman?" I countered.

He wouldn't meet my eyes. "Madam-ji said to keep him inside," he mumbled. Then he looked up, an expression of genuine dismay on his naturally taciturn features. "But he ran away from me – "

"All right," I said, "never mind." I was playing what I hoped would be a trump card, "Do you know that if the police come to know of what Sally-Madam is doing, you, Shammi, Laxman, will all be arrested?" Not to mention myself.

His eyes strayed anxiously this way and that. I felt bad putting him in a position where his loyalties were strained but I couldn't see any option. "Please," he was saying, "I don't know about that – but – I – "

He was spared any further responsibility by Sally's voice. She was standing at the head of the second stairway, her voice imperious. "Mrs Sen! Do you know the time?"

Sally hadn't disappointed me. She was wearing a gorgeous temple sari, deep crimson, stiff with gold brocade. She was decked in diamonds which flashed from her ears, her throat, the parting of her hair, her wrists. A gold belt showed around her waist. On her white forehead was a blazon of kumkum and her hair, silver in the light, was threaded with heavy chaplets of jasmine. The years had dropped away from her and she looked every inch a bride, a princess.

I took a deep breath, stepped away from Salim and said, "Oh ... hello, Sally! You look wonderful!"

She frowned, her eyes suspicious. "Mrs Sen! We have been waiting! Everything is ready!"

"Sally," I said, walking towards her, affecting a breezy manner. "I'm sorry about that, but I think there are still a few things left to discuss."

"Oh?" she said, cocking her head to the side, unsmiling.

"Sally," I said, "you must understand, I've never done anything like this before – there are things I need to ask you, things that I need to know." My mind was racing ahead of my words, searching for delaying tactics.

She frowned in annoyance. "Mrs Sen, I'm sure you are aware of realities in the tropics? We can't afford to wait long! He's not on ice!"

"Oh, it won't take long," I said tranquilly, "but I think it would be best if we went back downstairs into the drawing room. It's a bit hot on the roof."

"Mrs Sen, this is ridiculous!" She was now openly angry.

"Nevertheless," I said, "I think it would be best if you did follow me downstairs."

Her heavy silk soughed luxuriantly as she stepped up onto the roof and approached me. "Mrs Sen!" she said, her eyes snapping, "have you taken leave of your senses? You have a job to do! Subhash is already in place! You have to come *now! I order you!*"

I was concentrating on keeping Sally's attention. I knew that if I wasn't careful, she would dispense with me in favour of Salim or Shammi.

"I'm sorry, Sally," I said, "you called me here for a specific reason and I can't fulfil my function properly if I can't speak to you. It's important that we spend just a little while together, answering some vital questions – "

Her eyes were narrowed with impatience and uncertainty. She was the same height as me and could return my gaze without effort. "I don't believe there is anything I left out in my instructions," she said finally. "I can't imagine what you're talking about."

Salim was watching us, slack-jawed with disbelief. He wasn't used to seeing Sally's will being crossed.

"I can explain but we'll be wasting time, Sally," I said.

"Just go on," she said.

"Well, look – if you want me to be reporting on this, then you'll have to tell me more – " But she cut me.

"I believe I've told you enough, Mrs Sen!"

"Well," I said, "you mentioned, last night, about your husband's personal papers and his books – you said you'd show them to me, but you haven't! Of course – you couldn't have known he'd be gone before you had time, but ... "

It was a valid question and it gave her pause to think. She stared hard at me and I stared back, becoming conscious of the make-up she was wearing, the fine fur of foundation, under which her own facial hair was plastered down. The rouge and the virulent lipstick, the pencilled brows and the eye-shadow, were, at close range, overdone. But she had groomed herself for video posterity.

"This is a fine time to ask," she said.

"And ... and there's so much more you need to tell me! How you hit upon this particular method, who designed the Well, when it was constructed ... "

"It'll take too long!" she fretted, "and everything's there, in the notes, in his study – " She all but stamped her foot in frustration. "You should have got this done before! Not now, at the last minute! Really – it's *most* unprofessional – !"

"Sally, believe me – without these details, it'll just sound like a crank story! I won't have any proof of – of – the planning that went into your decision!" I was gabbling, saying whatever came into my mind. The only notion I had was that if I could only get her downstairs, I would have won the decisive battle. Nothing clearly thought out, just the feeling that anything would be better than having to grapple with her on a rooftop with no parapet wall.

"Just give me half an hour and I promise you – " I said. But I never finished telling her what I promised. From the courtyard there arose a wall of flame followed by a sound that registered as a fist punched into my eardrums. I was knocked off my feet, and lay dazed, while my mind shot ahead of me, down into the courtyard.

He must have been hiding there, I guessed. He must have seen Sally leave to come up to the roof. He must have scurried forward, in that silent, desperate way he had. He must have had an urgent, irresistible idea.

He must have turned the little wheel that he had seen being turned before. He must have crawled up into the well. He must have lain down. He must have waited a short while. Then pressed a small button.

Laxman.

Salim was the first to stand. He moved gingerly towards the inner edge of the roof, silhouetted against the orange light that was reaching towards the sky. The air was full of black confetti, a funerary carnival. Burning leaves fell out of the sky.

Sally, closest to the blast, was lying face down. Then slowly she lifted up her head. I saw her face and realized that I had forgotten, since the time when we first met, how old she was. The sari was grimed with ash and dust. "Subhash ... " she said, hoarsely, "Subhash ... "

Downstairs the French windows had been shattered by the blast, producing a shimmering carpet of glass underfoot. Between Salim and myself, we managed to get Sally down the spiral stairs.

We took her to her bedroom. Shammi and I undressed her, while Salim went to call Subhash's family, at my request.

Sally was like a mannequin in a shop-window, lifeless. We put her to bed and she turned over on her side, her eyes wide, seeing nothing. We washed her face and, without discussion, left the kumkum undisturbed. Salim came in to tell me that he had gotten through to one of the brothers, who said he would come by morning.

Back in the drawing room, the Well, visible behind the skeletons of smoldering rubber plants, was burning like an Olympic flame. It was still smoking late into the afternoon, while I supervised Shammi clearing up the glass and other debris. I despatched Salim to buy me a ticket on the first train out. The two ayahs and an advocate who had been handling Subhash's private affairs turned up to pay their last respects and to collect fees due to them. I told them that Madam was indisposed with grief and that they should return in a day or two.

Salim bought me a ticket for the next day. That evening, when I went in to check on Sally, I found her delirious, with a high temperature. She refused all food, weakly pushing away the spoon held to her mouth. Subhash's day nurse appeared just after lunch, looking disappointed at having missed the death. When she offered to attend to Sally, I accepted on Sally's behalf.

After my dinner I went to sit with her. She was quiet but conscious and agreed to have a little soup. Then she slept. Her fever was still high. I remained in there awhile, not speaking, till she fell asleep. Once or twice her eyes focussed on me, then slipped away again.

I called my editor and told him that there was no story after all and that I was coming back. He sounded tired. Then I called home to say that I needed to be collected from the station late the following night.

Sally was fully conscious in the morning, when I went in to see her. She said very little. I sat with her an hour and we may have exchanged a sentence apiece. I saw her once more just before leaving. Her mouth twitched, as if she would have liked to have managed a smile, even a mechanical one, but instead she lay back, exhausted.

That was my last sight of her.

I had planned to check on the Well just before departing but forgot in the process of bidding Shammi farewell. She was subdued but affectionate and wept when I gave her my address. I told her she must be in touch with me if she needed anything. Then I left. Salim drove me to the station in the Jeep. On the way, we passed a white Ambassador going in the direction from which we had come, bristling with Subhash's relatives.

Maybe five months later, I had a postcard from Shammi, written in Hindi, telling me that Sally-Madam had "passed on". Two brothers were living on the property with their families now, she said. They were tearing the house down and rebuilding it. She mentioned that she had also sent me a parcel. Something from Sally-Madam.

It followed, in a week. It was the colour photograph of Sally with the willows behind her. On a sheet of scented paper, in a tiny cramped hand, she had written me a note. "Mrs Sen," it said, "This is to thank you for your kind visit. I wonder if you could send this photograph to my family. I am enclosing some money for postage. You may keep the balance. Thank you. Sally." There was, in addition, twenty rupees in cash, an address in the U.S. and a telephone number which didn't seem to work. I wrote an investigative letter, but it came back to me stamped "Addressee Unknown".

So I keep the photograph on my desk at work, where I can see it. Every time someone asks me who it is, I pause, knowing that I could say anything, anything at all. I could build her up, I could play her down. I could call her an actress, a countess, a whore.

But I do nothing of the sort. I explain that she was

someone I met while out on a story, someone who made a deep impression on me. That she gave me this picture. That she made a charming dessert with China grass. A few more words is usually all she gets.

After which, she is forgotten.

EXILE

"Look – how bad can it be?" asked Rashmi, as she began the firing sequence on her sleek SuzDai Mini-Cruiser. "We've got to think of this so-called banishment as an *opportunity*. Not a calamity."

Her two fellow travellers remained, however, stubbornly silent. Her husband Siddhangshu sat beside her as co-pilot, while Lakshmi, her younger sister, was secured within the rear seat.

Rashmi sighed.

"So all right," she relented. "Mum *could* have told Kailash Uncle – step-dad Number Two – to back off. Everyone knows that. But it would've broken his little heart." Oo, catty! But perfectly human, surely? Not every parent sends his eldest stepdaughter off to the planet's Surface for fourteen long years. "Mum *hates* discord. She made a promise to him in a moment of tenderness and now he's taken advantage of her kindness. Or whatever. Who can say what lies behind Mum's decision? Maybe she believes it'll be good for her eldest daughter to spend a little time back on the Surface. Maybe she feels I need some perspective. After all, her foremothers put our home satellite into orbit at a time when most humans were still living on Earth. I-Udia was built to Mum's own specifications, it's part of her DNA. She's free to administer it any way she wants."

"Free to hand it over to her toy-boy hubby you mean," murmured Siddhangshu. "Him and his simpering little bimbette of a daughter …"

"Please, Sid!" protested Rashmi. "Bharti was designated as my replacement and as such, demands my unswerving loyalty – "

"Oh spare us the saccharine, sis," said Lakshmi. "Bro-in-law's right. It's a take-over pure and simple. You've always been Alpha Girl. How could you not be? Mum's never made a secret of the fact that she took an extra dose of gene-supplements when she had you. Which is *fine*, we're all okay with that, including Babs! But her Dad's super-competitive. Right until last week he imagined his little girl had a chance. Then Mum announced she was designating you as Chief Admin and he's been spitting fire ever since."

The little space-craft's secondary engines began to hum.

"But *why*?" asked Rashmi. "There's place enough on I-Udia to accommodate all of us and all our descendants for centuries ahead …"

The outer locks opened. The starlit blackness of open space yawned into view.

"Well," said Sid, as he snapped his visor down, "maybe *he* knows something *you* don't, about succession rivalry."

"That's rubbish," said Rashmi. "Everyone knows I feel only the deepest love and respect for all my – "

"*Counting down*," said the on-board computer. "*TEN* …"

"So that's you. Not the rest of the known Universe." Sid's voice was muffled.

"*EIGHT* ... "

"I guess we'll have a lot of time to discuss this," sighed Rashmi. "Comm links off – "

∽◦∽

Some hours later, having landed smoothly and been processed through the automated gravity re-training therapy, the three travellers found themselves hurtling downwards in a glass-walled elevator. They got out on what was called the "ground floor" though of course there was not a grain of soil or earth in sight. The surface on which they walked was faintly spongy and grey in appearance, formed out of synthetic tiling. The elevator shaft was a retractible tube which vanished upwards once it had disgorged its contents.

Up and around them, in every direction, was a tangled mass of giant, soaring struts and columns made of glass, steelcrete and plastinium. There were no plants or trees to be seen, not so much as a single blade of grass, yet there was something pleasingly organic about the glistening arches, the smooth planes and the long, swinging loops of cable that surrounded them on all sides. Here and there, tiny flashing movements betrayed the presence of free-moving minibots, that performed countless minor tasks of repair and maintenance. The air was filled with a continuous buzzing, clicking, chattering sound. Though entirely artificial, the effect was very similar to standing in the midst of a rainforest. The columns were supports for solar collectors which formed a canopy of flat panes rather like leaves. Between the panes, high in the distance, the sky showed itself, remote and blue.

Rashmi smiled, her head swivelling this way and that. "Hey team," she whispered, "this is kind of ...

awesome. Wouldn't you say? I can feel it in my bones: we're going to have a great time."

Siddhangshu refused to be impressed. "We're totally unprotected from the elements in a completely alien, hostile environment. I've not seen anything even remotely like a toilet. And we have no idea whatsoever of our ... uhhh ... co-inhabitants."

"Co-*what?*" exclaimed Lakshmi. She was more spontaneous and excitable than her sister. "I thought this whole banishment thing was about being *alone*!"

"Sure – alone with all the other low-brow riff-raff that never managed to emigrate – plus every desperadina who's ever been thrown off her home satellite with no other place to call her home but poor old Earth."

"Hush," said Rashmi, throwing a dirty glance in her husband's direction. He was as handsome and gallant as a man could be, but commonsense? Uh-uh. Not his strong suit. "Come on then – we had best strike camp before sun-down."

All three were clothed in light-weight, climate-controlled suits which gave them the appearance of being bare-skinned. All three were in their early twenties, tall, smooth-muscled and very fit. They carried their gear slung on their backs and attached to their waists, wrists and thighs. They also wore *smart*helmets that gave them the appearance of wearing ornate, pagoda-shaped headgear.

"The first priority is to locate a water source. I already checked it out on the GPS while choosing coordinates for our docking site." Rashmi flipped down a transparent electronic patch from her helmet and positioned it over her left eye, giving herself a 3-dimensional model of the surrounding terrain. "And here we are. It's *this* way," she said, striding forward in a south-westerly direction.

They constructed a temporary shelter for the night,

recognizing that it would be several weeks before they found a spot that combined access to food and water with functioning sanitary facilities. The Surface had been gradually abandoned as successive waves of the citizens chose to move up into orbiting estates with pristine eco-systems. What they left behind was a planet run entirely by *smart*machines. Fully automated factories, all underground, synthesized nourishment out of the planet's raw materials. Fuelled by sunlight and wind, the products created in the factories kept the orbiting havens furnished with an inexhaustible supply of food. Far-sighted developers had ensured that tiny cached stockpiles of food and water plus sanitation depots were maintained as public-access resources on the Surface, exactly so that off-worlders who wished to return for brief holidays would not go hungry or unwashed.

Between them, Rashmi, Lakshmi and Siddhangshu spent their mornings foraging for these stockpiled caches, the underground sumps containing water and the always too-well-hidden toilet facilities. They kept precise records of where they had already been in order to plan which direction to move in next. Documenting the abundant mechanical and electronic entities that kept this astounding inorganic paradise in continuous working order soon became Rashmi's primary pastime. Lakshmi, who was an accomplished draughtsman, devoted every spare moment to creating detailed views of the spectacular scenery that unfolded around them whenever they shifted camp.

Siddhangshu was the least fulfilled of the three. His skills lay in the design of multi-dimensional virtual wargames and in satellite-construction engineering. Here, in this enforced isolation where the three travellers were not permitted so much as a radio-connection to the life they had left behind them, he had little choice but to play endless games of solitaire on his hand-held or to search for functioning hardware from the computer-era which he could then attempt to refashion to suit his needs.

They'd had exactly one communication with their family since leaving and that was an extremely tearful video session with Babs. Reception was good and she'd set the resolution for 3D life-size. It was exactly the same as having her stand directly in front of them except that the tears rolling down her cheeks didn't actually hit the ground. According to her, she was devastated to hear that her beloved older sister had been sent away. It was not something she had wanted or asked for. There was no question of accepting the position of Chief Admin or ever occupying the hot-seat of the satellite's command centre. Alas, there was no question of relaying daily instructions: her dad's conditions, to which this video chat was to be the sole exception, included severing all comm-links. To the best of her ability, she, Babs, would administer I-Udia as she believed Rashmi would have. What else could she do? Then she broke down in further floods of tears.

"Of course, of course," said Rashmi, soothingly before asking about the health and humour of everyone else on the satellite. She was told that their mother Damini was still under heavy medication to counteract the stress caused by the entire banishment scandal and that the three wayfarers were sorely missed by family and staff alike.

"Ahh," said Rashmi, "fourteen years will pass like a dream! As for the banishment itself, I fear we may grow to love the Surface so much that we'll find it hard to return." She laughed lightly. "Only kidding! But seriously, it's more enjoyable than I expected. Please thank Kailash Uncle on my behalf for providing me with this unique learning opportunity."

Haha, thought Siddhangshu as he heard these words. *Speak for yourself, wifey dear. I'm totally losing my nut to boredom!* But he knew better than to express himself out loud. The record would show that he said nothing at all during this exchange. In the archives, the 3Dgrams revealed him looking perfectly serene and untroubled.

❧

Days turned into weeks and weeks turned into months.

As regards the other denizens of the Surface, the three satelliters maintained a low profile. A couple of encounters were friendly: an elderly hermit called Shabir, for instance, approached them with a unique gift. He had taken it upon himself to collect a store of vacuum-packed mango fruit-leather. It was not clear how he came to choose this particular item but his intentions were obviously benign. Unfortunately, he had also felt the need to sample each sachet, in order to test for freshness, thus effectively contaminating every single one. Rashmi accepted the tribute graciously regardless, claiming that the highly concentrated and desiccated strips of fruit pulp tasted all the better, now that they had been allowed to mature naturally. Lakshmi took one bite and immediately broke out in an allergic rash.

Much more typical however were encounters involving disputes with other dwellers over who had the right to a particular food cache, water sump, toilet or electrical power outlet. In most cases, Rashmi was so quick to assess the situation that she could either avoid a confrontation altogether or else successfully disable the electronic equipment of the opposing parties by remote control. Nine times out of ten, their outmoded gadgets were overwhelmed and died with a despairing bleep. Whereupon the owners turned tail and ran.

More rarely Rashmi had found herself fighting off an inorganic foe, some giant leviathan with sinews of steel and a chunk of silicon in the place of its heart. These beasts were programmed to be highly territorial, designed to dig up or renovate factory sites, recognizing no master but another machine. In two such situations, Rashmi had managed to outwit the monsters by rewriting their programmes using her trusty hand-held remote, until they turned against one another.

In a third case, she narrowly escaped with her life, by throwing her metal-detector down the maw of the gigantic tunneling machine that threatened to crush her under its unyielding bulk. The metal detector's magnetic core caused havoc inside the behemoth. With agonizing shrieks, the vast assemblage of steel parts began to lurch and flail, its dozens of electronic sensors blinking slower and slower until they could no longer detect Rashmi's presence, allowing her to slip away.

A year passed.

On the first anniversary of their arrival on the Surface, Siddhangshu had wanted to re-examine their meek acceptance of the banishment order. But Rashmi refused to be drawn. When Lakshmi tried to intervene on his behalf Rashmi stopped her. "Mum put me in charge of this expedition. The longer I stay here the more convinced I am that she wanted us to experience our ancestral home. I trust her intuition and am bound to abide by her wisdom." She allowed a pause of silence before continuing. "I didn't ask either of you to accompany me. This so-called misfortune was intended only for me. You chose to come. I must admit I'm a little disappointed that a year later you're both still in denial about the reality of this choice."

"That's a bit unfair," said Siddhangshu. "It's hardly 'denial', to question the extremely selfish, manipulative decision made by a step-parent! Enough's enough: it's been one year! I mean, *hello?* Thirteen years hence you'll be thirty-six. What about, you know, tick-tock and all of that?" He pointed to Lakshmi. "And your kid sister, what about her? She'll be an old maid by the time we head back and I don't need to tell you there aren't any debutante balls being held here."

Aside from the old hermit, all their encounters had been with other women.

But Rashmi had a faraway look on her face.

"I don't know if it's the advantage of age or what," she began. She was two years older than her sister and one year older than her husband. "The fact is, I'm okay with being here. I can't explain why exactly, but it feels right. I'm learning so much that I'd never get to know any other way. Yes, time's ticking away. So what? If I'm not fussed, you shouldn't be either. And if you are, well … bottomline? Get over it. Because I'm not leaving! And without me to fly the Mini-Cruiser, neither can you."

She ended the discussion by getting up and walking away.

Lakshmi glanced at Siddhangshu.

"Big Sis can be tough, huh," she said.

He shrugged, then chuckled good-naturedly. "Good thing I like tough women!"

Lakshmi drew in a breath.

"By the way," she began, but her brother-in-law stopped her.

"It's all right," he said.

"You can't know what I was going to say!"

"I can guess." He smiled. "I've noticed how you find excuses for going away and leaving us alone in the shelter at regular intervals. Don't think I'm not grateful. It's not necessary, however." He screwed up his face, as if acknowledging that he could be more upset than he actually was. "I didn't have any way of bringing this up with you before but Rashmi ... well, she discussed it with me even before we left I-Udia."

"Are you saying what I think you're saying?" Lakshmi looked incredulous.

Siddhangshu nodded. "She explained that the three of us would be a team. As a team, it would be lousy for morale if she and I, you know, *had relations* while you waited around the corner, humming a tune or whatever." He allowed himself another chuckle. "It makes a certain kind of sense. None of us has any training as obstetricians, after all! Fourteen years is an awful long time for a zero-error situation. So maybe I'm the one who needs to get his head examined, but I did agree to go along with her deal." He squeezed his eyes shut and flexed his neck sideways a couple of times. "I'm not saying it's been easy, I assure you! You're both extremely good looking ladies. And all that."

"Oh – *no*, I mean – no, Sid! Not me, not ever! Don't say that – !" She had covered her face with her hands and said, in a strangled voice, "I'm your *sister-in-law!* It's totally not okay to even bring this up."

"I'm sorry, I disagree. It's better to put it out there where we can all see it. And anyway that's all there is of it, I promise you. Just this conversation. Nothing else. Including thoughts. If I can resist Her Ladyship, then I can resist you too." He added quickly, "Not that it's a reflection on your, ah, charms or anything! Desire isn't the kind of thing that stays neatly at the end of a leash, you know? Once it's out, you can't control where it runs. So it's easier never to let it out. At all."

"Sid ... I think she's being terrible cruel to you. Really I do."

He was shaking his head. "Not really. No. The worst thing about her is that she *is* right. Always. Drives me crazy sometimes, I admit that too. But I've learnt to accept it about her. It's like today and the discussion – there was just no other way for it to go. So it didn't." Then he glanced over at his sister-in-law. "What's the matter? You look like you're bursting to say something."

Lakshmi nodded, quickly. Guiltily. "I've always wanted to know ..." She stopped. "You don't have to answer, okay? And we'll never have this conversation again, promise." There was another pause, during which she covered her face with her hands once more. From that position she asked, in a hoarse voice, "Sid, is Big Sis hot? I mean, considering she's always so poised, so rational, so ... so ... Miss Ideal Womanhood! Well. I just can't imagine her, you know, *letting herself go*." She removed her hands now. "I realize it's probably just my own extremely flawed personality. That I even want to know."

Siddhangshu had a slight smile on his face.

He turned to look at Lakshmi straight in the eye and said, "Yes, she's hot. Because that's the thing about Idealness – it goes deep, it touches every part of her being – and it includes being hot. So even when I want to feel sorry for myself and my deprivation, I know that she's deprived herself too and just as badly as me. But she's managed to turn her deprivation into something positive. She can do that. And by doing that she makes it possible for me to do it too." Then his smile broadened into a roguish grin. "Of course, there's one other little point I could mention here."

Lakshmi frowned. "What?"

"What would I know of 'hot'? I've never been with anyone else."

⚭

Two years passed. Then five. Then ten.

Ever since that first-year anniversary, there were no more discussions about leaving. The three satelliters became so accustomed to their lifestyle on the Surface that they no longer considered it a chore to pack up their kit and move to their next location every couple of months. Over time, they had learned to use local materials to build their shelter. As an added precaution, Lakshmi set up a force-field which was keyed exclusively to the bio-energy of the three residents of the fragile structure; other than themselves, no living thing would get through the field alive. Eventually, they became so expert at predicting where and how to locate their next food cache or making themselves invisible to the others who moved about in the shade of the towering solar collectors that they rarely faced encounters of any sort, hostile or friendly.

Each had worked out a set pattern. In the mornings, they planned their day. Afternoon was their time for exchanges of a practical nature while in the evenings, over the night meal they discussed broad topics about life, philosophy, the future of the Universe and the prospects for humankind.

Then in the twelfth year of their exile a change, like a cold shiver running through the entire region, began to express itself. One day Lakshmi said, "The strangest thing happened. I was out, as usual, trying to capture the play of light on a series of regular columns, when I began to imagine I was being watched." Rashmi whipped around, her expression tense. "Anyone else feel that way? After a while it made me so uncomfortable I actually packed my things and left."

Rashmi grimaced and clenched her teeth. It was very unusual for her to reveal any internal conflict.

"I hadn't wanted to bring this up, ever," she said now. "But some weeks ago I had an extremely disturbing encounter." It had happened, she explained, right before their last shift of camp-site. "You might both recall that I suggested moving suddenly? Well. It's because of what happened. I was in the South Quadrant – " they had named the various sections of the Surface according to their position on the planet "– when a figure stepped out from behind one of the columns. A man."

In all their time on the Surface, except for gray-beards such as Shabir, they had seen no men.

"He wasn't just any man," continued Rashmi. "At first glance I thought he was severely deformed. But it was surgical intervention. Elective self-mutilation." His front teeth protruded like a boar's tusks, causing him to drool; his forehead was low and deeply indented, as if he had spent his childhood butting cast-iron grilles; his skin was mottled with multi-coloured tattoos and all down his spine were spikes, embedded to look like the dorsal fin of a man-sized lizard.

"Yech!" said Lakshmi. "Sounds like a real freak."

"What'd you do?" Siddhangshu wanted to know. "And why didn't you tell us?"

"Because of what happened next: he stepped forward and without any preamble he – he – propositioned me!" Rashmi frowned, biting her lower lip. "He may have said something, but in the first place his speech was indistinct and in the second place, I understood his intentions perfectly. He literally staggered forward towards me with his male member, hugely distended, sticking out from his clothing, like a club. I acted completely instinctively. And rashly. Stepping back, away from him, and with one swipe of my laser-torch – you know, the one I use for breaking the vacuum seal on food-caches? I … *sliced it off.*"

Lakshmi and Siddhangshu both looked aghast.

"Omigosh," was all Lakshmi could say. "Omigosh. Omigosh."

"That's why I didn't tell you," said Rashmi, holding her hand to her forehead. "I've not been able to forgive myself."

"Forgive your*SELF*?" cried Siddhangshu. "Why – you clearly acted in self-defence – he gave you no options! I'd have done the exactly the same – "

"No, you wouldn't," said Rashmi. "Because in the first place, he'd never have approached you in that condition and in the second place …" She sighed. "That's just the thing. It all happened in a twinkling, as if we were both puppets in the hands of a malicious puppet-master. Whenever I think back, it's like watching a staged play." She sighed again. "He gave a terrible howl and fled, shrieking and cursing, spouting blood from his wound. I just stood there for a long while, rooted to the spot. Waiting to see if there'd be any repercussions. There weren't. After a while, I came home."

She glanced up at the other two. "I was literally too shocked and disgusted with myself to mention it. And that's the honest truth. I suppose I'm not used to admitting I've done something that embarrasses me. And I'm really, really sorry. I had hoped against hope that moving away from that area would be enough to prevent any follow-up action. But of course that is both cowardly and unrealistic. We'd better start discussing our options."

They spent the whole of that day and much of the next, talking through the implications of the man's presence.

"It would be too much to hope that he was solitary," reasoned Siddhangshu.

Young men were normally kept under tight social restraints. Access to and from the orbiting estates was based on bio-genetic keys. If once a family's signature genes became scattered through indiscriminate breeding, it was the same as broadcasting the password to a bank vault on an open frequency.

Rashmi shrugged. "Let's assume he belongs to a clan of off-worlders like us, visiting the Surface for private reasons. If so, we have the advantage of experience, because we've been here so much longer. Nor have we noticed them before the time of my incident and Lakshmi's feeling of being watched. What about you, Sid? Anything?"

He was about to shake his head. Then he stopped, narrowing his eyes.

"Hmm. Nothing threatening or suspicious, but ..." For years now, his favourite pastime had been to retrofit hardware that he salvaged from dump-sites dating to the silicon chip era of computer manufacture. "You know how I've been creating a very rudimentary surveillance network? Out of antique audio and video devices? Well, there's this one thing that's been showing up and I have no idea what it is. Here – " He switched on one of his salvaged monitors, a bulky box-shaped item with a vacuum-tube for a screen. "It's obviously some kind of minibot except that it doesn't seem to have any clear purpose. Just appears and disappears."

As he spoke, an image appeared of a mechanical object, about the size of a crow or a small cat. It had no visible limbs and was smooth, ovoid and golden in colour. It shot across the screen, vanishing behind a column. "I've tried increasing the screen resolution," said Siddhangshu, "but it moves too fast for this clunky old equipment to register any details."

"Very odd," said Rashmi, staring at the screen. "As you know, I've been compiling a registry of all the various inorganics that occupy this region. I've never come across anything like that." Over the years, her knowledge had grown encyclopaedic. She could recognize at a glance the make, manufacture and software generation of every little whirring gadget and suction-footed micro-widget that patrolled the Surface. They were all related in one way or another to keeping the external environment from succumbing to the planet's weather, but she had found ways of re-writing their software until she could get them to do her bidding any time she wanted.

"I've been wanting to catch it, to understand what exactly it does. But there's no predicting when or where it'll appear," said Siddhangshu.

"Would you say your first sighting was before or after our recent shift?"

"Oh, only after, definitely," said Siddhangshu. "Perhaps one week ago?"

Rashmi sat down in front of the monitor and studied the stored images of the darting golden object for a long time. Finally she turned away. "It seems to me," she said, slowly, "there's definitely something suspicious about this thing. Lakshmi and I have never seen it in all our wandering. Unlike any of the other minibots, it doesn't appear to have any function. Meanwhile, it pops up regularly on your surveillance cameras and seems literally to dance in front of them before vanishing. I'd say someone's specifically targeting you. Trying to catch your attention."

"What for?" asked Lakshmi. "If the Mystery Man's clan members wanted to take revenge, they'd come after you, not Sid."

Rashmi shrugged. "Who knows? Maybe the guy's family sent out scouts to find us, noticed Sid instead and got distracted." She smiled fondly at him. "I wouldn't be surprised. You're the only prince to appear on the Surface in all the twelve years we've been here."

Lakshmi wasn't smiling. "If that's the case then what's to stop them from tearing into our camp and taking him? After all, the man you met appeared to be mentally unstable as well as violent. Perhaps his family's even worse?"

Rashmi got to her feet. "We've got to assume they've not been able to disable your force-field. That doesn't mean they haven't been trying or that they won't succeed tomorrow."

Lakshmi got to her feet too. "I say we go out and confront them right away. We surely don't want to be surprised as well as out-numbered."

"Look!" cried Siddhangshu, pointing at the monitor. "There's the golden minibot – it's in front of a camera that's just ten yards from the camp entrance – " A pair of coordinates on the monitor revealed its exact location.

"Okay," said Rashmi. "We'll go right now." She snatched up her specimen net, GPS dial and laser-torch before dashing for the camp-exit.

Lakshmi, following close behind, called out as she left, "Sid – remember, it's you they want. Whatever happens, do NOT leave the field-area. We'll catch the minibot and be right back."

Her voice trailed off into the distance.

Siddhangshu was left standing at the entrance to the little shelter. They were always constructed using existing struts and overhanging platforms for extra protection. "I have a bad feeling about this plan," he muttered to himself. But there wasn't anything he could do about it now. He went back inside. On the monitor, the flashing golden minibot had of course slipped from view. Idly, he watched the glowing screen, waiting to see the figures of his wife and sister-in-law wander into the frame.

A minute ticked by. Two minutes. Five.

No figures.

Suddenly, his heart began to pound.

The camera was transmitting a loop, not a live image.

Siddhangshu sprang out again then skidded to a halt at the sparkling curtain of the force-field. Lakshmi's warning rang in his ears: *do NOT leave the field-area.* He clutched at his hair in an agony of indecision. They'd not had time to discuss alternative plans of action in case something went wrong. What if one or both women were attacked? How would he know? What action was he supposed to take?

Just then a fluting cry rent the air. It sounded barely human. Was it Rashmi? It did not sound like her. And yet ... and yet ...

Returning to the hut only long enough to snatch up his kit-bag, Siddhangshu ran towards the glistening barrier. He felt nothing as he passed unharmed through it.

"Rashmi!" he called, "Lakshmi – come back! It's a trap, it's a trap!"

But he had only taken a few steps into the clearing beyond the shelter when a blinding white light stabbed down from above, freezing him in his tracks. The glistening cylinder of a suction shaft whooshed down over him, trapping him like a fly in a giant's drinking straw. His feet lost contact with the ground. Blackness descended upon his senses.

☙❧

"Two things," said Rashmi, "are clear: one, we're going after Sid. Two, we will *not* apply to I-Udia for help in our quest."

Lakshmi nodded, but her face was a mask of grim despair.

"Won't be easy, Sis. All right, so we've located him, because of his GPS chip. But how d'you plan to break into the enemy estate?" It was an orbiting property similar in size and eminence to their own I-Udia, but positioned in geo-stationary orbit on the far side of the planet from where they were. It called itself L-Nka and was just as impregnable to assaults from outsiders as all other off-worlder facilities. "Even you can't possibly break open a gene-sequence code by brute computing!"

"No," said Rashmi, "nor would I wish to." She glanced at her sister. "The laws that keep modern human society free of the vicious, blood-fests of the past are clear on that point: we may not attempt to synthesize a code to break past one another's barriers. However, I believe there may be another way. It's sneaky. But I don't think there are any specific laws forbidding it." She smiled. "Come on. We've got a lot of work to do."

❦

Meanwhile, far away in L-Nka, Siddhangshu sat in an enormous hall, being plied with every kind of rich food and potent wine imaginable. One week had passed since his abduction. Every day he had been subjected to the same ritual: in the morning he was awakened by a team of fawning young boys, offering him a choice of bath oils and breakfast foods, and presenting him with a new set of clothes. Every morning he rejected everything that was offered, drinking only plain water and refusing to change out of his own clothes until it was time for his audience with the Chief Admin of the estate, a giantess by the name of Raveena. The rest of the entire day was spent in arguments, alternating between seduction and agression, to get him to submit to her will.

"Come on, cup-cake," said Raveena. "It's only a matter of time. Either you'll die of hunger and thirst or you'll come to your senses and accept my caresses. If it's the former, we'll have your DNA in a vacuum flask. If it's the latter, you'll enjoy every pleasure you ever dreamt of and then some *and* we'll have your DNA in a, shall we say, more hospitable location. For us, it's win-win either way. For you? I have to say there's only one option that's worth considering." She put on her most wheedling expression. "Come to Mamma, hunky-poo! All you need do is say *yes!*"

Siddhangshu looked the woman steadily in the eye. "Sorry. Not happening."

She was at least one foot taller than her prisoner and certainly twice as wide. Her skin was the color of white chalk and her hair was metallic blue, sculpted into enormous structures like rams" horns that extended sideways on either side of her head. Woven into this hair, she wore a dozen animated masks, six on either side, each one a caricature in minature of her own face. The masks were constantly in motion, sticking their long tongues out or crossing their eyes or else pouting their thick, red lips in simulated kisses. She had rivets instead of eyebrows and her enormous pale green eyes were outlined in flickering shades of flame. She wore diamond-encrusted chain-mail instead of clothes. Her spine ended in a long, tufted, muscular tail that she flicked this way and that, like a fly-whisk. It was not clear whether this appendage had been added surgically or was part of her heredity.

Raveena sighed and all her masks alternately boo-hooed and retched. "Dearie me. You're really beginning to tax my patience, pretty boy." She snapped her fingers in order to summon a tray of snacks for herself. She fed her masks before stuffing her own face. "So. Tell me again: what is the reason you continue to resist me?"

"Because I love my wife," said Siddhangshu, in a patient voice. "Because I will not be disloyal to her or her clan. Because I know that even if you succeed in squeezing my seed out of me, so long as it is without my consent, you will have broken the law – "

"The *law!* How quaint. And who, my darling, remains to administer any laws in our orbital dimension? Each estate is a law unto itself! You know that as well as I do. As for that little charcoal stick you call your wife, the one who attacked my beloved baby brother Suresh and who is the reason I discovered you at all – why, she's obviously forgotten all about you, hasn't she? We've not heard the faintest whisper from her." Which was a lie. Rashmi had been beaming messages towards L-Nka every six hours. They went unanswered of course.

Siddhangshu was unperturbed. "Even if that's so," he said, "it'll be for a reason. As for orbital law, there are conventions governing the conduct between estates. Breaking those conventions can cause repercussions which …" In measured tones he detailed the legal ways in which Raveena would be made to atone for her transgressions.

Every evening ended in the same way, with Raveena retreating in frustrated fury and Siddhangshu being administered a sleeping potion to knock him out. His attendants were all male, but a couple of them were Raveena's younger brothers. Early on, one of these brothers took pity on Siddhangshu and offered him food that had not been drugged or poisoned. He said that he found his sister's behaviour unutterably offensive, whereas Siddhangshu's dignity and nobility in the face of all the disgraceful pressure he was being subjected to were what he admired. And he poured off the sleeping draught so that the prisoner might remain in his senses through the night.

Siddhangshu lay awake thinking about the week that had passed. He was extremely grateful for the opportunity to be alone with his thoughts but it was certainly hard to suppress the sense of having been abandoned. Every day that went by without any idea of where Rashmi and Lakshmi were, or what they were doing, was an ordeal of forebearance. Gradually however, as he mulled these ideas over and over in his mind, he became aware of a faint sound. It was really very slight.

The room was in darkness, but the floor was so white that it gave off a slight radiance. He turned his head this way and that, trying to locate the source of the sound when he noticed a dark patch against the whiteness of the floor. It appeared to be moving slowly, a small flat blob about the length of his little finger. He began to smile to himself, in the dark. It looked very much like a black beetle but he recognized now that the faint sound he could hear came from the whirring of a miniature drive shaft: one of Rashmi's minibots. Siddhangshu placed a finger down on the floor. If his guess was right then the gadget would be one that had been trained to seek out his unique bio-signature and would come directly towards him. If it ignored him then it was either an actual insect or a toy created to look like one.

For a long minute the dark blob stopped in its tracks. Then very slowly but deliberately, it turned and homed in on the heat signature it had been programmed to seek. When it was close enough, he picked it up, turned it over and saw that there was a message glowing on the underside: *hang cool, bro!*, it said, *we're coming to get you out. lux*

∽

The army of minibots that Rashmi sent in entered the satellite estate through its garbage vents, its evacuation channels and its exhaust pipes. Being non-organic they set off no alarms. Once inside, they could be directed to follow Rashmi's bidding. She concentrated on sending in waves of minibots while distracting Raveena with verbal arguments and appeals to let Siddhangshu go. When the little machines had infiltrated in sufficient numbers, she and Lakshmi directed them to seek out power sources, to send her accurate plans of the interior of the estate and in particular to target the computers that kept the space station in functioning order.

There was no battle in a traditional sense. Over a period of days, mysterious breakdowns began to overtake the satellite until finally Raveena began to understand that an invasion of some sort was underway. It was much too late by then to counteract it. Under cover of darkness, one night when the moon's light was blocked by the bulk of the Earth, Rashmi's tiny forces turned the power off across the whole of L-Nka while simultaneously releasing a narcotic agent into the air. As the residents of Raveena's private domain sighed and sank to their feet in sleep, Rashmi and Lakshmi berthed their craft without the slightest opposition. Finding their way to Siddhangshu's quarters, they hustled him out and bundled him into the MiniCruiser. He was weak from his imprisonment but very glad to be alive. The campaign had taken a month. No-one had died or been physically harmed and in terms of the formal rules of engangement between estates, no laws had been broken. The tiny minibots were designed to self-destruct once their purpose was served, leaving behind only a trace of their presence. Even if Raveena understood the means by which her security had been breached, she would be unable to reconstruct the software or the chips with which she could launch a similar attack herself at some later time.

Siddhangshu regretted that the friendly young brother who had been of such support to him, had to be left behind. "Maybe some day he will find a way to escape his sister's control," suggested Lakshmi.

"Maybe," said Siddhangshu. "But where are we going? We should be starting our descent."

"Our work on the Surface is done," said Rashmi, "so we're going back to I-Udia." She'd called home once the campaign to save Siddhangshu was approaching its successful conclusion. "We've been away a little over twelve years. A lot's happened back there. Uncle Kailash has mellowed. Mum passed away. Out of grief, said Babs, who, everyone says, has kept her word about acting as my regent, not my successor."

The trio returned to I-Udia, to universal approval and celebration. For the girls, it was of course, a sad loss to be motherless but they were able to overcome their grief as part of the general celebration.

Some months after their return, when all their three lives had settled back into something approximating their normal pace, Lakshmi asked to have a private audience with Rashmi.

Her face was serious.

"What is it?" Rashmi asked. "I haven't seen you looking so grim since that time when we realized the golden minibot was a decoy."

"Listen," said the younger sister. "It's not my business. But there's been a whisper doing the rounds." It seemed that amongst the younger generation of staff members, an idea had been set loose about Siddhangshu's time on L-Nka. Orgiastic parties were mentioned, unnatural acts, chemical means of coercion. "There are those who want you to have him tested for chromosomal contamination. Or to subject him to brain scans to determine whether or not he betrayed your trust." Lakshmi shook her head. "I'm sure you won't want to do any of that, but then again ..."

"Then again – what?" Rashmi asked.

"Oh ... just ... the people need to feel confidence in their leaders" gene-pool. No?"

Rashmi shrugged. "Maybe. But I have no doubts. And that's what counts. What *I* believe."

"Wow." Lakshmi grinned. "That's *way* cool, sis. Put like that, it's so obvious, so easy. You totally rock."

"Yes," said Rashmi, sharing the grin. "I know."

THE STRENGTH OF SMALL THINGS

You know what I mean: you have a train to catch at four thirty, you start packing at three-thirty, and at quarter to four, you're all done. That's when you remember that you've forgotten to take your ticket. So you go to the big wooden almirah in the corner, the kind in which all important things are kept locked away, and you insert the little key in the key-hole with the worn edges and – the key refuses to turn.

Refuses to turn.

To begin with, you are calm, you move it back and forth in the hole, gently, knowing that it's just a small maladjustment, a little jiggling will do the trick.

But it doesn't budge.

You start to get a little anxious. The time is now ten to four. You need your ticket. The traffic is heavy between your house and the station. You will need time to find a taxi, time to give the driver the right change, time to check that the train is on the same platform as always, time to find your bogey and your seat.

The key doesn't shift so much as a millimetre.

You tell yourself, Look: the tongue of the key has

three little bumps and one depression; the lock has three little depressions and one bump; due to some minor dislocation, the bumps and depressions are not correctly aligned, therefore the key does not turn. It's only a *tiny* little sliver of metal which has caught against the wrong edge in the lock, it's really very small, it'll slip into place now, any minute now, just be patient, any minute now ...

No deal. The key feels as if it is turning against a cement wall.

Five minutes to four and you begin to lose nerve. You jiggle the key, you turn it hard, and your fingers, sweating, slip on the small flat loop of the head of the key.

Doesn't budge.

You lose control and hit the edge of the door of the almirah with the side of your palm. You shake the knob on the door violently. You start to pant.

You sit down by your suitcase in despair. You know that this is one of those situations in which the key will not turn until you have missed your train. You wipe your forehead, you feel cold panic down your spine.

That's when you begin to think of the strength of small things. One tiny edge of metal, pressed tight against another tiny edge. And that prevents the key from turning in the lock, which prevents you from opening the cupboard, and from getting the ticket and from catching your train.

The strength of small things.

Look at me, for instance.

I'm big. Six foot two. My mother used to feed me with her own hands until I was ten years old, telling me stories with every mouthful. My elder sisters might have been starving, or crying, or just waiting to have their hair brushed, but Ma would feed me first, make sure every scrap of food went in. Then she'd wipe my face and my mouth and call me a good boy and tell me that I would be big and strong when I grew up, if I always ate like that.

I used to adore my mother. Thought the world of her. Nothing was good enough for her.

She was small too, come to think of it.

When my father died, I was still just a boy. But I was already growing, I was already shooting up, just as my mother said I would. I felt big and strong when I was near her. She would stand near me and her head just came up to where the bulge in my biceps began and she would look up at me and I would feel my heart expand with love and pride.

She would say that I was all she had, her big boy, her only boy. She would rub the inside of my arm and she would say I must never leave her and I used to wonder why she ever bothered with saying it. I never would. Never did.

Not really. Well, I mean, of course, I had to go away to study. Went to the USA. My uncle paid for me. I studied to be an engineer. But she was always with me, my mother. I wrote to her every week, I thought of her whenever I wasn't thinking of anything else. She sent me food, she sent me gifts. She told me not to fool with foreign girls. Life was hard for her she said, while I was away. She had to live in my uncle's house, my three sisters had to be married off, a lot of money had to be spent on them. If I fooled around with any foreign girls, I would forget her and then – who would she have? Nobody. Nobody to look after her in her old age.

I used to feel like screaming when she wrote those letters, because I felt so useless to protect her, so far away, so futile. I knew I had to stick it out in the USA and that I had to earn my degree and I had to do well. Otherwise it would all be hopeless and I would be unable to do anything for her.

I was three years in the USA.

In the end, I did have girlfriends, just like everyone else – or, should I say, I had them, but not like everyone else. Some other Indians used to say that they felt bad, when their girlfriends would ask them if they would get married soon, if it was real love. But I never felt anything bad. I would tell every girl that I loved her, that she was the only one for me. They seemed to like to hear that. It made them extra-loving and caring. They would want to do all my cooking and washing and cleaning. Then after a couple of months I would tell whichever one it was that I had a rare tropical disease and that I hoped they hadn't noticed the symptoms of it yet.

They always left before I had a chance to describe the symptoms!

And in a couple of weeks, at some party or at a bar, I'd meet someone else and the story would start again. I didn't ever have to get involved. Those girls could never understand that for a man like me, even a thousand of them could not take my mother's place in my life. They could clean and wash and cook for a hundred years, even, but when the time came for me to go back to my mother, I would forget their names before the airport bus pulled away from the kerb. I would forget their faces, their bodies, their existences.

I didn't tell my mother about them, though. I think she would have been hurt. Or afraid. Afraid that I might not return to her because of one of them. She needn't have worried. I didn't want to do anything which would make her even more afraid for her future than she already was.

By the time I returned, two of my sisters had got married and one was being shown around. It helped her prospects now that I had returned from the USA, her big brother who was an engineer with a foreign degree. I would go with my mother to the homes of prospective in-laws, and I could see how impressed they would get, with my height and my new accent and my clothes. I would show off a bit, and sprawl on their sofas and tell them about the film stars I had met and the dirty movies I had seen.

We would tell them that, just as soon as I was married, we would be able to give them the sort of dowries they were demanding.

Some of them even offered to exchange their daughter for my sister! Free of charge!

I used to laugh at that. How will I look after my mother like that, I would say. Where is that money going to come from, huh? Who's going to pay for my mother's old age, huh? Your grandfather?

Fools.

Anyway. In the end, my sister ran off with someone, some rich boy, and we didn't have to pay a thing. We never met the boy or his parents, and I don't know where she is now or what she's doing. My mother said, in her gentle voice, "Good riddance! Now we have only to think of a nice girl for my big boy!"

It didn't take very long. I left everything up to my mother. I let her choose the girl and I let her decide on the price. I just went along with her to the homes of the girls, and I smiled at everyone and I showed off my credit cards. I even suggested that I had a green card and that we would live in California.

The girl my mother chose was not very tall, and nothing much to look at, but we had already agreed, my mother and I, that if a girl is very good-looking, she can also be very proud and cocky. The thing was to find someone who would be humble and who would just quietly sit in the house and look after my mother's needs. And mine of course, but my mother would be there to take care of me anyway.

We got married and the girl's family paid twenty lakhs in cash and another twenty in gold and jewellery. They bought us a Maruti and promised that in two years we would have a deluxe model. I said that I would prefer a Fiat NE 118. They said, Sure, sure, anything – but what about California?

I said, Everything depends on that extra fifty lakhs we talked about, remember? In dollars, payable in the USA?

That shut them up.

In two years, they said. When we marry off our son.

So there we were, three of us, living in a flat in Bombay. The flat belonged to the girl's family, and would belong to us, eventually. I started to work. The girl was a fairly good cook and she had done a secretarial course. She wanted to work, she said, she wanted to earn her own living, but my mother said no to that. My mother said, When a girl earns her own living, she gets the wrong ideas about life. She must stay home and look after her husband.

Then she was pregnant. My mother advised me that we should start a family quickly, to get that out of the way. Have two sons, she said, that should be enough.

The first pregnancy was of a daughter, we went to the doctor and they performed some famous test and so we got rid of that one. Why waste time with girls, my mother said.

The second time she was pregnant, my wife said she wanted to go to her parents' house. We wanted to do the test, but she escaped before it could be done. When she came back from her parents' home, we went to the doctor, but the doctor said that even if the test showed that baby was a daughter it was too late to have an abortion. It would be dangerous, he said. Dangerous for whom, said my mother. Isn't it dangerous to have daughters? Isn't it dangerous for families to have daughters? The doctor looked at her strangely and said something about old-fashioned views. I said we would find another doctor.

Finally, we had the test, it was shown to be a girl, and we got someone to do the abortion, but when the whatsit came out, it proved to have been a boy after all. Then my wife was terribly unhappy and she cried for months and wouldn't do any work in the house and my mother told me that she had a feeling that this girl was not suitable after all.

Then she got pregnant again. She said, This time, I won't have any tests. You can do what you like, I won't have any tests. My mother said, If you want to be like that, go to your parents' house and have the wretched brat. Why should we pay for your medication in vain?

She went away and she had a daughter.

The two years were up, by this time and I wrote to her family to say that my mother and I were waiting for the fifty lakhs to appear.

Her family wrote to say that, unless we took her back, there would be no fifty lakhs anywhere, anytime.

I said, Why? We fed her and clothed her for two years. Paid for all her hospital bills?

But there was silence from that side. I had not yet seen my daughter even once. Not that I wanted to, but still.

By this time, my mother said she had an idea. She said, someone she knew had a daughter studying in the USA, a girl who had got a green card. If I could marry that girl, I could settle abroad without all this trouble of waiting for my wife's parents to provide me with the dollars or of being saddled with an ungrateful wretch who refused to listen to reason and who kept running home to her parents at every slightest problem.

I said, But how will I get a divorce? I don't think my wife's family will let her give me a divorce.

My mother said, why bother with a divorce? Don't you read the newspapers? There's a much simpler way, and everyone does it.

I said, You mean ...

My mother said, Yes.

For the first time in my life, I argued with her. I begged her, I pleaded with her not to ask me to take this course. It's wrong, I said, it's sinful to take someone's life.

But she did not budge. She said, when you have a disease, you have to cure it by killing the germs.

I cried, I fought, I went down on my knees and touched her feet, I stopped eating my food. But she was like rock. She, so small, so frail, so white-haired, was like a great mountain made of solid diamond and I was like a dung-beetle in front of it, trying to make it move.

In the end, I gave in. What else could I do?

I wrote a sweet letter to my wife, telling her how much I missed her. I said, I was willing to settle for half the money now, in rupees, and forget the rest, we'd work out something. I said I needed her in the house and that everything would be different when she came back. I said that even my mother missed her. My mother helped me write the letter.

We have a smallish flat, just off Princess Street in Bombay. There are two bedrooms, one with a bathroom attached and one with a large verandah and some fresh air coming in. My mother had that one, because of her breathing problem. When my wife came back, she would have liked to stay in that one, because of the baby and the need for some more space, but it was important for the plan my mother made that we should stay in the same bedroom.

My wife brought the baby back with her. It was four months old by then and quite sweet. Sometimes when I held the baby I felt something shift inside me. Babies have that effect. They are so small, so weak, and yet they can reach into the hard places inside a human being and shift something there. I don't know how they do it. My mother told me not to hold the baby too much or else I would get attached.

My wife brought the money back with her in a suitcase. It was the old-fashioned type, the kind where the sides are stiff and unyielding, and the locks are the kind where there's a small flap which has a sort of flat loop in it. The loop fits into a slot on the lower front side of the suitcase. When the case is shut, the little flap is held down and the loop pushed into the slot, where it is held in place by a bar which can be slipped back and forth with the aid of a round button-shaped release-lever. When the suitcase is locked, the lever is fixed in place, so that the slotted loop cannot be released from the bar. You know the kind.

My mother's plan was that we would put some sleeping powder in my wife's cup of coffee at night, lock her and the baby into the bedroom and set fire to the room. We would leave cigarettes around, to suggest that my wife had caused an accident by smoking in bed. If we did it late enough at night, no-one would notice the smoke until it was much too late.

We decided to do it on the first moonless night after my wife's return. I was supposed to go away on a business trip, for which reason I had a couple of bags around, supposedly to take with me on my trip, but actually meant to carry the money. My mother would have to stay behind in the house, so that she could see that, before the fire came to anyone's attention, she could unlock the bedroom door, so that no-one would suspect anything.

Also, it would seem as if her own life had been in jeopardy, and that would convince people that a genuine accident had taken place.

Everything went as planned. My wife didn't suspect a thing. We had a hearty meal and my mother made a show of preparing the night-cap of coffee. The baby was a bit peevish that night and I was walking her up and down to make her sleep. I thought about what was going to happen to her. I felt bad about it. I felt I couldn't do this to such a tiny little thing. Then I fell to thinking about how it is that women, who are, after all, so much smaller, weaker, stupider, less important than men, still manage to survive in life. How they endure. Girl children get less food than boys, they get less attention from their parents, yet when you look around, there are so many old women around, apparently so many of them do survive. They say that women live longer than men.

I thought of myself, and of how big I am, and of how I'm not afraid of anything. I thought of how much more power I had than this tiny creature in my arms. I thought of how easily I could snuff her life out and how she could do nothing, nothing at all to harm mine. I noticed that she was asleep. Her lashes seemed to tremble slightly and her skin seemed fine and very delicate. I felt something shift inside me. I reminded myself that I was so much bigger than her, so much stronger than her and I took her quickly inside the bedroom and put her in her cot and shut the door behind me.

My wife said she would go to bed, because she was feeling tired. She offered to pack for me, but I said I would manage. She went inside. I sat in the dining room with the video on, waiting for her to fall asleep.

Soon all was quiet in the house, and in the building. It was already about one o'clock and my flight was by Air India, one of their cheap internal fares to Delhi. My mother came to me and said that we had better get on with the plan.

I got the suitcase out from under the bed. My wife stirred, but she was sleeping heavily. I could hear the sound of the breathing, long and slow. The windows were already closed because of the air-conditioner. The door to the bathroom was also closed. I wondered, as I lit a cigarette from my pack, and left it near my wife's side of the bed, whether I should use a little lipstick and hold the cigarette in my mouth, so that it would seem absolutely clear that she had been smoking it. Then I thought, it was a ridiculous detail, because surely the whole room would be burned up before anyone came to investigate?

I took one last look around, then I spilled a bottle of my wife's nail-polish remover on the carpet near the bed, let the cigarette drop onto it and noticed with satisfaction the flame spring up. I had about fifteen minutes to transfer the money from the suitcase to my two bags.

I put the suitcase up on the dining table, got out the key and unlocked both sides. I wondered whether my wife would wake up at any point or whether the fumes would get to her. I had arranged the bed clothes so that the rest of the room would burn before the flames reached her, so that she would die of asphyxiation.

I pushed back the button releases and – one of them refused to move.

I said to my mother, "It's stuck, I think it's just some rust. Get some of that oil – that oil you use on the sewing machine."

But it was useless, it just made the front of the case messy with oil. My mother said, "You should have done it before, I told you to do it before – "

I said, as patiently as I could, "I didn't want her to suspect anything. You know how she never let the case out of our bedroom, how she was so particular about it." It was true – she may have guessed something of our intentions, because she let me count the money but she insisted that it must be under her side of the bed.

My mother said, "Why don't you just break the lock?"

So I got out a big screw driver and I put it under the flap and pulled up with all my might. The flap bent upwards, but the small flat loop remained stubbornly inside the slot.

I tried again with the key. I turned it around to lock and unlock the release lever, but in one of my attempts I twisted the key so fiercely that it got bent and I could no long remove it from the lock. I began to sweat.

My mother said, "Why don't you take the suitcase with you? Why do you need to transfer the money?"

I sat down, with my head between my hands. "I can't take the suitcase with me because ...because ..." It seemed such a silly reason now, but I had thought it would seem incriminating, if I came back with that suitcase in tow. It was a huge bulky suitcase and I had thought it would be easier if the weight of the money were distributed in two cases.

My mother said, "And anyway, why can't you change your plan and take it with you now?"

I looked at her feeling the hopelessness welling up inside. "The ticket is inside," I said.

"Inside the suitcase?!!" screamed my mother. "You let that bitch put your ticket inside the suitcase!!"

It had seemed such a small, unimportant thing. My wife had received the ticket when it came from the agency and when I asked her where it was, she said she put it in the suitcase. I didn't argue with her, because she seemed to feel that the suitcase was her only refuge in the house, the only source of her power, and in a sense it was, and it seemed pointless to make a fuss about it. I didn't want to do anything to make her suspect.

"Break it open," my mother was saying, "take one of the big knives and break it open ... "

That's when I heard the sound of glass breaking.

It came from inside the bedroom, and for a sickening moment, I thought maybe my wife had woken up and was breaking open the windows. But even as I leapt up to go and listen at the door, I realized it couldn't be that, because surely she would have made some other sound, surely she would have tried the bedroom door first. I stood outside the door, listening, trying to understand what would make that sound.

And then I remembered the glass pane in the door of the bathroom. That must be it, I thought, that must have broken with the heat and the air pressure built up in the room.

I stood outside the door, undecided, wondering whether it would make a very great difference if the bathroom door was no longer air-tight. I tried to remember whether the window inside the bathroom, the window which opened onto the ventilation shaft was open.

Then I heard the baby. She had woken up and was crying.

She was screaming. Of course, I couldn't hear her very loudly, because there was a crackling sort of noise inside the room and the door was quite thick. But I could hear her. She was screaming in that way that babies have, half-way between rage and fear, she was screaming for her life.

Literally.

I remember that my mother tried to hold me back from going in to get the baby, to make her stop crying, but I was already opening the door. Or trying to. Of course, it wouldn't open. Too hot, right? Right. Some small piece of metal inside the lock, now expanded out of shape, no longer accepted the teeth of the key. Just a tiny bit, nothing much really, nothing compared to the size of my muscles or the strength of my fear, but enough. Enough to keep me from being able to open the door in time to stop the baby crying. Enough to ruin my life.

Because the baby's crying woke the neighbours up. Then they saw the smoke, coming in through the bathroom ventilation shaft. In panic they came up to our flat and when we didn't respond to the doorbell, broke the door down and found me and my mother and the suitcase full of money.

∞

My mother died of a heart failure shortly after the fire brigade arrived that night.

My wife and my baby survived, but of course they are no longer mine: my in-laws prosecuted me successfully and sent me to jail on the evidence of the neighbours, who were able say that they caught me in the act of trying to murder my wife.

And so I sit here in my squalid cell, which I share with seven other men. I watch the ants. So small and so industrious.

I think of how big I am and how, all my life, I was

brought up to believe that being big, and powerful, and confident – this was all that was necessary to be successful in life.

Then I remember that small bar of metal in the lock on the suitcase. And the small lungs of my baby. And the minor expansion of metal in the lock on the door of the bedroom.

And I am dazzled that these small things are – what is the word? – so steadfast, so incorruptible, so pure in their purpose. They have no task but to stay in place and to do the things for which they have been designed. And in their smallness, in their modesty, in their lack of ambition, they have strength.

The strength of small things.

STAINS

It was a tiny mark, barely visible. Yet Mrs Kumar was holding the sheet between her thumb and forefinger as if she feared that merely to be in the presence of such a sheet might mean eternal damnation. Merely to know of the existence of such sheets.

She said, "Blood."

Sarah said, "Yes," while wondering whether she should apologize. "I'm sorry," she heard her voice say, "I – I'm sure it'll go away." She could hear herself sounding one foot tall. "I mean – I'll wash it – "

Mrs Kumar said, "Come. I will show you." She turned and left the bedroom, still carrying the sheet.

They went down two floors and into the basement. There was a sink there, deep as a well, cold, cracked and forbidding. A pipe jutted out from the wall. A pressure-valve perched at the end of it. "Here," said Mrs Kumar, "here you will wash it." She dropped the corner of the sheet that she had been holding into the sink. "Wash now," she said, "it must not become. . ." She searched for the word. "Stain. It must not become stain." There was an antique cake of laundry soap congealed into a tin soap dish on the rim of the sink. "See – there is soap – "

She glanced up at Sarah, then turned again and left. What had the glance meant, wondered Sarah. There had been something there, something.... She shook her head and the bushy mass of her hair shifted on the back of her neck, feeling comfortingly warm and familiar. *Get this over with,* she thought, *just get it over with and don't let's think about it just now.*

She held down the release on the valve. A stream of liquid ice gushed out, biting straight through the tender flesh of her fingers and deep into the bone. She flinched, wondering whether there was any point to wetting the whole sheet. She picked it up and scrolled through it gingerly, looking for the stain.

It wasn't easy to find, what with the all-over floral print. Faux Monet. Ersatz Klimt. But it was a blue-based design and the stain was there, finally. A single pale petal of dried, graduate-student haemoglobin amidst the heaving water-lilies. Sarah positioned the spot under the outlet and pressed the release. More arctic water. She reached for the soap tray but it had become cemented to the rim of the sink. She hauled the stain-bearing area of the sheet over to the soap-dish and scrubbed the cloth into the soap, which was rock-hard with age. It was minutes before it grudgingly yielded up its suds.

Then she held the material between her numb fingers and scissored it back and forth rapidly, to work the soap into the stain. Wetted it again, just a little, enough to see that the petal was indeed fading. Scratched at it with her fingernail. Looked around for a brush, but there wasn't one. The fine scum from the soap was under her nail now. A faint blush of brown in the scum indicated that the stain was shifting. Minute particles of her being, her discarded corpuscles, were detatching themselves from the cotton fibres of the sheet, tearing free and riding up on the skins of soap bubbles so fine that she could only see them collectively, as scum.

She held the cloth under the stream of ice. The brown scum slid abruptly off the site of the stain onto that part of the sheet resting on the bottom of the sink. *Damn!* thought Sarah. She held the release of the valve down with one hand and tried to hold the sheet up so that the flow of water washed the scum clear of the sheet.

It was absurdly difficult. The sheet filled quickly with water, becoming heavy and unmanageable. There was a moment when she considered holding the cloth in her teeth so that the frozen lump at the end of her left arm could smooth away the traces of soap from the sheet while she held the valve open with her other hand. But she decided against it, ultimately. It would have looked ridiculous. And besides, she wasn't sure that her teeth could support the weight of the sheet, now several pounds heavier as a result of the absorbed water.

Ultimately she draped the bulk of the cloth over her right shoulder, held the valve open with her left hand and used her right to smooth away the soap. The stain itself had faded to a memory, its edges slightly darker than its center. But she rubbed it into the soap once more, flattened the cloth onto the palm of her left hand and scraped at it with the nail on her right thumb, scraped until it seemed to her that the blue of the underlying water lily was beginning to wear thin. Then, satisfied, she washed the scum away in the gelid water until all traces of soap had been obliterated from the sheet.

When she was done, she held the cloth up to look at it, stretching it between her two arms to do so. A film of water which had clung to the surface of the cotton gathered itself up into an icy rivulet which flowed straight into the warm space between her hair and her neck, down her back and into the divide of her bottom, resting only once it had reached right upto the threshhold of her most private self. It was like a cold electric finger tracing the length of her flesh, invading her warmth, violating her with its icy impertinence. Then it fell away and dropped to the floor.

She shivered. Realized that her nightie had got soaked and that she was standing in a dark, unheated basement, half-swaddled in a wet bed sheet. There was something offensive and illogical about it, all which she would have to examine and understand and file away. But not just now. Later.

She went to the laundry room by the kitchen. Mrs Kumar was already there, bending over, stuffing a damp and faintly steaming wash into the round open mouth of the dryer.

"Uh," said Sarah, "'scuse me?" Mrs Kumar did not seem to hear. "Mrs Kumar?" The old lady straightened up slowly. "My sheet. . ." said Sarah, indicating that she'd like to include it in the load going into the dryer.

For a moment it seemed as if Mrs Kumar hadn't understood what Sarah was saying. Then she shook her head, a quick bird-like movement. "No," she said, "no! Not here! Only down! In basement!"

Sarah said, "There's no place in the basement – " But she had been in a hurry to get away and it hadn't occurred to her to look.

"There is place," said Mrs Kumar and bent once more to her wash.

Sarah turned and went back the way she had come. Her mind was blank. In the basement, she looked around and saw that there was a light bulb with a dangling cord.

She pulled on it and in the resulting light, saw that a potential clothes-line extended across the room.

She hung the sheet, turned off the light and went up two floors to the bedroom. Shut the door. She was shivering. She wrapped her arms around herself. *What's happening to me?* she asked herself. She was shivering with anger, not cold. *What am I doing here?* she thought. *What am I doing amongst … these people?* There. It was out. The words that had been hovering at the edge of consciousness for three days now. These people. Deep and his mother. Indians. Not-us. Foreigners. Aliens.

But not him, she thought. *Only his mother.*

Or was it? After all, he had lived with his mother these many years. It had to have affected him. What would he say about the sheet, for instance? Would he find some excuse, some justification for his mother's behaviour? Or would he see her, Sarah's, point of view? And if he didn't – wasn't that the thing that made his foreignness a problem? The fact that, instead of automatically seeing her point of view, he would flip it over onto its back and expose its soft underbelly, expose it for just another cultural blinker. "Even you," he would say, smiling with his beautiful teeth, "have that Western bias which makes it difficult for you to see that there isn't anything intrinsically bizarre about being made to wash your bloodstain out of the bedsheet in a freezing basement sink!" And then he might cock his head to the side and say, "Remember the horse-meat?"

She bit her lip. The argument had started innocently. On their way up to Deep's home from Cornell, they had driven past a meadow dotted about with Holstein-Friesians and she had nudged him. It had been a joke, nothing else. "Wanna stop?" she had said. He had looked at her without comprehension. "You know," she had persevered, "stop by and say a prayer or – or something – ." But he had still not understood. It had begun to seem too silly to explain. "Never mind," she had said, "it's not worth going into." He had insisted, however. So she had said, "The cows, you know? We passed a meadow and it was full of cows and I thought. . ." His expression had been so blank that she would have laughed except that she knew he got hurt easily. So she stammered painfully on. "Well, you know – I thought – since Indians worship cows – " But it had started to sound ghastly, even to her ears.

He had begun to nod in that quick tight way. "You think it's funny, don't you?" he said, finally. "Just one more laugh-riot from the cosmic joke book – the joke book in which everyone who isn't a Bible-thumping, beef-eating, baseball player is treated like a court jester. Everything we do, whatever we find sacred, is hilariously funny just because it's different – " And then the final rebuke. "I thought you, at least, would understand."

"Deep," she had said, distressed, "you've got it wrong – "

"What else can it mean?" he said. "We've talked about this. I've explained it before." He paused and she could see the muscle in his jaw tensing. "About cows."

She said, "Deep – it's just that I saw them grazing and, and I – " She stopped. What had she thought? "I thought of a cathedral. I thought that maybe for someone who worships cows, a big barn must be like a cathedral is for us – " Was that really such an insulting thought?

He had said, "We discussed it just the other day. Didn't you hear me? When I told you that it isn't just any cow? That it is *specifically* the Indian cow?"

It had been her turn to look blank. "You mean, one breed?" she had asked, astonished.

His face convulsed with annoyance. "Don't be stupid!" he said. His face worked, as he tried to compose an answer which would make sense to her. "It's not a question of breed," he said, eventually, in a calmer voice, "it's more subtle than that. In an Indian village, cattle are the foundation of life, an integral part of the family. Here? They're just beasts! Milk dispensers! Meat!"

Sarah could feel a charge building up inside herself. *Why are we talking about cows,* she thought. *Why aren 't we talking about you and me?*

"Do you understand any of this?" he had said. "I mean – you look into the eyes of one of these animals here and you see nothing. Just a dull, stupid, unreflecting stare!" His upper lip had lifted in scorn. Sarah couldn't understand why or how it could matter so much to him. Then his expression had softened. "But – " he said, "you look into the eyes of an Indian cow and there – you see it. Consciousness! An Indian cow is a developed being. She has a mind, she has a life, she is a person – no, better than a person. A sort of living manifestation of the, uh, bounty, the giving spirit of nature." He looked at her, glancingly, as if expecting very little. "For the Indian villager, the cow's milk provides food and income, its dung is used as fuel and the bullocks are a major source of draught energy. And on top of all that, they eat almost anything – they're part of the garbage disposal system!" He smiled slightly now. "Does it make sense now? Do you understand the difference?"

Sarah had nodded. 'Yes," she had said, uncertainly, "yes, I think I can relate to what you're saying." She had grown up on a farm, till she was eight. She fought down a vague irritation she felt at the way he had described American cows. *How dare you insult our cows!* she had wanted to say. But instead she had said, "We have that kind of relationship too, with horses – "

That's when he had said, scornfully, "Oh yes! Horses!

During the war, you used to eat horsemeat! A truly nourishing relationship, wouldn't you say?"

"That's not true!" The words had whipped out of her. It was only the French who ate horsemeat!! Not Americans!! Never Americans!!! But the force of his contempt had drained her confidence. He was so often right about things like that. He seemed to store up tiny scraps of information just so that he could produce them at crucial points in an argument. "It – it's not typical behavior, what we did during the war – " Even as she said the words, there had appeared in her head a question mark. "*We*"?

He said, smoothly arrogant, "In India, there used to be terrible famines. But even at the depth of the famine, even when children were dying in their mothers' arms, there was never any report of cows being eaten. People were willing to die rather than eat their animals!"

"Well – " she had said, "well – I think that's stupid! It's just stupid to die rather than to eat what's there – "

He had said, "Oh? So – in a famine you'd eat your sister's flesh?"

"That's different!" But she had felt so helpless. He was implacable, when he had his teeth into an argument. "It isn't normal to eat one's own species – "

"But we've agreed that wars and famines aren't normal times – !"

It had gone on and on and on. There had been no resolution. He had grown increasingly cool and confident while she had felt her cheeks radiating a black light and had heard her voice grow shrill and incoherent. Towards the end of it, she had found herself saying that she couldn't respect a people, a culture which didn't have the sense to avoid famines. He said that a few famines were inconsequential in the face of five thousand years of civilization. She said that the ethical system to which she belonged could not view famines as inconsequential. Whereupon he had replied that he couldn't place much confidence in an ethical system which used, as its central icon, the tortured corpse of its religious prophet.

It had taken her a few seconds to understand what he had meant by that remark and when she did, it upset her so profoundly that her eyes stung with sudden tears. So she had turned her face towards the window. She didn't know what had bothered her more – that description of Christ or her reaction to hearing it. She didn't think of herself as a believing Christian, yet it hurt her to hear that description.

They drove the last fifty miles in silence.

Deep's mother lived alone in an old two-storey building surrounded by majestic elms. She had probably been standing at the window looking out for the car, because the front door opened even as the tires purred up the driveway. Deep turned to Sarah and said, "Will you be all right?" She was relieved to see that the sarcastic stranger with whom she had been arguing had reverted to being the familiar friend and lover of the last five months. She had nodded and got down from the car.

And yet ... standing at the window three days later, she knew that it hadn't been all right. That stranger, that alien, who had been at the wheel of the car dressed in Deep's body, hadn't vanished entirely after all. Having once appeared, he had continued to lurk, just at the outer margin of Deep's personality. Had he been there all along?

She hugged herself tighter. Why had Deep's mother wanted her to wash her bedsheet in the basement? What could possibly be the point of it? Then she thought of something. She thought of something she had heard her own mother and aunt talking about, laughing. A long time ago. She tried to focus on it, but couldn't. It had been too long ago and she had been a child at the time. She hadn't understood what they'd been talking about. But it triggered another area of thought. In primitive communities, menstruating women sat separately, sometimes in a special hut.

Is that what she's doing with me? thought Sarah. Avoiding contamination. Avoiding the unclean magic of a bleeding woman. *Unclean.* Sarah felt a current of power course through her. *That reminds me,* she thought. *Time to change.*

She went to the bathroom and pulled down her panties. A scarlet streak told her that she was just in time. She reached for the kit-bag in which she stored her tampons, while in the same movement sitting down on the toilet. She reached with her right hand under herself to find the string of the tampon, wound it around her finger and tugged, feeling all the while curiously self-conscious of all her movements. As if she were performing for some invisible camera crew. Twentieth Century Woman Removing Vaginal Insert. The tampon came out with a silky squish, and she released it, letting it drop into the toilet. Then stopped.

Why am I looking away at nothingness? she thought. *Why don't I ever look down when I do this? Why are all my movements so automatic?* And even as these thoughts appeared in her mind, a gush of simultaneous thoughts: *I shouldn't be thinking this way!* It was unseemly to look at one's menstrual products. It was unnecessary to think about what one was doing when one removed tampons. It wasn't proper. And yet ... why not?

She wiped herself with toilet paper. Then made herself look at the results. *It's a beautiful colour,* she thought, *red and warm, like – like Burgundy.* She wanted to giggle. *Imagine being caught sitting on the toilet and looking at my own blood!* she thought, then added, with surprise. *Why do I feel so guilty? Why? Even when I'm just alone with myself?*

As if to augment this thought, she heard, from the bedroom, the door open and Deep's voice. "Sarah?" he called. "Are you in there?"

"Yes!" she answered and quickly dropped the toilet paper out of sight.

He opened the door and said, "You're not dressed yet?" Then he caught sight of the kit bag with the tampons in it. "Oh," he said, "oh. Sorry." And shut the door. Sarah narrowed her eyes and smiled to herself. *Powerful magic, this blood!* she thought. *It can make a man apologize at ten paces, just at the sight of the equipment!*

By the time she was through with her bath Deep had already gone down. She found them, him and his mother, in the sunlit kitchen nook, with the remnants of breakfast on the Formica-top table. She didn't feel like eating anything and said so, pouring herself a mug of coffee. She could feel Deep's eyes on her but didn't look at him. He was encouraging her to eat what his mother had made, because, as he had already told her once before, it was rude to sit at the table and refuse food. *Too bad*, thought Sarah. *I'm not going to perform for him, for either of them.* If his mother could make all her meals without consulting her guests, then she, Sarah, could refuse to eat those meals without consulting anyone.

Mrs Kumar started to speak to Deep, in Indian. Deep responded, muttering. He seemed to be arguing with her, but it was hard to tell. The language sounded that way. *A bit like Klingon,* thought Sarah. Full of explosive consonants. Deep said, in English, "My mother says, it's not safe to go hungry in ... your condition. She says she prepared this – " he pointed to a disgusting looking mush "– especially for you. To build you up."

Sarah turned what she hoped was a blank look in his direction. "What 'condition'?" she asked.

The corners of his mouth were twitched inward in irritation. "You are bleeding heavily, she tells me. Apparently you stained the sheets."

Sarah said, "Sheet. It was one sheet. And a very small stain." She turned to Mrs Kumar. "Mrs Kumar, I'm sorry, but I'm not hungry just now." She spoke distinctly and slowly. "Thank you for making something special, but I really don't need it." Turned back to Deep. "If it's all right with you, I'm going for a walk just now." She smiled tightly and got up from the table, taking her mug of coffee with her and went out, walking slowly.

The front yard was fenced in with wooden palings. Sarah walked down the driveway and onto the road. There was no sidewalk. Deep's father had been a surgeon with a good practice in this small rural community in northern Pennsylvania. He had died four years ago, leaving the property and a fortune in investments for his widow and son to live on in comfort for the rest of their lives.

Sarah's breath, augmented by the heat of the coffee, steamed busily out onto the crisp air. *They do well here for themselves,* she thought to herself. *These Indians, these aliens.* She was trying to see what it felt like to view a minority group with race-hostility. She was mildly amused to see that she couldn't do it easily, that she felt guilty thinking thoughts like that. Even though, going by the typical logic of race-hostility, she had reason to feel embittered about the soft life that Deep's father had afforded for his family.

Her own childhood hadn't been easy. Her father had grown up on a farm and later managed to buy himself a garage. He had struggled to put his five children through school. Only she and her sister had gone to college. Two brothers were still in school and one brother had died at eighteen, in a car accident caused by his own drunkenness. *Aliens! Aliens!* she thought, *But isn't it funny that I can't even think up a cuss-word for them?* Maybe they hadn't been around for long enough to be absorbed into the vocabulary of racial abuse.

She hadn't been walking for long before she heard quick footsteps behind her. It was Deep. "What's the matter with you?" he said, panting slightly. He never wasted time with preliminaries. "You've been acting strange since this morning."

"It's your mother," said Sarah. "It's the bedsheet. I don't understand why she made me wash it like that." She would have liked to add that it was more than that. It was the horsemeat, it was the prophet-corpse, it was the revelation that there were chasms between them, which would never be bridged. She didn't think that the visit was working. She would rather leave right away and not stay for Christmas.

"You're so hung-up," said Deep, calmly, his face showing no sign of any emotion, his voice flat. "She's just an old lady. Why is it so difficult to do something different for a change? To bend yourself just a little?"

"Deep – she wanted me to wash the bedsheet in a sink, in the basement, in sub-zero water! It's not just something different! It's something so stupid and unreasonable I don't know what to do with it! I mean, I thought we'd agreed that there's enough illogic in the world without having to add crazy out-dated customs to it!"

"What I don't understand is why you stained the sheets at all," said Deep.

Sarah said, "One sheet."

"All right, one sheet, then. But why did you have to do it? It's not as if you don't know how to ... be careful! I don't think it's at all ... polite to do that sort of thing."

"Polite!" She laughed, gusting a thunderhead of white breath. "What's polite got to do with anything! It's not polite for your mother to sneak around looking at our sheets either, you know!"

"It's your fault for not having made the bed in time."

Sarah turned on Deep. "I don't get it! Why does she have to come into our room at all? We're grown up, aren't we? I was still in my nightie, I hadn't even left the room and she was in there and making the bed!"

"Sarah – " he sighed. "My mother's just a lonely old lady. She has no-one to talk to or fuss over when I'm not here. I don't think you can see how important it is for her to be able to do things for us – "

" – for you, you mean!" said Sarah. "It's not for me she's doing it, it's for you! Her little son!"

He shrugged. "Okay, for me, then. But she's lonely – don't you see that? She needs to be needed. She needs to feel useful. Why do you make such a big deal about it? Why does it matter so much?" He was affecting to sound tired of it all. The weary male worn out by the bickering of females around him. "You're a feminist when it comes to young women and to women of your culture. But when it's my mother, who doesn't speak much English and isn't sophisticated, she's suddenly the enemy, the oppressor – "

"Deep, she's playing a power game," said Sarah. "Anyone can play it – you don't have to be a man or – or – white, or American. You won't see it like that, because she's your mother and the game works in your favour. But all these little things – the making of the beds, the not letting anyone else wash dishes or cook, she doesn't let anyone touch any of it – it's her way of maintaining control. Don't you see that?" She drew in a breath, sharply, the cold air hurting her throat. It was a hopeless discussion, because she knew he would never be able to see it her way. But she tried nevertheless. "It's clear enough to you, when it comes to world events, when it's Russia controlling the flow of arms to Uzbekhistan – or the US controlling patents in the Third World. But when it's your mother controlling the flow of my blood onto our sheet? Oh no! Then it's tradition! It's being polite!"

He said nothing for a few moments. They were walking on the grassy verge along a larger street now, up a slight incline. The cars coming over the crest of the low hill seemed to respond to the sight of the two of them by swerving sideways, like skittish horses. Sarah wondered idly what the drivers thought. *Do they see a couple walking along,* she wondered, *or do they see a racial statement?*

Deep said, in a quiet voice, "I thought we had something special."

Sarah waited a space before saying, "We did. We still do – I think – but – "

"But you've moved out of my reach. You're seeing me as a foreigner, as an alien."

Sarah's head was swaying from side to side. "No, Deep, no! It's not like that! Really!" Even though it was.

He said, "I'm not stupid, you know. I mean, it's interesting to me. I thought you'd be different, but you're not, really."

Don't react, thought Sarah to herself. *Be still now. He's going to say something. Hurtful. Brace yourself.*

He said, "I thought being black must mean that you're more sensitive – but that was stupid of me, huh? Another kind of racism. When it comes to the important things, you're just an American. Just a Westerner." His face was expressionless and his voice was perfectly bland. He could have been reciting the multiplication tables, for all the emotion he showed. But that was just his inscrutable, Oriental way. "I thought you of all people would understand what it means to be an outsider. To be excluded from the mainstream – but obviously I was wrong."

He continued for a short while, during which they were passed in succession by two Corvettes, a Datsun and three battered-looking station wagons filled with dogs and children. Sarah felt like a guest at a stranger's cocktail party, listening to the conversation with comprehension but no involvement. *I should feel insulted*, she thought, *why don't I feel insulted?*

They had reached the crest of the hill now and had stopped. Deep said "What are you thinking?"

Sarah said, "I want to go back. I need to change my tampon."

⚭

During lunch, the dull ache in Sarah's lower abdomen became a concentrated mass of pain so fierce that she found herself gasping softly to herself, hoping that she couldn't be heard. As soon as she could, she excused herself to the bedroom and lay down. It felt good to be on her back, but the pain didn't let up. It was a small hard fist of pressure, a living presence. *It's just got to do its thing*, thought Sarah, *it's not actually malicious*. She thought of the lightless inner world of her pelvis and the mute scream making its inexorable way out of the avocado-shaped muscle in which it had been held captive. *Come out*, she spoke to it, in her mind. *Don't be afraid. I won't deny your presence.* Instead of running away from the pain, she would disarm it with attention. *Come,* she thought at it, *let me look at you, let me understand your structure.*

It was dark, she decided, and glossy. A glossy pain. A deep, rich blue, royal in its own way. Forceful. Powerful.

She could see it as a male entity, a strong, husky bellow. *But I don't resent you,* she thought, *isn't that interesting?* It was possible to look steadily into the centre of the pain and in some undefined way, celebrate it. It was a trial by strength, a specialized type of wrestling match between her body and itself. There was no victor or loser, the struggle itself was everything. *You fill me,* she thought. *Here I lie, supine, while you, confined as you are to a passage no thicker than a pencil's lead, no longer than an AA battery, are able to irradiate my entire being so that I feel your heat from the farthest limit of my toes to the roots of my hair.* She thought of the sparking network of nerves which, moment to moment, sent in their bulletins of sensation from locations around the multiple dimensions of her existence, yet none of them could drown out the roar being broadcast from her uterus, from her cervix.

She smiled, her eyes shut, concentrating on fashioning something positive out of her pain. She didn't see Deep enter the room, walk silently around the queen-size bed and stop when he was by her side.

She opened her eyes.

"Why are you smiling?" he asked in a whisper.

She paused before she answered, not certain that it was wise to share her secret. Then she relented. "Because," she whispered back, "I'm in pain."

"Pain?" His face puckered immediately in concern. He sat down, causing the edge of the mattress to buckle under his sudden weight. "Is it serious? Have you taken anything for it?" His voice was suddenly loud.

"No!" she whispered, lifting her head off the pillow in her earnestness, "no! I'm sort of ... enjoying it ... " She relaxed once more, taking his hand in hers.

Deep stared at her, frowning. "I don't understand you any more," he said. He had the kind of expression on his face that men get when they start to ask themselves whether the woman in front of them is experiencing a mind-altering hormonal storm. "How can you enjoy pain?"

She said, "I'm trying it out. You know, an experiment. I can visualize it, I can sort of imagine it as a – a – kind of – "

He said, "How do you know you're not seriously unwell?"

"I'm just bleeding. It's a normal, natural event."

He continued to look suspicious and unconvinced.

She shifted to her side. "I don't know why, but it's different this time. It's not just blood coming out, but sort of *chunks* of stuff. So – of course it hurts. The pain is from expelling solid matter, from pushing it through the narrow passage – " She saw the expression of distaste on his face and stopped. "What's the matter?" she said. "You look as if you're going to be sick!"

He turned his face away. "In India," he said, "we don't talk about such things. Women's blood. We just don't talk about it."

She allowed a spasm to pass through her before answering. "But Deep," she said. "This isn't India, this is here." She paused. "I don't mean America, either. I mean, this is Here!" She patted the surface of the bed. "The special space we make between us, the space of just our own reality! No immigration officers, no bureaucrats to tell us what to say or how to sit and stand! We're the authorities Here, we're the ones who decide what we want to talk about!"

His head was moving about, he was hunching his shoulders in discomfort. "It's not realistic," he said, "to think that way. We're private individuals as well as social entities, affected by and affecting the realities within which we live." He looked at her. "You're not just Sarah, my girlfriend. You're also a – an American black, you have your history and your separate destiny. If I took you back with me to India, people would stare at you, they'd stare at your hair and your different race and my own relatives would reject you. Reject my choice of you – even though we're almost the same colour." He looked at her now. "I've told you this before but I don't know whether you've really understood it. I'd never be able to take you there. I'd never want to expose you to that kind of ... humiliation."

Sarah said, "Deep, is that how you think of me? As a Black Woman?"

He shrugged, trying to wriggle away from the simple trap she had laid for him. "I see you as Sarah. And as a woman. And as an African American." Then he turned it around. "You do it too! You see me as a foreigner, as an Indian! Admit it – the novelty is part of what attracts you!" He shook his head wearily. "We can't wipe away our colours and our bone-structures! When we try to, we risk losing things which are important, we risk becoming cultural zombies – " He swept his arms wide, indicating the whole country, perhaps the whole western hemisphere. "Isn't that what the West is suffering from? A loss of meaningful tradition?"

Sarah turned her face into the pillow and breathed a few times to suppress the giggle which she knew would upset him if he could hear it. She had had an irreverent thought and wasn't sure whether she had the energy to express it or not. Then she looked up. "We have TV," she said. "We have K Marts and Hollywood – " But he was already shaking his head. "We have Star Trek and Superman. Freeways and credit cards – "

"No!" he exploded. "It isn't the same! It isn't the same at all!"

She said, "– the only difference is, it's not old, it's not gilded with time – "

He said, "This just shows how impoverished you are!"

Sarah said, " – and we haven't had generations of historians to show us how unique and precious what we have is – because we still have it! It's not lost under some ocean or sunk under centuries of poverty! It's in the Coke bottles and in the chewing gum and the neon lights and – and – all the things that you sneer at so much!"

He paused a moment. "And anyway," he said, "where do *you* fit, in this world of Superman and Star Trek? Those are the white man's myths – you can't claim them as your own!"

Sarah tucked a pillow into her belly and curled around it. A new fist of pain had begun to form and was forcing its way down and out of her. She would have liked to moan softly, but it would have created too much of a response in Deep. She didn't want to give him that satisfaction. She wanted to end the discussion. She closed her eyes and made her voice sleepy. "Sure I can claim them!" she said. "I'm American, right? They're part of me … even when I'm not a part of them." She patted his hand away. "Now leave me to sleep."

He waited a few moments to see if she meant it, then got up and left, saying nothing. She continued lying on her side for a while, thinking about their talk and about the pain inside her, wondering whether it was abnormal after all and at what point she should seek medical help. She asked herself what she had liked about Deep in all these months. He had seemed gentle, she decided, that was what had attracted her. He wasn't a big burly jock. He didn't come on strong. He was cool, soft-spoken and always thoughtful. His colour was ... well it was there, an added factor, but it was only colour, nothing else. It didn't go deep. She smiled at the pun on his nickname. Deep, short for Deepak. He said his name meant "light". A tiny flickering flame. When he had asked her what her name meant, she had said she didn't know. He had teased her and at the time she had thought nothing about it. But now she realized, it must have been of consequence to him, one more sign of her inferiority on the scale of traditional values.

Something he had told her long ago returned to her mind. He had been speaking about his parents, how his father had come to the US. He had come as a student, stayed to become a citizen, set up his practice and then, when he had a respectable income, had gone home to India to have a bride selected for him. He had married Deep's mother after having met her once, formally, surrounded by all their relatives, unable to exchange more than two words of conversation. "Tea?" she had asked him and he had answered, "Yes."

It had bothered Sarah, that story. She had asked Deep what he thought about it, whether he thought it was right for two complete strangers to get married. He had shrugged and said that they weren't really strangers. They both came from similar families, with similar customs and similar food. Aside from the detail of personality, they were very much alike.

Sarah had laughed at that phrase "detail of personality." "But personality's *everything*," she had exclaimed, "not just a detail!" Deep had got offended then and said that every culture had its traditions and it wasn't right to laugh at his. She had asked him if he would get married like that. And he had said, shuddering, "No! Never!"

But she wondered about that now. He's American, she thought to herself, he's a citizen and yet it's only on the surface. Inside, he's this other thing. He had explained once that to be born into a strong tradition was to know the steps to an intricate dance which started with birth and ended with death. "When you know all the steps by heart, you don't have to think any more – you are the dancer and the dance," he had said and she had loved the mystery, the poetry of it. It hadn't occurred to her to ask him what happened when a dancer found himself alone on the floor of a different tradition. Could the steps of one dance fit the music of another? Could classical ballet perform to rap?

The pain, having reached a peak, began to subside. She fell into a light sleep, awakening to dampness which demanded immediate attention. She rolled over the side of the bed to avoid bringing her bottom into contact with the bed and went to the bathroom. Blood darkened the crotch surfaces of her panties, her panty-hose, her jeans. It took her twenty minutes to wash away all traces of it. She started to hang the clothes up in the bathroom, then stopped.

Deep's mother might well come in here and find the clothes. She'd know at once what they meant. It was highly likely that she would demand that all Sarah's clothes be washed by hand, by Sarah, in the basement. *Once you entered the logic of clean and unclean blood, you could find your way around the maze fairly easily,* thought Sarah. The bleeding woman is penalized for being in that "state": the correct condition, of course, is to be pregnant or nursing. Older women, like Deep's mother, had the loss of their own fertility as an added reason for wanting to punish younger women.

Sarah wrung her clothes out carefully and packed them into plastic bags. She started packing the bags into her backpack and then, without really thinking about it or planning anything, packed her other stuff as well.

Downstairs, the house was silent. Deep's car was not in the driveway. Maybe he had gone shopping with his mother. Sarah let herself out the front door, checking behind her to make sure that it was locked. Then she set off. Overhead the sky was grey. There were random snowflakes gusting about, but no storm had been forecast. Within an hour she had boarded a bus and was on her way back to Cornell.

It was evening by the time she got back to the apartment she shared with three other women. There was a message on the answering machine for her from Deep. "Call me," he said, "as soon as you hear this. I need to speak to you. Are you all right?"

So she called him.

"Why did you leave?" he asked in his direct way. "My mother was very upset. She said it was bad for you to travel while you were bleeding like that. She says you might get very sick. You don't understand her at all. She's really concerned for you."

"Tell her," said Sarah, "that I'm all right. Tell her I like to bleed and that I especially like to travel when I'm bleeding. Tell her that I got stains all over the seat of the bus and that everyone knew, by the end of the trip, that I was bleeding because I had to stop so often to get off and change my tampon. Will you tell her all of that?"

Deep said, "She asked me if I was going to marry you."

Sarah said, "Oh yeah?" and there was a silence.

Deep said, "She told me that it was all right if I wanted to, that she liked you, that she felt you were right for me." There was another silence. "Sarah," he said, "what's the matter with you? Did I say something wrong?"

"No," said Sarah, shutting her eyes.

"Look, Sarah – " said Deep. "You know what I said? About not taking you to India? Well, I was thinking about it, you know and I can see now that it could be all right too. I mean things have changed, even in India. My mother accepts you and that's a big thing. I think it could be different. It *would* be, I'm sure of that, perhaps."

Sarah said, "Do they wear tampons there? In India?"

There was a pause before Deep said, "Sarah, I don't think you realize yet what a powerful statement we can make by being together – "

Sarah said, "You didn't answer my question."

He asked her to repeat her question and she did. He said, his voice sounding stiff, "I don't know. I don't know about those things."

Sarah said, "Well, how about your mother then: did she wear tampons?"

Deep said, "Sarah, I don't think these are proper questions."

Sarah said, "… or Maxi Pads? You could tell her that I'm thinking of changing from tampons to pads because I no longer want to hide my blood from myself."

Deep said, "Sarah, you *know* these are not proper subjects for discussion."

"I don't know anything," said Sarah, "just now, except that it matters very much to me to have answers to these very things. Because – you know what? I've decided that the only level of culture I care about is the kind which makes my own life reasonable and intelligent. Listening to music and hanging paintings on the wall is all very well, but if at the end of the day someone wants me to hide my blood underground and to behave like an invalid – forget it, you know? If that's what tradition means, then I say, take it off the shelf. Leave it out. My packet of ultrathin, E-Z wrap pads and what it represents to me about the journey my generation of women has made, is all the tradition I need."

"Sarah," said Deep, "are you comparing five thousand years of civilization to … "he choked on the words "… feminine hygiene products?"

"Yes," said Sarah and put the phone down.

FEAST

The vampire strolled into the Arrivals Lounge at New Delhi's Indira Gandhi International Airport, a faint smile on his face. He looked like a man of means, silver-haired, clean-shaven, handsome and tall. He had concealed the extreme pallor of his skin with touches of rouge, giving himself a complexion befitting a European traveller who spends his summers idling on the sunlit sands of expensive beaches. He was dressed in a light summer suit, pushing a luggage trolley with two cases on it, one large and one small, both in black hand-tooled leather.

It was three a.m. yet the brightly lit hall was seething with people awaiting the arrival of their friends and family. Metal barriers had been set up to create a channel through which the newly-arrived could pass through the hall. Standing right up against the barriers were a number of young men holding up placards with the names of arriving passengers variously scribbled by hand or printed out, in large black capital letters, in English.

A thin trickle of fellow passengers straggled along

beside the vampire, their faces turned towards the waiting crowd, looking for anyone familiar. *So plump!* thought the vampire, as he too looked out into the throng, though not because he expected to recognize anyone. *So eager. So innocent.*

A moment later he had caught sight of a signboard with ANDREW MORTON inscribed upon it. He had chosen to affect a plain-sounding, forgettable name. The young man holding the board wore a dark maroon uniform with gold-embroidery on his pocket announcing the name of the establishment to which he belonged. A hotel: the Maurya Sheraton.

"Ah –" said Morton, broadening his smile as he inclined his head towards the young man. "For me, I think?" He had an excellent repertoire of accents but had chosen, for this trip, to affect a culture-neutral Anglophonic voice.

In another few minutes, the young man had introduced himself as "Satish, driver" and was trotting industriously ahead of the vampire, pushing the luggage trolley. The mass of hot, sweating bodies parted briefly to let the two of them through before surging back to fill the breach. To the monster's finely attuned senses, the scent given off by the entities around him was as ripe and heady as tropical fruit, pungent with a quality he could not quite identify.

Was it uniquely local? he wondered. *Or did it vary from one principality to the next?*

There would be time enough to find out.

Then they were outside the terminal building and the mild humidity of the interior of that over-bright Arrival Lounge was revealed to be an air-conditioned version of the sauna conditions outside.

"Oh... *my*," said the vampire, temporarily nonplussed by the viscous quality of the air. He dabbed his mouth with a fine white handkerchief. The atmosphere was practically liquid! It was unlike anything he had ever encountered before. Unpleasant, yes, but also intoxicating. Exotic. Rich with chemicals, human air-borne ejecta, germs, dust particles, scent molecules, pheromones.

Astounding!

A minute buzzing distracted him briefly. He snapped his head around to discover its source and saw a tiny insect coasting like a surfer on the current of warm air that flowed off Satish. Indeed, there was a cloud of them trailing the young man. *Mosquitoes,* thought the vampire. *How quaint!*

Of course he had encountered such creatures before, but there was a subtle difference. Here, in the third world, they were still a force to be reckoned with: carriers of disease, minuscule assassins. As he had no scent, they paid no attention to him.

Then he was once more within the temperature-modulated environment of the vehicle that Satish Driver was currently in command of. Once they were on their way, the young man attempted to engage the vampire in conversation, asking about his family, his home, his country. Morton listened and responded absentmindedly. His keen intelligence was sucking in information about this new and unfamiliar environment with the same avid hunger that he turned upon his victims when he fed. *Why has it taken me so long to come here?* he wondered. *Why have I never thought of visiting before?*

The city streets were shrouded in darkness, streetlights spaced at long intervals. There were broad avenues lined with trees and bushes. Behind the trees reared the silhouettes of tall buildings, punctuated by the vertical strip of their lighted stairwells. Other vehicles careened by on either side. But whenever his own car paused to acknowledge a red light, permitting the vampire to sample his surroundings, he could sense the presence of countless warm bodies lying unguarded in sleep on the sidewalks. They revealed themselves as long and low bundles, giving off a faint glow.

The hotel was like a fist of brightness, thrust up against the night sky. Satish saw Morton to his room, collected a juicy tip, and agreed to return the following evening in his capacity as driver and informal tour guide. By this time, it was close to dawn so the vampire drew the heavy drapes across his windows, turned off all the lights then went into his bathroom and lay down, fully clothed, in the tub. It was the closest thing to a coffin he would find while travelling and he greatly preferred it to the suffocating embrace of a bed. He lay in the cold white container, listening to the murmur of water rattling in the plumbing and entered into that state of suspended animation which passed for sleep amongst entities of his kind.

For the next three evenings, he went out in the company of Satish Driver to the most densely populated areas of the city. Chandni Chowk was the name of one. The area around the shrine of Nizamuddin Aulia was another. The third was an underground shopping mall called Palika Bazaar. He immersed himself in the fragrant, living heat of his prey, stoking his hunger like a child teasing a caged animal, enjoying its keening protests.

In places where the teeming hordes were especially dense, squishy soft bodies pressed against him on all sides with a surprising lack of reserve. He had never before encountered such uninhibited yet anonymous physical contact. In Europe it was unheard of for strangers, even in the grip of football hysteria or Oktoberfest revelry, to tolerate intimacies at this level. When he managed to persuade Satish to introduce him to a commuter train, bursting at rush hour like a pod full of human peas, he practically swooned with the intoxication of being squeezed butt-to-butt, thigh-to-thigh, chest-to-chest against dozens of fellow passengers. With their slick-skinned brown faces inches from his own, the aroma they gave off filled him with quivering delight. Cardamom and clove, onion and ginger, mustard oil, pepper and ... something else.

In the beginning he decided that it was *innocence*.

Yes. It was innocence that produced a fragrance as precise and particular as that of a spice.

Returning from the third foray, sitting in the passenger seat beside Satish Driver, the smile on Morton's face as he acknowledged the pressure of the need building within his body had grown into a grimace. Every individual hair-follicle was tense with longing. His hands were literally twitching in his lap. In his belly, the furnace of his craving burned so hot and bright that it was all he could do to avoid crying out. As it was, he had to keep his lips parted to allow him to pant softly. His canines thickened and grew long within his mouth, throbbing painfully as he reined them in, keeping them concealed.

At the hotel, he invited the driver to come up to his room. Within minutes of entering the chamber and locking the door, he had turned upon the lad and accomplished the deed. Satish didn't resist at all. He closed his eyes as the vampire embraced him, allowing himself to be bent backwards. Even as the gleaming white teeth punctured the soft, yielding skin of his throat, the driver merely stiffened and let out a tiny gurgling moan. Nothing more. For long minutes, Morton's senses reeled with the familiar blinding radiance that blotted out all thought, all awareness. He knew nothing of his surroundings until he had drained every last drop of the sweet, rich, life-sustaining elixir complete with all the other liquids that animated mortal frames. Only a dry, rattling husk remained in his arms when he was done.

Then he lay back on the carpet, sated.

Ah! he thought. *Ahhh. It has begun.*

His reign of passion in this new country. His personal, private bloodfest.

∞

In his suitcase, he had a small electric saw with which he sliced up the late driver's body. The tub was an excellent location for the operation. Once he had rendered the body down to a series of two-inch-thick slabs, he packed the bits into sealable plastic bags, then scrubbed the tub clean of corpse-litter. He transferred the now unrecognizable remains of the driver to his cases, called for room service, went down, hired a taxi and checked out of the hotel.

By evening, he was in the Taj Man Singh, with a new alias and a passport to match.

He waited till after midnight to go on a long slow walk, carrying the sealable bags in his backpack and emptying a few of them into garbage dumps as he passed them. In order to avoid attracting attention, he assumed the shrunken frame of a scavenging beggar, complete with matted hair and dirty, swarthy skin. Changing shape always required an enormous expenditure of energy and by the time he had completed his task for the night, his stomach was growling again.

He was perhaps a half-mile from the hotel. Keeping to the deep shade of the shrubbery and creeping along the boundary wall of one of the gracious mansions lining the avenue, he came upon a sleeping human form, curled up like a dog on a patch of jute sacking. He did not attempt to find the tramp's neck, but bit down into the wrist at the pulse point.

The rank scent of the skin, unwashed perhaps for weeks and sticky with oozing wounds, did not deter him for even a second. He took his pleasures where he found them, which was frequently amongst the poor and the destitute, defenceless as they so often were.

When he had recovered from the storm of his own delight, he resumed his own shape, rearranged his clothes and rested for a few moments, with his back against the brick wall. Once again he had tasted that flavour, the one he had initially identified as innocence. It was sharp, sweet and unmistakeable, like a citrus fruit that concentrates all the passion of summer within the plump grains of its flesh. But what *was* it? He, who had drained countless containers of human blood in the course of his unnaturally long life, could not remember encountering this quality before. Was it connected to the climate? Or something specific to this culture? And if it was culture, then how curious that he could detect it even upon this castaway, this stinking derelict with no discernible society to call his own!

Leaving the desiccated remains where they lay, the vampire returned to his hotel feeling thoughtful.

In the course of the next couple of weeks, he continued his forays into the city's night-time streets. He was astonished at the ease with which he found victims. The best locations were near garbage dumps, inside the many ruined tombs that dotted the city and under park benches. But public toilets and the stairwells of apartment buildings were equally well-populated by unresisting targets. Never yet had he encountered such extreme submission, such a total absence of struggle. It was true that he'd always had a gentle touch, an almost surgical skill at locating the exact point on an artery that would produce the swiftest results and with the least discomfort to the owner. Even so, it amazed and slightly unnerved him that he should have such easy success.

Equally astonishing was the fact that no reports of mysterious deaths had appeared in the press. He had been expecting to cover his tracks with meticulous care, as he had done with Satish. But it wasn't necessary. If an encounter took place in a park, he buried the remains in a pit he dug in the same location. If in a building, he folded the dry husk into a sack and carried the small bundle away to the closest convenient water tank. He had even, on a couple of occasions, affected the appearance of an Indian coolie carrying a head-load in broad daylight. No-one turned to look twice at him.

Though he fed only under cover of darkness, he no longer hid inside the hotel during daylight hours. Instead he travelled in buses and trains, walked through bustling market places and plunged into the crowds flocking outside shrines and other places of worship. He assumed a number of different disguises, finding that a young foreign male back-packer elicited the most positive responses from ordinary people. He talked to anyone who looked friendly, trying in various oblique ways to find answers to the questions that could never be asked directly of any mortals: *What is the meaning of this unique local taste? Why have I not encountered it before? Is it possible for culture to impart an actual physical fragrance? And if so, why have I never heard of such a thing before?*

In the hotel, he sought out fellow Europeans now and then, just to confirm that the scent or flavour or whatever it was did not stick to them. And it did not. Only long-time expatriates gave off a slight trace of it. Twice he'd been invited to Embassy receptions and had mingled with crowds of his own compatriots, feeling nostalgic for the familiar, uncomplicated scent he associated with European victims. It amused him to contemplate luring a fellow guest into the bushes for a quick nip, but he easily resisted the temptation. On the one hand, he was sated with daily feeding. On the other hand, he guessed that a disappearance from an Embassy party might result in alarm bells being rung. The tell-tale wounds would be recognized for what they were and the hunt would be on, with all the frenzy associated with it. How many years had it been since he'd last had to save himself from imminent exposure or fight off an attack from someone armed with The Weapons? He couldn't remember.

Back in Europe, he had got used to living so frugally, so mindful of the dangers associated with being a vampire that months would go by when he fed only on vermin, stray cats, crows plucked out of the air and even, on occasion, raw meat bought from a supermarket. He shuddered at the memory of the last time he had been driven to suck sustenance out of an inert lump of dead flesh bought at a Safeways counter. He now wondered how he was going to adjust back to his home environment. He'd grown flabby during his stay in this country, not just in terms of his physical dimensions, but in the loss of his vampire instincts. He simply didn't have to worry about exposure here. The majority of citizens were apparently unconscious of monsters of his kind and therefore had no defences against him.

But his six-month visa was running out and the stack of Euros he'd brought with him had dwindled alarmingly. He could not own credit cards or any other financial instruments because of the peculiar problems associated with immortality. Not only did he need to suppress bank records which revealed the unnatural length of his life, but Morton, or Martin Payne as he now called himself, routinely struggled when handling currency notes that made direct reference to the religion of his culture. US dollars, for instance, were out of bounds for him because of that pernicious line: "In God We Trust'. He had to wear gloves in order to avoid coming into direct contact with the notes before picking them up.

Sipping a cup of coffee in the hotel lobby restaurant one morning, fretting over the prospect of returning to Europe, he became suddenly aware that the hair on the back of his neck was prickling. He turned in his seat, to find a blonde woman standing near him, smiling in the way of someone requesting permission to join his table.

"May I?" she now said, as she came around to the empty chair opposite his.

Taken by surprise, Payne could not muster excuses quickly enough. "Why ... uh ... yes, I suppose so – of course –" he said, beginning to stand up.

The woman stopped him. "Oh, don't bother," she said, sitting down. She was a little over middle-age, with fashionably streaked hair and an amethyst necklace around her neck. Her crisp white linen jacket and skirt partnered with an ice-mauve silk blouse, spoke of expensive good taste.

"My name's Cindy," she said, in an accent that owed more to America than England. "Cindy Wright." She did not offer her hand for shaking. "You needn't bother looking around to see if there are empty seats elsewhere," she said. She paused for him to absorb the implications of her remark. "I'm here because I think I know what you are."

The vampire raised his eyebrows. "Oh?"

Already his mind was racing, estimating his chances of success if escape became necessary. Already he was berating himself for his lack of preparedness, his loss of caution. In a crowded room, in broad daylight, the only option was an extreme change of form – a bat, for instance –

"Relax," said Cindy, as if she perfectly understood his train of thought. "I'm not about to expose you." She paused with that annoying, knowing smile playing upon her lips. "I've been shadowing you for a couple of days so I'm pretty sure." She shook her head at him as he continued to look blankly at her. "Come on! Surely you've not lost *all* your instincts?" She leaned forward now and very quickly, in a gesture that shocked him because it was so unexpected, she flicked her upper lip with a finger, just enough that he could see one of her canines. Sure enough, there it was: the sharp unnatural point, unmistakeable even in its sheathed and quiescent state.

Relief flushed through Payne. "My goodness!" he gasped. "For a moment I thought...'

"I know, I know," said Cindy. "It happens to all of us. Exposure Panic Response! But that's the least of your worries. Don't just sit there gulping like a fish! Do you mean to say you really don't have the slightest idea what I'm talking about?"

"Well – I – " stammered Payne. "This is so unexpected! I've not met anyone else for such a long time that I'd stopped hoping. One of us, I mean. Are ... are there many? Of us?"

"Yes and no," said Cindy. "Very few with active teeth."

"Huh?" said Payne, his eyes narrowing. "I don't understand what you mean."

Cindy glanced away. "It's one of the final signs," she said, "that we've been here too long." She looked back at him. "Mine stopped descending after my first year.

But there are other signs. Just the fact that we're both sitting here in the open, in daylight, for instance. Didn't that surprise you? No? You'll find that fresh-flowing water isn't much of a problem anymore either. As for the reflections in mirrors, well?" She tapped one of the shiny metal spoons lying on the table. "Pick one of these up and surprise yourself!"

Payne sucked in his breath, feeling deeply disturbed. "What about ...?"

Cindy pre-empted him. "Each of us is different," she said. She held up her right arm. "Can you look at my charm bracelet?" Payne winced and averted his face, but not before he'd seen the small gold cross dangling from her wrist. "There you go. You're still sensitive. But I can wear one now. You'll be able to as well, if you stay here long enough."

"But ... why?" said Payne in a hoarse voice. "It makes no *sense*!"

"On the contrary," retorted Cindy, "it makes all the sense in the world. We're products of a very specific belief system – I won't name it, since you're still too sensitive – and all our dark powers, even though they're forged in opposition to that system, require our absolute belief in it." She stopped abruptly, staring at him with a searching expression. "In fact, just by telling you this, I might be weakening your powers. Do you want me to stop?"

"No, no ..." said Payne, in a low voice. He was finding it difficult to control his breathing. "Please continue. I have indeed been puzzled and curious. Whatever it is, I need to know."

"All right," said Cindy, "you asked for it." She was no longer smiling. "The belief system we belong to is an austere one. Think about it: one immortal soul, one life on earth, one chance for heaven or hell. Right? Within that system, by choosing to suck the life-essence out of our fellow creatures, we gave up our rights as mortals. In exchange we acquired supernatural privileges such as immortality. But in order to maintain our powers *we must uphold our own belief system!* Are you beginning to get my point? In order to be culture-specific monsters we ourselves have got to be True Believers!"

She gestured at the brightly lit, bustling hotel lobby in which they were both sitting. They were surrounded by guests and employees, a majority of whom were Indians. "In this culture, the rules of faith are completely different. There's no precise heaven or hell. There's no immortal soul – not in the sense we understand it – and there's no single ... uh ... divine authority. Instead there are infinite births, infinite deaths, infinite divinities. It doesn't really matter whether they formally believe in reincarnation or what names they give their deities or whether they even believe in anyone or anything. Just by being here they get recycled. So when we come here, we're exposed to a system that's directly opposed to our own. Instead of a single life and a single fate, there's a raging torrent of lives and fates, truths and deaths!"

Payne listened intently, saying nothing.

"Within this system, though they have monsters, even one they call 'vampire', there's nothing fixed and definite about them. Some say their feet are on backwards and that they lurk in lonely places. But there are no crucifixes or silver bullets with which to dispatch them, no well-defined appearance or behavior. They're not feared in the same way we're feared back home." She shrugged. "After all, if one life slips away courtesy a ghoul or demon, there's always a chance of having better luck the next time around! In the *next* life. The *next* incarnation." She sent him a searching look. "It's a system based on infinite abundance, in which nothing and no-one matters because there's always more where it came from. So when we, who belong to the one-life-one-chance system, come into contact with a multi-life-multi-chance system, we begin to drown. Not right away, but slowly, over time."

Payne said, his voice plaintive, "But they *succumb* to us! How can we be their victims?"

Cindy was shaking her head. "Numbers matter. All they have to do is keep on succumbing until, finally, our resistance is overwhelmed. That sweet flavour you've noticed? It's not just a tropical spice. It's a lack of fear. They don't fear us because they *know*, in their deepest hearts, that their sheer numbers will prevail. Without active fear to define us, we cease to be monsters. Our powers wane. We begin to die."

Payne could feel a churning sensation within himself. Already, he could sense the truth of what Cindy was saying. His teeth were aching strangely for instance. "Surely it's reversible?" he whispered. "Surely when we return to Europe we get our powers back?"

"No idea," said Cindy. "I've only met those of us who've chosen to stay."

"But – but – *mortality*!" said Payne, grimacing. "Don't you mind dying?"

"Ahh," said Cindy, stretching luxuriously and leaning back in her chair. "You get used to it after a while. And besides, once you've been here long enough, you find yourself starting to hope..." She was smiling once more.

"*Hope!* Hope for what?"

"Better luck next time!"

THREE VIRGINS

A young cousin once asked me the meaning of the word "virgin". I was fourteen at the time, she was ten and we were both attending another cousin's wedding, in Bombay.

"It means a lady whose son turns into God," I said at once.

"What?" she asked, looking confused.

I didn't want to be the one to break the news to her that men did disgusting things to women in order to coax the next generation into being. Or that "virgin" was the name given to those who had not yet experienced these horrors. As for why a term was needed to describe a condition which was defined by its loss? Well. Nine years in three different Catholic schools in three different countries had still not provided me with an answer to that puzzle.

By the time I graduated two years later, the implausibility of the virgin birth and my own attempts to find explanations obsessed me so much that the merest reference to Christmas caused lurid images to spool through my brain. Hymens made of rhino-hide; lecherous, inseminating angels; white-haired apostles poking their indecent curiosity up a young woman's private parts in order to determine whether or not she was "pure".

∽

I engineered my own journey past virginity as a conscious campaign. I couldn't bear to wait, passive as a dandelion seed, for a masculine wind to shake me loose and sweep me away. I wanted to choose rather than be chosen. I wanted to be the captain of my fate.

I was eighteen years old, living with my parents in Bombay. I was in Elphinstone College, with Economics as my major. A casual acquaintance whose name I have forgotten introduced me to her brother, Gai, in the canteen one day. Then she left us alone. She had no idea of my plans.

I studied him. He was an intermediate-year science student, while I was his senior, in the first year of my BA. His skin was the colour of oiled teak and his hair had a curling kink to it, parted on the right, lending an attractive asymmetry to the shape of his head. One of his two front teeth slightly overlapped the other. He wore wire-frame spectacles. He was maybe two inches taller than me and held himself very taut, like a bow tensed to receive an arrow.

There was no-one else within hearing of our conversation.

I told him I was interested in finding a one-time-only sexual partner.

He shrugged and said "How about me?"

His face had interesting moulding and shadows, broad at the cheekbones with an angular jaw. His nose was sculpted with a generous hand. As he aged, it would probably become a promontory to be reckoned with, but in youth it had a pleasing earthy quality, like a shapely potato.

His surname was "Singh" but he was an Indian Protestant, not a Sikh. So there would be no point asking him whether he believed in the Virgin Birth. Or how it came to be that two thousand years of religious doctrine depended upon the intactness of one woman's secret membrane.

We exchanged numbers. I told him I'd find us an appropriate place and time.

It was the home of another friend's aunt, an elderly Parsi lady. The aunt had gone to the hills to escape the pre-monsoon heat and her maid had gone with her, leaving the keys to an apartment filled with Belgian lace and Austrian crystal with Zarine, my friend.

I told Gai there was a time constraint as a result of which promptness was of the essence. Actually there was no time constraint: the aunt and her maid could not possibly return in time to catch us in the act because in those days there was no railway connection to Matheran, the hill station they had gone to. And Zarine had taken the precaution of speaking to her aunt on the phone that very morning in order to confirm that she and the maid were both firmly a day's journey away.

Gai rang the bell at precisely half-past two and that pleased me. I dislike the military and the violence, mayhem and destruction it stands for while nevertheless admiring its reputation for precision. I liked to think that what I was doing was sober and unromantic, conditioned by the ticking gears of well-oiled clocks rather than the unruly urgings of my hormones. I wanted to believe that I was taming the fearsome beast of uncertainty whose jaws gaped wide before me as I stood with one foot on the threshold of my future and the other foot still wearing the fuzzy slippers of my childhood.

I opened the door and led Gai through the gleaming apartment with its marble floors and the frantically barking toy Pomeranian called Shadow who was actually the reason that Zarine had been entrusted with the key to the apartment. Shadow had to be fed and watered during the two-day absence. I had done the needful, then locked him into the kitchen.

I led my visitor to the book-lined study that Zarine and I had designated as the appropriate location for my tryst. It had no windows, but the air-conditioning ducts ensured that we would not die of asphyxiation. There was a cushion-strewn divan that may have been custom-designed for late-afternoon dalliance. There was a lockable door in case of unforeseen emergencies.

I had placed a white bedsheet on the divan and beneath the sheet, a towel. All the literature supported the notion that there *would* be a spilling of bodily fluids even though I expected none.

The atmosphere was inescapably Emergency Room. Zarine had asked if I wanted music, because the aunt had speakers all over the house. I preferred silence, I said. No distractions. I had disconnected the telephone and checked for alarm clocks.

He reached into the pocket of his jeans and brought out a strip of three Government-issue condoms in their jaunty yellow-and-red packets. "I got these at the railway station," he said.

I glanced at them, nodding. I had asked him to get them, though I had a packet of my own, in my handbag, as extra insurance. I had been monitoring my monthly cycles and so far as I could determine, there was very little risk of pregnancy on that particular date. I sat down and began undoing the clasps on my sandals. I did not look at him.

"So. You'd like to just get down to it?" he asked.

"Of course," I said. "That's why we're here."

He was wearing a tee shirt over jeans. I didn't watch him undress, but instead concentrated on getting my outer clothes off with a minimum of delay, a blouse and jeans. I had dithered a great deal over which precise blouse to wear, ultimately choosing one that opened down the front, for ease of removal. When I was in my undies, I lay down. I have long curling hair and I arranged it fan-wise across the pillow under my head. Only then did I looked up at him.

He was down to his briefs.

"I think you should lie down now," I said.

It was, as it always is, a shock to be right up close to another person's face. Perhaps because I am short-sighted, I don't normally notice the pores on someone's skin or the precise pattern of small hairs as they rise along the edge of a temple and merge into a brow. The irises of Gai's eyes were dark and it was only at close quarters that I could see his pupils, fully dilated, like a cat's eyes in dim light. He had showered before coming over and I could smell the shampoo in his hair.

"Is this really your first time?" he asked, his voice breathy.

I had grown up in a highly sociable milieu, surrounded by my family's friends and relatives, my diplomat father's official guests and the army of domestic help that kept our various official residences well-dusted and polished. I was trained not to let emotions out unless they served a positive function. Smiling was good whether or not it was sincere, whereas crying, screaming or indeed ever raising my voice was not acceptable under any circumstance.

When I'm in an unfamiliar situation however, my face becomes an expressionless mask.

"Yes," I said, in answer to Gai's question. He could have no idea whatsoever that just under the surface of the skin of my face, a hurricane was in progress. Winds of unimaginable speed were whipping through my brain, uprooting houses, trees, cars, trains, whole libraries of books, whole villages of thought. It was like being on several roller coasters at the same instant. An unpleasant sensation about which I could do nothing except wait for it to stop.

Gai removed his briefs with one hand.

He whispered in my ear, "Have you seen one before?"

His breath had started to splinter into short fragments. I had heard this panting before, the sound that a man makes when he is aroused. It had alarmed me, the first time I heard it, while necking at a college picnic with a friendly but clumsy philosophy major. It was the voice of the body, not the mind and it had unnerved me. I had pushed that boy away after a few seconds, claiming ant bites as the cause.

"Only in museums," I said.

Gai shifted his weight slightly, so that I could look down.

The sight surprised me. Pornography involving pictures of men was not easily available those days nor had it ever occurred to me to look for it. Even in museums, gods and heroes were all that I had seen, not priapic satyrs encircling Greek drinking cups, not the heaving mountainous members of Japanese sumi-e paintings. In genteel European art, men's sexual parts look soft and harmless, small pink cornets of puff pastry. Even though I knew, from text book descriptions, that there would be a dramatic change of appearance, my imaginings had only produced smooth featureless cylinders. Surgical instruments rather than living organs with contours, bluntness and mass.

The item I could see now, even without my glasses on, looked rude and insolent, like a one-eyed eel, bouncing and wriggling according to an agenda of its own.

I took my undies off. He put on a condom. Then it was time.

All the accounts I had ever read about the act of sex suggested a vaulting up into another sphere of experience.

What I felt was the polar opposite: an absolute immersion in the here-and-nowness of the vessel of muscle and bone that is a body. There was no pain, no breaking-and-entry struggles, nor anything I would have described as pleasure. Everything I had anticipated was wrong.

That other body had its own urgency, its priorities, its heat, its weight. I was overwhelmed by the extreme otherness of its physical being – I couldn't think of it by a name, a context, or even a gender. Gai became just A Body. My own body threw aside its name and gender and history. It revealed itself as having its own existence, practically unknown to me, distinct from my mind, my thoughts, my feelings.

The tornado-atmosphere inside my brain had snapped off. My eyes were open, I was conscious and curious. It amazed me, for instance, to be pressed right up next to another being, crushed by his weight upon me, smelling the sharp raw scent of his body, hearing the moment of his orgasm, yet knowing nothing of his mind's interior. It was sublimely unavailable to me, just as mine was unavailable to him. It may seem paradoxical that I found this isolation pleasing, but I did. It told me that my mind was my absolute domain, that it could never be invaded or colonized except with my consent. It was a wonderfully liberating realization.

The rest was mundane: washing up, dressing, engaging in small talk, letting Shadow out of the kitchen. Saying goodbye. I did not meet Gai again. I don't know whether he resented the clinical nature of our connection.

I felt grateful to him even though I was disappointed by the experience. It had not answered any of my questions. Not really. What was there about this astonishingly prosaic event that deserved such attention? So far as I could tell, the abstract notion of chastity does not excite special interest in the world outside the Semitic religions. Morality is understood only in the context of society. If an act causes no social repercussions it is simply irrelevant. According to the Kama Sutra, a woman is considered a virgin if she has not yet been betrothed. I do not recall any referrence to sexuality in discussions with my parents or larger family circle. Everything about a young person's behavior was assumed to be controlled by our social activities, the fact that we were almost never alone, the fact that we were expected to be respectful of authority, never questioning the choices made for us.

Ironically, it was my convent schools that focused my attention upon the channel between a woman's legs in a way that suggested otherworldly dimensions of sin and ecstasy, both.

∞

When I was in my mid-twenties I began a series of paintings that would bring notoriety down upon my head. I had always been able to draw realistically. Portraits of friends, of street people, of taxi-drivers and waiters. I had always enjoyed drawing people. After my BA, with the help of some friends in art school, I held a couple of exhibitions. They were so successful that I decided to leave the degree in Law I was pursuing as a preamble to sitting for the competitive exams leading to Government Service, to become an artist full-time.

It was never my intention to be blasphemous. I had just begun experimenting with oil paints when I found myself returning in painting after painting to a woman's figure, slightly elongated, with her arms parted. She wore flowing white robes and a blue shawl over her head. Of course she was the Madonna. That was obvious to me from the start. What had never struck me before was that the familiar image was an especially poetic rendering of a woman's nether corrugations. By no coincidence, since this was the late seventies, feminist art was flooding the world's media with kite-shaped images representative of vaginal folds and frills.

In my depictions, the Madonna's gentle face was the clitoris, her outstretched arms were the outer labia, her central region represented the swollen interior void that is so uniquely and problematically the source of feminine identity while her feet were the homely fundus of the human digestive tract.

The show was what might be called a catastrophic success. Riots and demonstrations were staged by different religious groups outside the Jehangir Art Gallery, across the street from what had been my college for the BA. The Christian minority believed that I, a non-Christian with a Hindu name, must surely have intended to trample on their sentiments. But conservative elements from both Hindu and Muslim groups also denounced the paintings as obscene abominations. Not only were they tainted with Christian iconography but the depiction of That Which

Must Never Be Revealed, i.e., the female pudenda, made them especially vomitous.

In my interviews with the press I stammered incoherently about being areligious, about chastity and the symbol of the Perfect Woman. The elegance and beauty of her pose suggested that her female body is a portal to a higher plane of experience, I said. Her arms are spread wide in a gesture of loving invitation, generosity and hope. Her entire being deifies the female condition, with the blue of her veil representing the heavens, the white of her robes purity and the stars rimming her head the promise of eternity implied by sexual union and reproduction.

But the younger journalists gaped at me without comprehension while the older ones snickered and turned away. My preoccupations were regarded as eccentric at best and perverted at worst. My best friends encouraged me to do the city a favour and close the show before it opened. I listened to their advice. Meanwhile the paintings were sold in international auctions at ten times my original asking price even before they were removed from the gallery's walls. So it was a good time for me professionally, though I had to return to doing commissioned portraits for awhile.

It was during this period that a friend called Ork asked a difficult favour of me.

We had been close friends in college, staying in touch post-graduation even as our career-paths sent us in different directions. We had never had a romantic connection though he had once sent me a note written in code expressing a carnal interest in me. He never followed up in any way however. I tried once later on to push beyond the limits of platonism by propositioning him directly.

We were both living in Bombay at the time.

"Ork," I began. He had been coming over almost every day, spending a couple of hours talking over increasingly tepid mugs of tea, on the balcony of my parent's spacious flat. He was no longer the long-haired, lean-cheeked youth of college, whose nickname had been a back-formation from "stork", on account of his angularity and his height. He had the standard clean-shaven good looks of many another young North Indian man: chestnut brown eyes lavishly endowed with up-curled lashes, honey brown skin and wavy black hair. He looked up at me over the rim of his mug. "Ork, I think we should have an affair."

And he said, "No."

Just like that, without a moment's hesitation. Or even surprise.

"No. It would be a disaster," he said.

My mind went blank with shock.

"It would lead to marriage and *that* would be awful. I mean, being married to me would be awful. For you."

I refused to feel insulted. "Don't be silly," I said. "You know very well I'm not interested in marriage." Which was true. I was not then and had not been, from a very early age, ever willing to think of marriage as a viable future for myself.

But he shook his head resolutely. "You don't understand. It isn't that I'm not attracted to you. It's that I don't want to *marry* you. If we had an affair, we'd end up getting married and I'd lose you as a friend. That's what I don't want."

He was perfectly serious. I was flabbergasted. After a slight pause we continued talking, laughing and sharing anecdotes as if nothing had happened. When he went away that evening, it was just the same as on any other evening and he returned another couple of times. Then he went abroad to work in an older cousin's bank in

London. We kept in touch through letters and cards. We met when we could, sharing confidences, eating dinners together. Remaining good friends.

Several years passed. I attained my minor notoriety and moved into my own apartment in Churchgate. Ork returned from his travels to live with his parents. He earned a good salary as Assistant Branch Manager at Grindlays in Worli.

One day, over lunch, he told me he was engaged to be married.

He'd never before this talked of any girlfriends. I had assumed he'd had some but that he'd chosen not to mention them to me. Out of delicacy perhaps. I didn't talk to him about my boyfriends either, even though I'd had a couple between my proposition to him and this lunch-time revelation.

He stopped me from saying that I was happy for him.

"Wait," he said. "It's not what you think." He meant, it wasn't a romance.

He told me that when he'd returned to Bombay to live with his parents, it was with the realization that the scattershot approach to a private life wouldn't work for him. He'd seen too many of his contemporaries crash and burn while chasing after the Western romantic model: finding a girl, falling in love, proposing and then getting married with neither a dowry nor the collective blessings of a supportive clan. Even traditional Indian marriages were crumbling, but love-matches in particular were doomed. Starting as they did without the family's capital investment or social approval, their failure rate was hitting the 80% mark.

He had asked his parents to fix a match for him and they had gladly agreed. He said that he'd met a couple of girls before deciding upon The One. She had a childish nickname: Kiki. He liked her because of that name, which suggested that she didn't take herself too serious. She was keen to be married, attractive without being spectacular. She worked as a receptionist at a corporate office, but expected to give up her job once they were married. He showed me a picture. A pretty little face looked out at me, with a sharp nose and careful smile.

I had always despised the notion of arranged marriages and Ork certainly knew this. But he was also an old friend. So I accepted his decision for what it was and refused to feel disappointed about his lack of idealism. I had understood by then that most Indians made choices about their personal lives based on the patterns set for them by their parents. Regardless of what they said and however they behaved in college and even for a few years after college, when it came to the big decisions about which profession to follow or whom to marry, one by one they buckled themselves into the family harness. If I was different, it was only because I had grown up away from India and lacked the protective colouration that would have allowed me to blend in.

Over the next few weeks, Ork kept me informed about the progress of his project. Kiki lived in Delhi, so he didn't often get to see her. She visited Bombay occasionally, staying with relatives while accepting invitations to meet him at his parents' apartment in Worli. He described how, on one occasion, his fiancée had worn a flowered cotton kurta which so matched the fabric with which the living room sofa was upholstered that when she sat down on it, "she disappeared!" When describing her he used words like "cute", "girlish" and "quiet".

Late one afternoon, he called me from his office, requesting a walk on Marine Drive. That wasn't his usual style. He was not an outdoorsy person and the long drive across the whole length of Metropolitan Bombay would cost him more time and money than he was normally willing to spend. I wondered what was on his mind. The sun was low over the horizon. We walked towards the NCPA at the southern tip of the Drive, reversed direction and walked back the way we'd come. He waited until we were at the traffic light at Veer Nariman Road, five minutes from my apartment building, before saying, "This is very difficult for me."

The awkwardness and the time of day and maybe also the time of his life allowed me to guess what was coming. Which was a good thing, because when he did force the words out, I had already planned my response. "You probably don't know this about me – or maybe you do – but anyway, here's the thing: I'm twenty-nine," he said. "I'm a virgin. And I'd like not to be. You know. Now that I'm getting married. So I wondered if … if …"

And I said, "Of course."

We were buddies. I would never deny him.

We set a date and he came over to my apartment, in the afternoon. His parents' flat was out of the question, obviously, but I had a live-in cook who had been installed by my parents specifically to spy on me. I had to send her away on an errand on the other side of the city in order to be assured of privacy.

I was overwhelmed by the sense of responsibility. This was going to be the end of a relationship, not the beginning of one. In a couple of months, Ork would be married and in all probability would vanish from my life. I had reached that age when socializing with married couples as a single woman was becoming uncomfortable. So I did not expect to gain anything from the event other than the satisfaction of knowing that I was doing a good friend a favour. In the back of my mind, I was also terrified that I might instead be the cause of a sexual trauma that would scar him forever.

We normally sat in the drawing room or the small kitchen-pantry but now I invited him into my bedroom, to my queen-size bed. I had set up the room for intimacy, drawing down the white venetian blinds and peeling away the onyx-black tribal rug to reveal pristinely white sheets below. I had bought them for him, knowing that he was squeamish about bed linen.

I suggested getting in half-dressed, to save ourselves the introductory embarrassments.

He agreed without discussion.

There were no unpleasant surprises or disappointments. He was, as I expected he would be, perfectly well-equipped to perform. And he did. We were both contented at the end of it. He smoked a cigarette with the sheet wrapped around his chest and me snuggled into his side, as we talked in soft tones. If there had been a camera to record the moment, we would have presented a Hollywoodian portrait of post-coital ease.

I was impressed with myself for having been a sterling example of a true friend.

But I had misjudged the results.

Ork's marriage lasted less than six months after which he disappeared from my life for several years. When we caught up again, he told me that he had been a fool to think one episode in bed would tell him anything about being a husband to a wife. He blamed himself for having approached me for help but he blamed me even more for behaving like a professional courtesan.

"It wasn't real, what we did," he said. He wore reading glasses now to look at the bill of the restaurant we were in. He had a slight paunch and there were tufts of hair growing out of his ears. But he had remarried and was very happy with his second wife, also a divorcée. "The first time's about risk. About pushing past the fear. You weren't helping me to push past the fear. You just wanted me to have a nice time. At any cost."

I stared at him, open-mouthed with dismay.

"You wanted to pat yourself on the back for a job well done. I know you too well not to know that." He smiled, shaking his head. "I'm not blaming you. I was an idiot for asking. You were an idiot for agreeing. We were both young and ridiculous."

He was right.

The bodies in a bed are not buddies. They are combatants. Sometimes they're fighting on the same side, for the same goals. Other times not. Either way, they are alone.

Especially when one of them is a virgin.

〜

Some months ago, a friend whom I shall call Om, got back in touch with me after a lapse of many years. I had known him when I was in my final year of college, in Bombay. After Gai, that is and long before Ork.

At the time I met him he told me categorically that he had a steady girlfriend, that he loved her and that he expected to marry her. She had gone to the US ahead of him to continue her higher studies and he was getting ready to join her. He wanted me to know that there was no romantic capital to be gained from our friendship but that didn't mean we couldn't enjoy a little friendly barter before he left.

I did not believe in either cheating on a boyfriend or being party to another woman's betrayal. Why? Because

I didn't think that the emotional chaos caused was ever balanced by the pleasure gained.

Nevertheless, I was attracted to Om. Too attracted to step away. I hated to see my own rules bending and snapping in the wind yet I could not switch my attention off. I met him only every third weekend, but we talked on the phone every day. We had been a couple of times for walks at Juhu Beach, for swims at the United Services Club in Colaba and once or twice he had come home for tea. Whenever we talked, our conversations were of the kind that remained glowing and twitching in my memory for hours afterward.

Some of you reading this will recognize the symptoms: I was falling in love.

But was I ever going to admit such a thing to myself? Of course not. I had brought the case before my own internal Committee for Romantic Acquisitions and I had turned myself down. Om was, by the terms of my own Evaluation Council, unavailable to me on account of his fiancée. Being the bureaucrat's daughter that I was, I could hardly go against my own regulations.

Still. I wasn't ready let him go. So I created a loophole. Under the heading of Research and Exploration, my internal Committee could sanction a Physical Encounter. That was how I thought of it. Any other approach would have been dishonourable and unconstitutional. The terms of my loophole specified that I could not love him, nor do anything to keep him interested in me.

I remember a particular evening when we were driving back to the southern tip of Bombay, where I lived, after spending the late afternoon at Juhu, in the north. In those days, the beach was practically deserted. Om had drawn diagrams in the sand, in the slanting amber light, to explain internal combustion engines to me.

As an Economics major, I was fascinated by the sciences and wished I knew more. He talked about a performance at his college of *Waiting for Godot* and of how, during the interval, he had walked through the crowd saying, "Spade ... spade ... spade ..." while holding a spade in his hands.

I was acutely aware of the outgoing tide sucking the sand away from under my bare feet as we strolled along the shoreline. My sandals were in my hands, the wind was blowing my hair into my eyes and he was just a few feet away from me. He was taller than me, and lean, his movements elastic. He wore a loose white *khadi* kurta over white pajamas. I could feel the heat of his body speaking to me across the space that separated us. I could feel a spark of electricity igniting the chamber of charged air that contained us on that open beach. I could feel an engine of desire turn over and start to hum within me.

So in the car, going home, I said, "Would you like to sleep with me?"

"Sure," he said.

He lived in an all-men's hostel while I was still in my parental home, where there was never any question of privacy. So I organized a place and time: my friend Bena's room, in mid-afternoon. Her own parents were out at work and the servants were off taking their siesta.

Om arrived at the appointed hour and the three of us made small talk for a few minutes.

Then Bena muttered her excuses and left.

The moment she exited, a guillotine descended between Om and me, slicing the room in half.

The spark I had felt at the beach was extinguished completely. In its place were the clean white sheets, the small sterile room on the ground floor. The sun nuzzling its way in through baby-pink curtains. The humming air-conditioner. The sounds of traffic from the street outside.

There was nothing either of us could do to improve the situation. We undressed, lay down and got the action over with quickly. It was like a medical procedure, a brief storm after which we sat up, got dressed and we went our separate ways. I remember feeling like an actor who has dropped a whole scene of dialogue from a play, causing it to end an hour earlier. We did not meet again after that day, though we talked on the phone a couple of times. The events in Bena's room were never referred to, not even obliquely.

Then his exams were upon him. Then his departure loomed. Then he flew away and we did not exchange addresses.

For a long time afterwards, the memory of him remained buzzing and stinging within me like a swarm of bees caught in a fine nylon net.

He had not said or done anything out of order. He had not lied to me nor misled me. Yet I felt burgled. Even though I couldn't see what had been taken, what had been lost, I felt as if something vast had been siphoned out of me leaving me with a dense, impenetrable emptiness.

I tried to blame myself for my own inadequacies on that final afternoon – the silence, my impassivity – but I couldn't make the guilt stick. He would always have vanished westwards. The distances that had been inherent in our story would have remained obstinately in place whatever we might have said or done differently that day.

In the intervening years between then and now, we met twice, in the early eighties, while I was still in Bombay. He had divorced the girlfriend for whom he'd left India, then married twice again. I had the show that would alter the course of my professional life for the better.

Then twenty years passed.

Last month, when he got back in touch with me, the changes in both our lives were more profound than they had ever been before. We are both in stable relationships. He lives in San Francisco, working as an environmental consultant. I live in New Delhi, an established artist with the controversies of the past nacred over by my financial success.

We talked on the phone and met a couple of times for dinner. The bitterness and pain that I had felt at the time of his first departure to the West had dissipated so completely that I could smile at the dark energy of youth without feeling the least twinge. We exchanged e-messages, we Skyped, we SMSed. I did not think of these communications as especially consequential.

Then a few days ago, he called from a hotel in Cairo.

He had an unlimited supply of international minutes on his cell phone. Or maybe the UN was paying. It didn't matter. We embarked upon a light, lazy conversation which started as an exchange of anecdotes about getting through security in US airports before veering towards the past.

We talked about the visits to Juhu, about his diagrams in the sand, about calling a spade, a spade. We had always, to some extent, talked about the past. This time however, he referred with no preamble, directly to Bena's room.

"I don't remember her name," he said. "Your friend at whose house we met. The last time. Before I went away."

My centre of gravity shifted within me. It was true that I no longer felt resentful towards him but to talk about it was to be reminded of the tremendous waste of energy that takes place in youth. The way that we place our emphasis on the least consequential of things.

I tried changing the topic but he refused to be distracted.

He said, "Do you remember what you were like? So stiff and so unyielding. Like you were in a hurry to get it over with." His tone wasn't one of rebuke. It was as if we were both watching a film together, one that only he and I had ever seen, critiquing it.

I shrugged on my side of the conversation.

"Yes," I said. "I remember. And I *did* just want to get it over with."

I could have mentioned the screaming vacuum I'd felt in the months that followed, the charge of anticipation that had preceded the encounter and the complete voiding of my senses during it. But I was still holding myself to the contract I had written for myself at the time, in the ink of indifference. To have claimed any passion, even a negative one, such as anger, would have been inappropriate.

"We were so young and inexperienced – " he began.

"Not you," I said at once. The snap of accusation was audible in my voice. "You were older than me. You had a steady girlfriend – "

"Yes, yes," he said, cutting in. "*But you were my first.*"

His first lover. He had been a virgin.

"*No,*" I said. "*No.*"

The boundaries of time and space dissolved around me.

I was returned to that small neat room in Bombay. I remembered the smell of his hair, his mouth. The plain bright light. The ticking of a clock.

For thirty years, that scene had remained inside the archives of my mind, irrefutable and unchangeable, showing Om as user and me as usee. But it was the early seventies and his fiancée had not considered sleeping with him before marriage. I, belonging to a different generation and indoctrination, had not even dreamt of that possibility. It had never once occurred to me that maybe he, not I, had been at the greater disadvantage. That perhaps he had been fearful and embarrassed, or awkward and clumsy, or incoherent and lacking in élan because he really did not know anything else.

Within the space of two seconds the weight of that memory shifted, trembled and vanished altogether. It was gone.

In its place was a hint of stars.

Virginity is invisible. It has no mass or atomic number. It has little to do with membranes or bloodied sheets or pain.

It means nothing to those who do not seek truth.

"I hadn't told you," he said. "I was too proud. I should have."

I was literally speechless. I could not push a single word out of my mouth.

In all this time, after countless girlfriends, one-night-stands, misadventures, divorces, call-girls, marriages, clandestine affairs, wives and daughters he had nevertheless maintained one tiny fragment of a distant memory intact. He knew he possessed a single electron of information that he needed to transfer to me. He wanted to confirm that however alone, apart and separate we had been then and had remained ever since, we belonged to that cohort of seekers which values truth.

It mattered to him that I should know.

Though neither of us could really say why.

A CHRONOLOGY OF
THE STORIES IN THIS BOOK